Cinnamon Gardens

By Anna Jacobs

THE PEPPERCORN SERIES

Peppercorn Street
Cinnamon Gardens

THE GREYLADIES SERIES

Heir to Greyladies
Mistress of Greyladies
Legacy of Greyladies

THE WILTSHIRE GIRLS SERIES

Cherry Tree Lane
Elm Tree Road
Yew Tree Gardens

Winds of Change

a&b

Cinnamon Gardens

ANNA JACOBS

Allison & Busby Limited
12 Fitzroy Mews
London W1T 6DW
allisonandbusby.com

First published in Great Britain by Allison & Busby in 2015.

Copyright © 2015 by ANNA JACOBS

A CIP catalogue record for this book is available from
the British Library.

First Edition

ISBN 978-0-7490-1712-5

Typeset in 11/16 pt Sabon by
Allison & Busby Ltd.

The paper used for this Allison & Busby publication
has been produced from trees that have been legally sourced
from well-managed and credibly certified forests.

Printed and bound by
CPI Group (UK) Ltd, Croydon, CR0 4YY

Chapter One

Australia

Nell Chaytor waited until they were all sitting at the kitchen table. She smiled at her three sons, fine lads but a little lazy. She'd spoilt them because she loved them so much – and she hadn't loved herself enough. She understood that now.

She'd been seeing a counsellor for a few months because she'd felt lost, needing a better purpose in life. They'd discussed the family dynamics, especially her worries that her two youngest sons didn't seem to be making any attempt to become independent of her now they'd finished their education and got decent jobs.

She'd read about grown-up children who stayed at home well into their forties. That didn't seem right somehow. And it definitely wasn't enough for her to act as their unpaid housekeeper. They'd even objected to the amount of food money she'd asked for.

Where had she gone wrong with them?

And even though her oldest, Robbie, was married, he was only just starting to pull his weight in that relationship now that they were expecting a baby. Her daughter-in-law had told her so bluntly a couple of months ago.

'Your son's a kind guy and I love him to pieces,' Linda had said, 'but you've spoilt him rotten and he expects me to do the same. We've been having a few battles over him doing his share of the housework and I blame you for that. Well, he's not getting away with ducking out of chores, even if we have to quarrel about it from dawn to dusk.'

That had hurt Nell. It had been a struggle at times, but she'd brought her boys up with very little help from their father, who had left her for another woman when they were small. Except for the financial contributions. She would grant Craig that much. He might forget to attend a school cricket match or a parents' evening, and he hardly ever took the boys out, but he'd always paid the maintenance and his share of the mortgage on time.

As if that was the only thing that mattered in bringing up kids!

Well, things were about to change with the two youngest, which was why she'd called a family meeting. She hoped her eldest son would take note of what she was doing, though.

'Well, Ma?' Robbie asked impatiently. 'What's the big fuss? Why didn't you want Linda to come with me tonight?'

Nell's stomach felt shuddery with nerves now that the moment had come to speak out. 'I have something to tell you, and it's very important to me.' But the next words didn't come easily, because she knew she was going to upset them.

'You're not ill, are you?' Steve asked quickly.

Trust Steve to worry about that. He'd lost a friend to cancer last year and it seemed to have turned him into a worrier . . . when he wasn't partying as if there were no tomorrow.

'No. I'm not ill. It's just . . . I'm going back to England.'

'If anyone deserves a holiday, you do,' Nick said quietly. Her middle son had always been quieter than the others, even as a child.

'It's not exactly a holiday. You know I've always said one day I'd go back to the town where I grew up. Well, now I'm going to live there for a while – a year or two, at least. I have to sell this house anyway, now that Steve's finished studying and got a job, so it's a good time to go.'

'Why do you have to sell it?' Nick asked.

'I think your father's waited long enough for his share of the money, don't you?'

He frowned. 'But Dad said he'd let you buy the other half of the house on easy terms. He and Jenny aren't short of money, you know.'

'I don't want to buy this house and I definitely don't want the burden of a mortgage at my age. So I'm selling. And your father's signed the contract to sell with the estate agent, so he'd better not change his mind now.'

They exchanged puzzled glances so she tried to explain in a way they'd understand. 'Look, I stayed here mainly because you boys needed a home big enough for each of you to have your own bedroom. Robbie moved out a while ago and you two keep telling me you're grown up, so I thought you could get a flat together. You're both earning enough to pay your way. You can have some of the furniture to help you get started and—'

They all tried to speak at once and she stopped trying to make herself heard.

After a minute or two Robbie yelled at them to be quiet, as she'd known he would.

'What will you do in England, Ma?' he asked. 'No, shut up, Steve, and let Ma speak for herself.'

'I don't know exactly. I just . . . need to get in touch with my roots, so I'm going back to Wiltshire. I've been wanting to do that for a while now, actually. I'm going to be fifty next year and I reckon it's time to do a few things for myself.'

Robbie frowned. 'How will you manage if you leave your job? And where will you live? You aren't going to spend the money you get from this house, surely?'

'That's the beauty of it. My Great-Aunt Fliss left me her house in Wiltshire a few months ago.'

Three voices shouted almost as one, 'You never told us!'

She shrugged. Fliss had left her some money too. She doubted anyone in the family had realised how much her aunt had put by for a rainy day because Fliss had lived quietly once her husband died, not making a fuss about being on her own. She'd always managed without anyone's help, rather like Nell herself.

Indeed, one of Fliss's favourite sayings had been: *I can manage, thank you.*

Nell didn't intend to tell her sons about the money or they'd pester her to use it to buy the other half of this house and might even expect her to share the windfall with them. If she did that, the money would vanish like snow in summer. It meant security for her old age, that money did.

None of her sons seemed prepared to wait for anything. They wanted it all, even if they had to get into debt to buy the latest electronic gadget or whatever.

As for her ex, Craig was a cunning devil where money was concerned. If he knew about her windfall, he too would try to persuade her to buy her share of the house from him – which would be much easier for him than selling it.

Well, too bad. She wasn't going to let any of them near her money.

Her sons were still looking at her, so she said casually, 'I'll probably find myself a part-time job. I'm still a British citizen, after all. If I don't have to pay rent, or buy food for your bottomless stomachs, I won't need to earn a lot. I can do some sightseeing, enjoy myself.'

There was dead silence but all three were frowning. Were they concerned about her or about themselves? she wondered. Both, probably. They did love her, she knew, in their own selfish, immature way. Yes, immature. None of them had yet taken full responsibility for their own lives, even Robbie, who left management of his finances to his wife.

It was hard, but she had to do this. Tough love, people called it.

Steve broke the silence. 'Where is it, this house of yours?'

'In Sexton Bassett, a small town south-west of Swindon. I used to stay there with my great-aunt when I was a child. I stayed for the whole summer holidays most years because my parents couldn't afford to go away. I loved being there and I loved Fliss.'

She fell silent for a moment or two and they waited. 'I got in touch with her again as soon as I left home. You remember how my dad refused to contact his family after he emigrated. No, perhaps you don't. You weren't all that old when he died. Anyway, Fliss was in her seventies by the time I got married, but she'd already learnt how to use a computer. I found out her email address by writing to an old friend of hers.'

Steve's face brightened suddenly and from what he said, he'd only been half-listening to her. 'Hey, we could come and stay with you there. Have a family holiday together. See a bit of the world.'

'You've just started a new job. You won't have any holidays owing and you don't have any money saved. I'm not subsidising you for an expensive holiday.'

He shrugged. 'Call it a loan, then. I can always get another job when I come back and repay you. I rather fancy living in England for a few months. What's your house like? Is it big enough to fit us all in?'

'I doubt it. I've never seen it, but when she turned eighty-five Fliss wrote that she was going to sell the house because it was too big for her to manage. She was moving into a small cottage instead.'

'Didn't her lawyers send you photos of the house when you inherited it, or give you details? Didn't you even try to find out, Ma?'

'I was a bit busy at the time. It was when Steve broke his arm and I was typing his final assignments for him, if you remember.' He'd always needed more help than the others with his studies. He was better at working with his hands, but Craig had insisted he get a qualification, so he'd gone to the TAFE institute to do a more practical course in IT. He hadn't enjoyed the theory, though he'd enjoyed working with computers.

She'd stayed up till all hours after work to do them from his recorded dictation while he went to bed or watched TV.

10

Oh, she'd been such a fool over the years – a loving, kind, stupid fool.

'Were you Fliss's only remaining relative? Is that why she left it to you?'

'I don't think so. There ought to be several cousins still living in the area. My father might have fallen out with his family, but I'm going to get in touch with them.'

'You will be coming back to Australia to live eventually, though, won't you?' Nick asked.

She shrugged. 'I'm assuming so, but I can't seem to plan that far ahead at the moment. I have to sort things out this end before I can leave.'

And then it burst out, the excitement, the freedom, the sheer joy of it, and she beamed at them. 'I feel so gloriously free. I'm going to recharge my batteries first – it's been a hard year at work. And then I'll do some genealogical research, and I'll drive around, get to know England again. After all, I was born there, even though we came to Australia when I was a child.'

She smiled. 'I've not been back since before Robbie was born, and even then, it was only a few days as part of a whistle-stop tour your father and I made around Europe.' Actually, Robbie had probably been conceived in England during that tour.

She and Craig had had a lot of fun together until the boys were born. He hadn't enjoyed being the father of small children, and the fun had gradually stopped. 'Over twenty-seven years since I've been back. It's been too long. It's part of my heritage, you know. And I still have dual nationality.'

There was dead silence again. Steve opened his mouth

to speak and Nick dug him in the side, so he shut it again.

She stood up, 'I'll make us another cup of tea, shall I?'

Robbie looked at his watch. 'Er, no. I have to go.'

'Oh, stay and have a cuppa,' Nick said. 'It's not often all three of us get together.'

She knew that while she was in the kitchen they'd be discussing what to do to stop her taking such a drastic step. Let them talk and manoeuvre as much as they wanted. They wouldn't change her mind.

The first step had been hard, but she'd done it, told them what she was going to do.

When she went back with the tray, they were waiting for her. Nick took it out of her hands, Steve pushed her gently into a chair and Robbie leant back, as if dissociating himself from what they were going to say.

'We've worked out what to do,' Steve said. 'It's obvious, really. You can take Dad up on the mortgage, then Nick and I can rent this place from you and maybe rent out another room to a friend. That way you'll have somewhere to come back to and the mortgage will be paid while you're away.'

'And once you move out, in a year or two? Who will pay the mortgage, then?'

Nick leant forward. 'That's the beauty of it. When you come back, you can sell the English house and pay off the mortgage here. *Voilà!* Problem solved.'

'I'm afraid not, boys.' She used the excuse her counsellor had helped her prepare and rehearse. 'I don't want a mortgage hanging round my neck ever again. You know how I feel about getting into debt. And I won't want a house this big when I'm on my own. Too much maintenance.'

They all started protesting at once.

She held one hand up in a stop-the-traffic signal they'd all recognise from when they were children. 'There's something else. You might not realise it, because you were very young when your father and I split up, but this house has some bad memories for me.'

It was Robbie who muttered, 'I remember you and Dad quarrelling a lot.'

She'd never told them all the details but it was time for the truth. 'He slapped me around towards the end, you know.'

The two younger boys exchanged horrified glances.

'He didn't!' Nick protested.

Robbie surprised her by stepping in to support her. 'He did. I heard him thump her a few times. I heard her crying sometimes, too.'

Steve scowled at him. 'Well, I never heard anything. Dad was probably just angry. He does have a bit of a temper. He didn't mean to hurt you, Ma.'

Robbie came over to put his arm round her shoulders and give her a quick hug, then turned to his brothers. 'You were too young to realise what was going on, but Dad did it too often for it to be an accident.'

Nick stared at her in horror. 'Why didn't you say?'

Nell spoke up again. 'It was between your father and me. I couldn't do much to stop him, he was so much bigger than me. I was glad when he met Jenny and left me.'

'But you're still angry at him,' Nick said. 'Why? Isn't that old history now? He's changed. Time to let it drop.'

'He's changed because he got counselling about his violence after he married Jenny. She threatened to leave him if he didn't. He refused to see a counsellor when I asked him, several times he refused, and when I threatened to leave, he told me to go. Only I couldn't. I had you three to look after.'

'That's the real reason why you don't like to see him, then, even now,' Steve said slowly.

'Exactly. Even if I were staying in Australia, I'd sell this place. I don't want to be in debt to your dad. I don't want to be in contact with him in any way once I leave. I intend to be done with him completely and finally. I'm not going to come between you and him. That's a different relationship. But I want out, completely out.'

Craig was still a control freak and even now, after they'd been divorced for fifteen years, he sometimes acted as though he had a right to tell her what to do.

The boys stopped trying to persuade her to keep the house, ate most of the cake she'd baked for them, then Robbie went home and the others vanished into their bedrooms, as usual.

But she knew it wasn't over. They wouldn't give in so easily.

Over the next few days Nell's two younger sons tried several times to persuade her not to sell the house. She could get a mortgage from the bank, no need to be in debt to their father.

Craig came round and cornered her in the garden one day after work. 'We need to talk.'

'So talk.'

'It'd be better to do this inside.'

'You're not coming in.'

He leant against the wall of the house and folded his arms. 'You are such a bitch about it. It is half my house, you know.'

14

She shrugged. 'And you know how well I've looked after it. Now, hurry up and say what you have to. I've got things to do.'

'The boys are worried about you, Nell.'

'They're more worried about living on their own, having to do their own washing and cleaning.'

'They're worried about you. And so am I. You've always been an impractical fool. For heaven's sake, stop this stupidity. Go over to England for a little holiday, by all means, but don't burn your bridges here. You'll soon want to come back once the English summer's over and the cold weather sets in. What will you do if you don't have a home here any longer?'

'I can always rent somewhere till I decide. I've got a house of my own in the UK now. It may be small but it doesn't have a mortgage on it. I'll probably stay for a year or two.'

'So the boys said. What sort of a house is it exactly? A terrace? A bungalow? I can look it up on Google Earth if you give me the address.'

She stiffened. What did he know about English houses? He'd only once visited the country. She'd met him when she was backpacking round Australia. He'd been tall, lithe and suntanned, fun to be with. She'd been dazzled by him, and he was still good-looking, the rat. 'What has my English house got to do with you?'

He shrugged. 'Just thought you might need some financial advice.'

'I don't. And if I did, I'd not ask you for it.' She looked at her watch. 'I have to go out soon, so get on with it. I can't stand here chatting all day.'

'Let's go inside and talk properly.'

'You're not due an inspection, so you're not coming inside.'

He breathed deeply and scowled at her. 'I'm not letting this drop. You're making a big mistake and for the sake of our sons, I think you should—'

She went quickly into the house and banged the door in his face before he could push in after her. She leant against it and took several deep, slow breaths. She didn't let him ride roughshod over her any more but even so, it was always an effort to stand firm against him as he loomed over her. She wished she'd been born tall and strong.

It had been a big effort to be so tough with the boys, too.

She wondered if she'd ever do that sort of thing easily.

The dreams started that night. She was walking round a garden, a beautiful place. It had a sundial in a walled square that was like a garden room, and a shabby summer house to one side. It was a very English garden, with masses of soft flowers, like living rainbows. She loved gardens like that.

Beyond the summer house were some tall old trees because the garden seemed to back on to a park.

There was a house, too, but it was only a shadowy outline, and however hard she tried, she couldn't see it clearly.

She could hear voices, women chatting. They were too far away for her to make out what they were saying but the sound was soothing.

For the next two nights she had the same dream, each time seeing another part of the garden: a huge vegetable patch, a few old fruit trees, a rather neglected rose garden in full bloom. She still couldn't see the house the garden belonged to or the women, but she kept hearing them chatting, laughing, clinking their teacups.

'Who are you?' she called out to them on the third night.

There was soft, musical laughter and a voice said, 'We wondered if you could see us yet. I'm the original lady of this house. You'll visit it when you come here. Hurry up. You're needed.'

'I can't come to England till I've sold my house in Australia.'

More gentle laughter. 'In two days it'll be Lady Day. You'll sell your house then. Very appropriate, don't you think, Nell, for a nice lady like you?'

The dream began to fade, and she woke, feeling comforted by the thought of selling this house quickly and by their compliment. She snuggled down and fell asleep almost immediately.

All day she kept remembering the garden. It had been so beautiful, she wished she could go and walk round it. Why hadn't she been able to see the house, though? One day she would, she felt quite sure of that.

How stupid! She was acting as if that garden and those people in it were real. Who believed in dreams? Not her. She was a modern woman, more used to computers than spooky stuff.

Out of sheer curiosity – she didn't believe you could foretell the future, no way! – she checked Lady Day on her favourite search engine: *Lady Day, March 25th, tied in to the Equinox*. It was the end of the financial quarter and had been the traditional time for signing annual contracts between landowners and tenant farmers in England.

And it was the day when her house would be open for the first time, for inspection by potential buyers. That must be what had sparked the dream.

She hoped the house wouldn't take too long to sell. She was eager to start her new life.

Angus Denning sighed in annoyance at himself when he realised he'd been speeding and the police were signalling him to pull over. He was only five miles above the speed limit, but it was enough to earn him a fine. He groaned when he saw who was getting out of the police car: Edwina Richards.

He'd played cricket with her father, Eddie Richards, on a small local team for years. They'd never got on, though, and had quarrelled frequently about politics, the latest news, other sports; you name it, they could quarrel about it.

Eddie was a redder-than-red socialist and hated anyone with a title on principle. Not that Angus had a title, exactly. He was just an Honourable, and most of the time he forgot about it. He'd put Eddie out of his mind, too, when his old antagonist had transferred to Bournemouth prior to retiring there.

The trouble was, Eddie's daughter Edwina had carried on the family tradition and joined the police force, and she'd been posted to the district once her father left. She seemed to be carrying on the other Richards' tradition, too, of making life difficult for the owner of Dennings. The old house had been in his family for generations and Richards had seemed to resent the mere idea of that.

Angus pulled over and opened the car door, surprised when she reached in to pull out his keys. What did she think she was doing – apprehending a criminal who might try to start a car chase?

'Well, if it isn't the Honourable Angus Denning,' she mocked.

He ignored the sarcasm, had given up telling the Richards family that the term 'Honourable' was never used in speech. He was the youngest son of an earl, so he had no chance of succeeding to the title, and thank goodness for that. But tradition had lumbered him with the prefix 'the Honourable', whether he liked it or not.

'Can I help you, Officer?' he prompted when Edwina continued to gaze scornfully at him.

'You were speeding, sir.'

'Was I? Sorry.'

'We'll have to give you a—'

The other officer nudged her. 'It was only five miles over the limit, Edwina. We can let him off with a caution this time.' He turned to Angus. 'Have you had anything to drink, sir?'

'No. I don't drink and drive. Ever. But go ahead and breathalyse me, if you have to.'

She had the gadget out already.

He blew into it, not surprised by the zero reading. He resisted saying 'Told you so!' in case it further upset her.

Edwina scowled at the gadget, then shrugged and turned back to Angus. 'Please be careful how you go from now on, sir, whether you're nearly home or not. Speeding can kill . . . not just yourself but other people. And make sure you keep this car roadworthy. It's rather old and battered. In fact . . .' she studied the vehicle.

Damn the bitch! That was a below-the-belt blow. She knew perfectly well his wife had been killed in a car accident

19

by a drunken lout three years ago. He summoned up his most upper-class accent, the one he used when telling jokes against the aristocracy, knowing it would gall her. 'Yes. I certainly will be careful, Officer.'

He looked at the male officer and spoke more normally, 'Warning duly noted.'

'I believe in letting people off with a warning once,' the man said. 'Not twice, though.'

'I'll remember that.'

'And you should keep an eye on those tyres, sir. They're getting near the end of their useful life.'

'Yes. I will.'

Angus watched them drive off down the country lane. Not until they were out of sight did he get back into the car and continue in the same direction, heading towards Sexton Bassett. He wove his way through the streets on the outskirts of the small town, then turned left, approaching his house via the rear entrance, which had been used by tradesmen in the old days.

He was still simmering with anger. That officious bitch had mentioned drink-driving on purpose to hurt him, he was sure. And had succeeded. He and Joanna had had a great marriage and he still missed her.

He drove even more slowly along the dirt track that formed the rear entrance to his two acres of land. He knew how to avoid the worst potholes and rode out the bumps by going slowly, feeling as if he were on a ship.

The main drive, which led in from Peppercorn Street, was gravelled and in better condition but still not good. He wished he could afford to do some work on it before it deteriorated further still. It was only a hundred metres or so long, but it'd cost too much to resurface it while his finances were in their current state.

Inside the house, which was far too big for one person, all the unused rooms were dusty and cobwebs graced the corners. Fortunately the roof was sound. One day he hoped to be able to do something about the general shabbiness, but he didn't want to spend the money to get proper domestic help to keep such a big place clean, not at the moment.

He'd been over the moon when he was offered voluntary redundancy a couple of years ago, because a small specialist app he'd developed in his spare time had just taken off. It hadn't made him rich, too specialist for that, but together with the redundancy payment, it'd given him enough money to stay away from paid employment for a few years.

His daughter looked down her nose at the way he was living, but he wasn't changing his lifestyle to suit her. Ashleigh was into motherhood and social climbing, in that order, with grandson number two expected in a few weeks.

His son was backpacking round the world and was in Australia at the moment. Angus hoped Oliver wouldn't stay away too long, or decide to settle in one of the faraway countries he'd visited. His cheeky lad had left a big hole in his life.

The house had once been full of laughter and young people. Angus missed that era so much it was like a physical pain. The joyful energy had all seemed to ebb away after Joanna was killed. And after Oliver left home, it was worse.

He didn't enjoy living on his own, but what alternative was there? The house had been in the Denning family for over two hundred years, was named after them:

Dennings. He didn't want to sell it, he loved it too much. It was . . . home.

Parking the car near the back door, he lugged in his groceries, and once he'd put them away, he forgot about everything else, setting the timer to remind him to stroll down to the pub later to meet his friends.

He always enjoyed eating there. He wasn't helpless, knew how to cook a few basic meals, but he was usually in a hurry to get back to his computer, so he made do with whatever was quickest when he cooked for himself.

Thank goodness for his work. He'd be lost without that.

Nell had arranged to take the next day off work to get the house ready for its first viewing on the Saturday. Her estate agent said the house was unlikely to sell quickly, because March was the end of the main buying season, but Nell intended to give it the best chance she could. If she could leave for England soon, she'd have the English summer in which to settle down.

On the Friday she went through each room in turn, making sure they were immaculate clean and looked as good as possible. She'd bought a couple of showy pot plants to prettify the downstairs room.

The only places she didn't touch were her sons' bedrooms. If she tidied them today, they'd be in chaos again before tomorrow.

When Nick and Steve came home from work, they whisked in and out of the house at the speed of light, eager to go out for their regular Friday evening on the booze with their mates. As she'd expected, they didn't seem to notice what she'd done to the house.

When they came to say goodbye, she barred the way out. 'Listen carefully for a moment, you two. I'll want you to get up early tomorrow morning, by seven o'clock at the latest.'

Steve stared at her as if she'd lost the plot. 'What? On a Saturday?'

'The house is going to be open for viewing. Remember?'

'Of course I remember. But that's not till noon. We won't need to get up till eleven, give or take.'

'You're getting up at seven and you'll be off the premises by nine because I want to clear out your rooms. They're like pigsties. You're not to come back till three o'clock at the earliest.'

'Yeah, yeah.'

Their father said that when he wasn't really listening or didn't intend to do as she asked. It annoyed her that they'd picked up the habit recently. She didn't argue now, though. Just wait till tomorrow, she thought after they'd gone. You two are in for the shock of your lives.

She put her cleaning things away and strolled along the street to her friend's house for their usual Friday night glass of wine and natter. But she didn't stay late.

She couldn't settle to anything. It was so important to sell her house.

Only then would she be truly free.

Chapter Two

The next morning Nell woke her sons at seven o'clock as she'd threatened, dragging the covers off, ignoring the fact that Steve was naked. Well, she'd seen it all before.

When he tried to get the covers back, she raised the spray bottle of iced water she'd brought with her and gave him a good squirt.

His yells echoed down the corridor.

'I meant what I said, Steve. Get up now!'

Nick must have heard because he was up by the time she went into his bedroom. He was wearing a sagging pair of jocks and looked bog-eyed. He raised his hands in mock surrender. 'No need to squirt me, Ma. I'm out of bed.'

She brandished the spray bottle. 'See you stay up, then.'

'That was cruel of you.'

She grinned. 'Only way to get Steve going after a booze-up.'

They both came along to the kitchen shortly afterwards,

expecting her to make them a cup of coffee before they started getting ready.

She stood guard in front of the kettle, arms folded. 'You're not getting anything to eat or drink till you've had your showers.' She didn't budge, staring them down.

It gradually dawned on them that she was deadly serious, so they fought their way to the bathroom they shared. Nick won by a short head.

When they came back, fresh-faced, with hair still damp, they reminded her for a moment of how they'd looked as little boys after their evening bath and her heart softened slightly. But her determination didn't.

Steve announced, 'As it happens, I can't go out today. I need to do some stuff for work on my computer. They're paying me overtime. But it's OK, Ma. I'll just sit quietly in my room. If anyone comes to look round, they'll not even notice I'm here.'

She slapped their breakfasts down on the table. Scrambled eggs on toast. 'You'll be out of the house by nine at the latest if I have to drag you out by the hair. I want you and your cars gone. You can do the work tomorrow.'

He opened his mouth, caught her eye and gave an aggrieved sigh.

When they'd finished eating, she shooed them along to their rooms. 'Tidy up now. Any mess you leave goes straight into the bin. Put every single thing away, including your clothes. I mean it.'

They rolled their eyes at each other and she left them to it. She smiled as she went back to the kitchen to clear up their mess. They didn't think she meant it about the dustbin, but she did. Oh, yes. She was fed up to the teeth of their slobby ways.

When they came back, she thrust the newspaper into Nick's hands. 'There. The property pages. You need to start looking for a place to rent. I've marked some possibles. What if I sell the house today? I'll have to be out in a month and I'll be off to England straight after that. Where will you two live then?'

Steve let out a snort of laughter. 'Sell it today! You may not realise it, Ma, but there's been a downturn in the property market for a while and this is an old place. It'll be months before you sell it and you'll probably have to drop your price considerably. Minimalist is in fashion now in houses, not tumbledown colonial.'

He might be right. But even so, every time the house was open she intended to make sure it looked as attractive as possible.

When they'd left, she breathed a sigh of relief and went to do their rooms. She found dirty clothes tossed in heaps in the corners of both bedrooms, a worse mess than she'd expected after all her warnings.

She'd kept the lads moderately tidy as youngsters, but how did you force grown men to put things away? Heaven knew, she'd tried hard enough. The effort had driven her to this state of desperation.

Grimly she piled up the clothes and anything else lying around. She hadn't really been going to toss them into the bin, in spite of her threat, but when she found remains of food going mouldy in takeaway wrappers under the beds, she changed her mind.

She didn't even separate the clothes, just hurled

everything into the big plastic rubbish bags, including the food scraps, then tossed them into the bin.

'See how you like that!' she muttered.

She wiped away a tear. They hadn't even tried. That hurt.

The estate agent, Stacy, didn't turn up until five minutes before opening time. By then, two cars were parked in the street. Nell kept peeping out of the living room window, checking them. No doubt about it, they were waiting to view her house.

Even as she watched, one couple got out of their car and came to study the front garden, pointing things out to one another.

Stacy came rushing into the house, after dumping a 'House Open' sign on the grass verge. 'Didn't expect anyone to come looking so early, Nell. That's a good sign.'

She turned in a circle on the spot, staring. 'Wow, it looks great in here! You must have worked really hard to declutter. Didn't you have time to put some coffee on? And what about playing music, as I suggested?'

'I don't want to play tricks on people.'

'It's not tricking anybody, it just puts clients in a better mood.'

Nell shook her head, still unwilling to do this. She didn't know why, just that it felt like cheating.

Stacy shrugged. 'Well, I'll do my best anyway. The house and garden are looking good, and that's the main thing.'

Nell stopped at the door. 'Just one thing. If my ex-husband turns up, don't let him inside and don't say anything to him about offers or anything else financial. He may tell you he's handling the business side for me, but it isn't true. I wouldn't trust him to do my grocery shopping.'

'Yes. You said that already. Several times.'

'Just reminding you.'

Stacy patted her hand. 'Calm down. It won't be the end of the world if we don't sell today.'

Nell took a deep breath. 'Sorry.'

Stacy's voice grew gentler. 'I'll do my best. I realise how important it is to you.'

As she went out to her car, Nell passed the couple who'd been studying the garden, so on impulse she stopped for a moment. 'Lovely day, isn't it?'

The woman, who was rather pregnant, smiled. 'Yes. And you've got the garden looking beautiful.'

'It's a very rewarding hobby. Take a look at the veggie garden at the back while you're here. I supply a lot of my own food, all organically grown. I had the soil checked.'

The woman's face brightened. 'I grow my own food too. You actually had the soil checked?'

'Yes. My agent has a photocopy of the paperwork.'

Stacy's voice floated across to them. 'We're open for viewing now, folks.'

Nell realised she was stopping them going inside, so smiled again and walked on.

She spent the next hour in a nearby park, sitting peacefully under some trees, not even bothering to read the magazine she'd bought. She'd worked brutally hard yesterday and this morning. Now, she just wanted to rest.

She felt as if time was suspended and she was waiting . . . hoping . . . Oh, she was so ready for a change!

When she got back to the house, the car of the couple she'd spoken to was still there, so she didn't go inside. Surely that was a good sign?

She was so lost in thought, she jumped in shock when someone tapped on her car window.

Sighing, she wound it down fully. 'What are you doing here, Craig?'

He looked at her scornfully, as if she'd said something stupid. 'I do have an interest in selling the house, or had you forgotten?'

'It's you who's forgetting something.'

He wrinkled his brow in the exaggerated way he had of showing puzzlement.

'I meant what I said last time. You aren't getting involved. I have the legal right to control the selling, as long as I don't sell the house for a ridiculous price. Your only rights are either to sign the contract or veto the sale on the grounds of price. And, of course, you take fifty per cent of the money after costs.'

'I know that. But—'

'If there's any news today, I'll phone you.'

'Yeah, yeah. Just tell me why you're waiting outside. What's gone wrong?'

That was where Steve got it from, the dismissive phrase that irritated her so much. She jabbed her forefinger towards the parked car. 'Nothing has gone wrong! That car belongs to a couple who were here at the beginning of the opening and are still here. I'm waiting for them to come out. I don't want to interrupt them in case they're negotiating.'

'Ah. Well, now that I'm here, I might as well stay and see how things go.'

'Then wait in your own car and leave me in peace.'

'Aren't you ever going to call a truce between us?'

'No. I still remember what it was like.' She mimed punching something.

He glared at her and strode off down the street to his own vehicle, a brand-new one, all gleaming silver.

It was another ten minutes before her estate agent came out of the house with the young couple, waving them goodbye, then picking up the 'House Open' sign and putting it into her car boot.

Nell hurried across to Stacy before Craig could get out of his car again. 'How did it go?'

'Really well. These two have been here for the whole hour. Might have an offer for you later. We had a good turnout today, actually, and quite a lot of serious interest.'

There were footsteps behind them. Nell turned to glare at Craig and he stopped a few paces away.

'Persistent, isn't he?' Stacy murmured.

'Still wants to control my life and finances – especially the finances – even after we've been divorced for fifteen years.'

Stacy looked at her watch. 'Look, I don't want to be late for my next opening. I'll phone you after five.'

'On my mobile.' If her sons picked up the house phone and found anything out, they'd share it with their father.

'I'll come back around five,' Craig said at once.

'I won't be letting you in,' Nell told him firmly.

'But you might need my advice and—'

Stacy shot her a look of sympathy, wound up the car window and drove off.

Without saying a word, Nell walked past Craig towards

31

the house. He followed her, of course, still trying to talk persuasively, but she slammed the door in his face. Hurrying to the back of the house, she did the same with the kitchen and laundry doors.

She smiled as she listened to the front doorbell ring . . . twice. Then he started hammering on the door, shouting, 'For heaven's sake, Nell, can't we even talk?'

Even though it was a pleasantly warm day, she didn't unlock any of the doors till he'd driven away.

She knew he'd obtained a copy of the new door key from one of her sons, though both denied it. She was also aware that he still came into the house sometimes. Never while she was here, of course.

She'd had a lock fitted to her bedroom door, a lock to which only she had the key so he couldn't find out anything about her personal affairs.

Craig wasn't going to get involved in the house sale, whether he enlisted the help of her sons or not. All he had to do was add his signature to the contract when it was all over.

'Did you see any nice flats?' she asked when Steve and Nick returned.

'We saw a few from one agency, Ma. No point in going on looking, though. Have you any idea what rent they're asking for anywhere half decent?' Steve looked at her indignantly, as if that were her fault.

'Of course I have. I've been keeping an eye on the rental market for a few months so that I could advise you.'

'If we get a place as near the city as this, we'll not have enough money left after living expenses to do anything at the weekend.'

'You'll have to get a place further out, then. They're a lot cheaper.'

He shuddered at the mere thought. 'I'm not living further out. It'd cost me a fortune in taxi fares.'

'Or you could stop drinking so much and drive yourself home.'

'What's the point in going out if you don't get smashed rotten?' He folded his arms. 'Dad says that we should refuse to move out. He says it'd make an excellent rental property, so why don't you reconsider and let us rent it from you? Eh, Ma?'

'If your father buys out my half, he can do what he wants with it, even rent it to you. You can suggest that next time you discuss my affairs with him – something I've asked you not to do, as you might remember. But I wouldn't rent a place to you and I bet he wouldn't either, for all his big talk.'

'Why the hell not?'

'Because if I wasn't on your case, you'd be living like pigs. You don't know how to look after a house and you've refused to learn. You won't even let me teach you how to cook a few easy meals. My investment would go downhill quickly if you two were left here alone.'

Nick had the grace to look ashamed.

Steve shrugged it off. 'We'd change. We've got time to learn to cook a few things before you go and you can leave us a freezer full of stuff.'

Nell lost it then, really lost it, as she hadn't done for years. 'I have had ee-bloody-nuff of running round after you two. You will move out as soon as I sell this place, even if I have to hire someone to throw you both out into the street physically.'

'But, Ma—'

'And don't think I wouldn't do it! You can plot with your father all you like but you won't change my mind about selling the house. He's only taking your side because he wants to take the easy way out. But I'm selling now. Get used to it.'

They looked surprised by her outburst.

She glanced at her watch. 'There are still a couple of hours before closing time. I'll ring Stacy's property guy and see if there's anywhere we can view today.'

She ignored their protests and made the call, smiling triumphantly at them as she put down the phone. 'He has several places to rent in your price range and is happy to work late to show us round.'

'Work late on a Saturday?' Steve asked in outrage. 'He's a loony.'

Nick said nothing, just turned meekly to follow her out to her car.

Steve grabbed her arm before she got to the door. 'Mum, I don't have enough money for the deposit. And I've got a few . . . you know, debts.'

'I'll lend you the deposit. And unlike your father, I won't charge interest, but you may need to get a weekend job to pay back the debts. I did warn you about living beyond your means.'

'Everybody does it.'

'Well let "everybody" help you pay your debts off, then. If you want my help, you'll do it my way.'

Steve flung himself into the back seat of her car and took out his mobile phone. Nick got into the front with her.

As they set off, he asked quietly, 'Why is it so urgent to

do this today, Ma? Can't it wait till you get an offer?'

'I may have one already. It's . . . um, not certain yet, though it's looking hopeful.' For some weird reason, she felt quite sure she'd get an offer from that nice couple. Just as the dream had said.

Their faces fell and they exchanged distinctly apprehensive glances.

Her heart went out to them, but she tried to hide that. It was always hard to be pushed out of the nest and be totally responsible for supporting yourself. In the past, men had simply been passed from mother to wife, and had always been looked after physically. Most of her sons' generation had to fend for themselves and share the marital chores, as Robbie had found out.

She sighed. She was too efficient and could get the housework done more quickly on her own. It would have been better to have given them regular jobs around the place when they were younger and insisted on the jobs being done before she handed out spending money.

But would they have done the jobs even then? They had refused point-blank to learn how to cook, as their father had before them.

No, she had no alternative now but to give them tough love. For their sake as well as her own.

But it was so hard to actually do it.

It only took until six o'clock to find them somewhere to live. It was much further out from the city centre than they wanted and small, but at least it was on the side of the city nearest to where they worked.

When they tried to refuse it, she winked at the salesman. 'We'll think about it, Matt, but I can't see us improving on this flat in their price range. I'll be in touch on Monday morning. Give me first refusal until then.'

'It's yours.'

'That place was horrible,' Steve said urgently once they were outside. 'Tiny and shabby, and it hasn't got any furniture. It looked out onto a car park, too.'

'It's all you can afford and it's clean. I told you I'd give you some of my furniture. You can have everything from your bedrooms plus the kitchen table and chairs. The flat won't look as bad when it's furnished.'

But they had to press for more. 'What about the lounge suite?'

'It's nearly new and I have a buyer lined up.'

Steve scowled at her. 'You didn't waste any time, did you, Ma?'

'Do I ever?'

She tried to drop some gentle advice in their ears. 'You need to start small, save your money and work your way up to renting something better. That's a good rule for life, too. You can't get the best of everything straight away, you know.'

'Yeah, yeah!' Steve pulled out his smart phone again and began to text someone.

Nick had already slipped in some earbuds and was nodding in time to the music.

Once they got home, they tried to talk her into refusing the flat, then gave up and went to their rooms. The sulky expressions on their faces meant they hadn't really taken what she'd said on board. Nick was usually more reasonable than this, but it was what she'd expected of Steve.

There was a yell of outrage from the boys' end of the

house and she braced herself as Steve came thundering down the stairs to confront her.

'What've you done with my clothes and my other stuff, Ma?'

'Exactly what I said I would do with anything left lying around in your bedrooms: I've thrown them into the dustbin. You know I always keep my word.'

He went to find them and came storming back a second time. 'They're all crumpled and smelly now, and I was going to wear those jeans tonight to go clubbing.'

'Unless you want the smell to linger, you'd better wash them before you go out.'

'Aren't you doing any washing this weekend?'

'Nope. I told you that, too. If you leave any dirty clothes lying around from now on, they'll go straight into the rubbish bin – whether it's due to be emptied that day or not.'

She wouldn't actually have let their clothes be carted away, couldn't have gone so far, but he wasn't going to be sure about that, not after today.

He took a deep breath, glared at her again and stormed off to his room. Each of them was out of the house within ten minutes, picked up by friends, so Steve must have found something to wear. The stinking clothes were lying on the laundry floor, as if they still expected her to wash them. She took them up to their bedrooms again. Let them enjoy the pungent smell.

Only when the second car had pulled away did she call Stacy back. She'd felt the phone vibrate while the boys were getting ready to go out, but hadn't answered it then because she didn't want anyone listening in.

Stacy never wasted her time on polite chit-chat. 'It's looking very promising.'

'What does that mean exactly?'

'Well, we have two interested parties and a bidding war going on. That's all I can tell you for the moment. I can't stay on the phone because I'm expecting one of them to call.'

'Have they actually made an offer?'

'They've both made offers, and we're now into counter-offers, so I haven't nailed down a winner yet. Bye.'

Nell fumbled her way to the bed and sank down on it, her heart pounding. It was happening. It really was.

At nine o'clock that evening her mobile rang. She looked at the display. Stacy again. Taking a deep breath, she answered the call. 'Yes?'

'Took a while because both buyers were keen. It surprised me how keen.' Stacy chuckled. 'I got you $10,000 more than your asking price.'

'What? But that sort of thing doesn't happen with houses round here.'

'It's just happened for the first time, then. You do have a larger-than-average block of land, you know. One couple wanted to knock the house down and build a bigger one, while the others wanted to redo your place in full period style and enjoy a large organic garden. They won.'

'Are they the ones who were leaving just as I got back?'

'Yes. She's a really keen gardener. My boss is delighted. He's heard of one or two other bidding wars in the area recently, so it looks like this is going to be the next über-desirable suburb.'

'I . . . can't believe it.'

'There are conditions.'

Her heart sank. 'What?'

'They want you out in two weeks. The wife is pregnant, as you no doubt noticed, and wants to do some of the renovating before she gets too big.'

'Is it possible to settle so quickly?'

'It is if the husband works for a big bank and can pay cash. He says he can also push through the inspection and other stuff more quickly than usual. They've just been transferred back to the city, apparently, and he doesn't like staying with the in-laws but they'd be offended if he moved to a hotel.'

She waited, then added, 'Are you all right with moving so quickly?'

Nell found her voice. 'All right? I'm thrilled to pieces.'

'Is it too late to come round and get your signature tonight? I do like to make a contract offer binding as soon as possible and the buyers are waiting up to hear from me.'

'I'll have to ring Craig, because you'll need his signature as well. I'll contact you if I can't get hold of him.'

'Craig?' She could hear the sound of voices in the background. 'Sorry to disturb your social life.'

'Nell? Is something wrong?'

'On the contrary. I've sold the house.'

Dead silence, then, 'How much did you have to drop the price?'

'I didn't. We got $10,000 over the asking price.'

Another silence, then, 'You must have a good agent.'

'And I did a lot of work on the house. Remember, you

agreed to pay half the bills for that. I have all the receipts for paint and so on. I won't charge you for my time.'

'How generous of you.'

'Anyway, what I rang for is to ask if you can come round now to sign the contract. Stacy wants to tie the buyers down.'

His voice became heavily sarcastic. 'You mean you'll let me into my own house?'

'On this occasion, yes. Don't muck me around, Craig. Do you want to sell at this price or not?'

'I'm on my way. I'll be there in five.'

He was there even before Stacy. Nell let him in and gestured to a seat. 'Sorry to drag you away from your friends.'

He grinned. 'Selling the house is much more important. I put a bottle of good champagne in the fridge for when I get back.'

To her relief the doorbell rang and she didn't have to sit and make conversation with him. 'Stacy, come in. You've met Craig. He's come to sign the contract to sell.'

Her agent got out the paperwork and handed them each a copy, then waited for them to check it through.

'Two weeks is cutting it fine,' Craig muttered. 'Can it be done?'

'With this client, yes,' Stacy assured him.

He went back to the contract, nodded and looked up. 'All right. I'll sign it.'

When he'd done that, Nell wrote her signature neatly beneath his scrawl and stood up. 'I'll show you out, Craig.'

He glared at her but began moving. 'We'll need to discuss the boys.'

'We can do that tomorrow over the phone.'

She returned to Stacy. 'Thank you for being so efficient. I've got a particularly nice bottle of Chardonnay in the fridge. Would you like a glass to celebrate?'

'I'm driving. Well, just half a glass, maybe. It is a good result, isn't it?'

When her agent had gone, Nell sat on till nearly midnight, sipping a second glass of wine. She couldn't stop smiling. Fate seemed to be on her side for once. She was moving, leaving this house and its unhappy memories. At last.

It suddenly occurred to her that her dream had come true, just as the voices had said. What a strange coincidence!

Then the efficient side of her kicked in and she got out a pad and started making lists. She'd need to give in her notice at work, book her plane ticket to England, start clearing out the house . . . and get the boys settled in their flat.

The pencil fell from her hand. Could she do all that in two weeks?

She most certainly could. She was famous for her efficiency. For her, the title 'Office Manager' wasn't a fancy word for secretary. She managed a staff of five, servicing the administrative needs of four legal partners and their suite of offices. They'd miss her but she wouldn't miss them.

She heard Nick arrive home at two o'clock. She was woken at three o'clock by the sound of a taxi pulling up and Steve's slurred voice talking to the driver. Clearly the need to save money hadn't stopped the boys from making a night of it and coming home in style.

She'd been feeling regretful about what she was doing

to them, but now she was even more certain that it was necessary. They had to learn to handle themselves and their money if they were to become useful members of society.

She'd save the news about the sale for the morning, however. They'd be in no state to hear it now.

Chapter Three

The next morning Nick got up first, as usual, but not till ten o'clock. Nell stood to one side of the kitchen with her arms folded, not offering to make him a cup of tea.

After a puzzled glance in her direction, he went to switch on the kettle and get out the instant coffee. 'How did the house opening go?'

'I'm not giving you any information till Steve gets up.'

'Aw, go on, Ma. Tell me now. I can see you're full of news.'

'I am, but I'm not repeating myself. I'll tell both of you at once.'

He fidgeted around for a few minutes, drained the mug of coffee, then stood up, leaving it on the table.

'Hey! You forgot something.' She pointed to the mug. For a moment she thought he was going to refuse to clear it away, then he shrugged, rinsed it and put it on the draining board ready for his next cup.

'I'll go and wake Steve or he'll stay in bed half the afternoon.'

She waited and heard shouting, then a few minutes later Steve followed his brother into the kitchen, looking like a sleepwalker. She let him take a few gulps of coffee before she said, 'Right, then. Sit down and we'll talk.'

They both joined her at the breakfast table, Nick looking wary, Steve yawning and bleary-eyed.

'I've sold the house.'

Two mouths fell open, like little birds waiting to be fed.

'Did you hear what I said?'

Steve's voice came out croaky. 'But you can't have! Dad said it'd take ages.'

'Which just shows what he knows.'

Nick's eyes were overbright and he blinked furiously. 'You really are leaving us and going to the other side of the world, then?'

'Yes. Didn't you believe me?'

'Dad said you wouldn't do it.'

'He never did understand me. At the risk of repeating myself, I need to do a few things for myself now you two are off my hands.'

Nick looked hurt. 'Well that's it, then.'

As one they stood up, both looking angry.

'Don't go yet, boys! There's more.'

They turned back.

'What else?' Steve snapped.

'We have to be out of this house in two weeks. You'd better take that flat we saw yesterday. I'll pay for the deposit and the first two weeks, starting straight away, to give you time to shift your things. Anything left here by the time I move out will be sent to the charity shop.'

Steve glared at her. 'We can't do it.'

'Why not?'

'It's . . .' He waved one hand round vaguely. 'This is our home. We've never lived anywhere else. We can't just up sticks and leave at the drop of a hat. We aren't even used to the idea yet.'

'You've no choice about leaving. I've already signed the contract and that makes it legally binding.'

Silence, then they pulled out their reserve card. 'Dad won't agree to it.'

'Your father came round last night and signed the contract to sell with me. He's very happy with the offer, believe me.'

'How much did you have to drop the price?' Steve asked.

'I got ten thousand above the asking price.'

'No way!'

'Would I lie to you about something so important?' She watched him pull out his mobile phone. 'What are you doing?'

'Calling Dad. Checking whether you can do this to us.'

He put the phone on loudspeaker mode so that his brother could listen, so she heard the conversation as well, smiling grimly as Craig's voice grew sharper and he too set his sons right about the need for them to move out.

They sat staring at her afterwards as if she was guilty of ill-treating them.

'You have to grow up and take responsibility for your own lives and money, boys,' she said gently.

'You mean we have to go and live in a hovel and be short of money?' Steve said. 'Well, thanks for nothing, Ma!'

Nick tugged his sleeve but he shook his brother's arm off and stormed out of the room.

She looked at Nick.

He shrugged and followed his brother out.

She felt guilty, but she knew she had nothing to be guilty about. This was the right thing to do.

Their reactions hurt, though. A lot.

Her phone rang and she glanced at it. Craig.

'Can you talk?' he asked. 'Or are they still there?'

'They're in their rooms, so I can talk.'

'They're taking it badly.'

'Yes.'

'Um . . . what are you going to do about them? Where are they going to live? I'm not having them living with me and Jenny.'

'No. I've noticed that. You didn't even have them to stay with you if you could help it. Well, I've found them a flat, so they can go there, but it turns out Steve has debts.'

'Well, I can't help him. All my money is tied up at the moment.'

'Oh, come off it. You're about to get half the house sale money.'

'Why can't you help them, then? You'll have the other half of it.'

'I am helping them. I've paid the first two weeks' rent and the deposit on the flat for them.'

'Well, you can help them with the debts as well, can't you, give them hints about shopping and so on?'

'I've tried. They walk out. They're in denial. I'm not doing it all, Craig. Anyway, I shan't be here. I'm going to

England in two weeks' time, leaving on the day I hand the house over.'

She hesitated, then added, 'They're going to need help, Craig, and maybe they'll take it better from you, man to man. Heaven knows I've tried, but they live like pigs, they refuse to change their sloppy habits and they've no clue about managing money.'

He was silent for a moment or two, then sighed. 'I don't know where they get it from. Neither of us was ever extravagant. I hope you'll grant me that, at least.'

'Yes, I will. You've always been good with money.'

'Very well, then. I'll keep an eye on them after you leave.'

'Thanks, Craig. I'll let you know the exact settlement date.' It was as amiable a conversation as they'd had in years.

She put down the phone and looked round the kitchen. She might as well start clearing the cupboards out. She'd make sure the boys had enough crockery and she'd put a few of her favourite possessions into storage.

She heard their voices as she passed Steve's room, not their usual loud tones but sounding low, almost conspiratorial. Then she heard the sound of the ringtone Nick favoured. That'd be Craig calling him, she guessed. Well, she hoped it was. It was more than time her ex took some responsibility for his sons' metamorphosis into adults.

The boys would learn to cope, surely? They weren't stupid, just . . . selfish and hedonistic. And young.

They might be angry now, but they'd come round after a while.

The sale of the house made her feel as if the heavy load of responsibility she'd carried for years was growing lighter and would soon be lifting off her shoulders.

Well, more or less. Did you ever stop feeling protective about your children, even after they'd grown up?

While he was working at his computer, Angus heard his phone ring and cursed under his breath. Should he ignore it? No, better not. It might be someone wanting a small job doing.

He'd put together a few simple websites for local businesses over the past couple of years, which wasn't hard to do. He didn't go out hunting for business, but he got referrals from the satisfied customers and did updates to some of their websites every now and then. It was easy work and made useful chunks of money to spin out his severance pay. The original idea for another app had developed into a suite of related apps, and was coming along nicely.

The caller was his friend Scott, so he settled down for a chat.

'Have you heard the news, Angus?'

'What news?'

'I thought you wouldn't have heard about it yet.' Scott paused for effect.

'Get on with it. I'm busy.'

'You know that huge old house in Peppercorn Street whose owner died last month? The one two houses away from that new street, what's it called, yes, Sunset Close? Well, the old lady's son has sold it to Gus Nolan. He didn't waste any time, did he? Nolan is going to knock it down and extend the over-50s housing development into another little street. Well, he will if he can get the house next to it as well once the new owner shows up.'

'And I should be interested in this why?'

'Aren't you even vaguely concerned about what's going on along your street, Angus my lad?'

'Not really. I don't feel as if I live on the street.'

'Your address is number 1 Peppercorn Street and you walk or drive down it into town regularly. I despair of you sometimes, Angus. You're becoming a damned hermit. You need to get out and meet people. And talking of meeting people, my main purpose in calling was to check that we'll be seeing you in the pub tonight.'

Angus glanced at his computer, sighed and said, 'I can't come this week. I've got too much on.'

'Either you turn up at the pub or Tom and I will come over to Dennings and drag you to the Red Lion. Don't think this is an idle threat. Our wives only allow us off the leash one night a week and we can't party without you.'

'Party! How long is it since any of us have done that?'

'A good many years. That's what having children does to you. Stops the wildness.'

Angus smiled. 'You were never wild, even in your youth, Scott.'

'Listen who's talking. You were the first to get married. You'd no sooner met Joanna than you were engaged.'

'I knew a good woman when I found one. Only took me two days to fall in love with her.'

'Well, maybe having a quiet drink with the lads is all the partying us men in our fifties are capable of.'

'We're not fifty yet.'

'We're nearly there.'

Angus didn't like to dwell on how old he was getting. 'I've got a lot of work on and—'

Scott's voice softened. 'You'll regret missing the weekly get-together if you don't come tonight, my lad, you know you will. All work and no play . . .'

'Oh, all right. I suppose someone needs to keep you two in order.'

After he'd put the phone down, Angus ran his hand through his hair and frowned at his reflection in the mirror across the room. He needed a haircut. Badly.

He kept meaning to move that damned mirror, which made him look pale and ill, only it'd probably pull some plaster out of the wall if he took it down. The thing must have been up there for a couple of centuries and he wasn't game to disturb it without expert help.

He glanced at his reflection again. It still shocked him sometimes not to see dark hair topping his face. It shouldn't have done. He'd gone completely grey by the time he was forty and now his hair was pure silver at the front. At least he still had hair. His father and grandfather had gone bald by this age, so he was doing better than them.

The silver hair had diminished his confidence where women were concerned. It shouldn't have done, but it had. Or maybe he'd never had much confidence. He and Joanna had married young, so he'd never played the field.

Since he'd lost his wife, he'd dated a few times, but he'd not met anyone who attracted him and he certainly didn't go round looking for another woman.

After a year had passed since Joanna's death, Scott and Tom's wives had started introducing him to eligible women, one after another – eligible in their eyes, not his. The only thing he'd had in common with them so far had been age.

They'd all been in their forties, most of them divorced and angry about it.

The wives seemed to have run out of single females now, thank goodness, but he'd bet Dawn had nudged her husband into suggesting online dating the other week. Tom would never have suggested that off his own bat.

Well, Angus drew the line at putting himself up for sale online.

Oh, hell, where was all this introspection coming from? He turned away from the mirror, did a few stretching exercises and ran up and down on the spot. He didn't want to damage his body by sitting in one position in front of his computer all day, so he was careful to take regular exercise breaks.

He walked round the ground floor of the house for good measure, trying not to notice how shabby it was looking: faded wallpaper, dusty old furniture and sagging, threadbare curtains. He wished he had the money to do it up a bit, but he'd never earn enough to bring it back to its glory days, however hard he worked.

He sat down at his computer again. He couldn't afford to waste time. His voluntary severance money wouldn't last for ever and he wasn't getting any younger.

But he really did believe he was on to something with the new software programs he was writing. Maybe he could hit the big time with this suite – well, bigger time than his first app, anyway.

And it was interesting to try. It was Scott's mother who'd given him the idea. There weren't a lot of apps catering for this market.

* * *

At teatime Angus strolled down Peppercorn Street towards the town centre to join his friends at the Red Lion pub. As he passed the old houses Scott had mentioned, he slowed down to study them. Edwardian, probably. The first one he came to looked tired and sad, well past its use-by date. The other two were nearly as bad.

He moved on a few metres to the small group of new-build houses. They were nearly finished and he paused again to study them. The tiny cul-de-sac was called Sunset Close. What a ghastly ageist name! If he ever chose to live in over-50s housing, he'd be leading a campaign for a street name that didn't signal old and on the way out.

The houses looked too small for comfort, huddled together in three tight little groups of three, with narrow strips of garden in front. What were they building here? A twenty-first century ghetto? A future slum? Prison cells for oldies? They didn't look like desirable residences to him.

He carried on to the pub, pausing for a moment in the doorway, his spirits lifted by its bright, cheerful atmosphere and happy buzz of voices. Suddenly he was glad Scott had insisted on him coming tonight, as he had been on a few occasions before. His family home got too damned quiet sometimes. Perhaps he should sell it. He'd had offers.

No, he shouldn't. The Denning family had held on to that house for over two hundred years. The cousin on his mother's side who'd left it to him had stipulated in the will that he should keep it in the family, if at all possible.

He hadn't needed that instruction. He loved the old place, had done since he first visited it as a lad.

* * *

The two weeks till settlement flew by. Nell stopped work immediately, only able to do that because she'd already trained her successor. They still didn't like it, but too bad.

There was a lot to clear out and give to her sons or sell before she could leave for England. To her amazement, Craig came round and helped a couple of times, chivvying their sons into working more quickly and paying for the removal of their furniture and other belongings.

He stood at the door as he said goodbye to her – or was it to the house? She could have sworn there was a look of sadness on his face. But only for a moment.

'Have a good time in England,' he said. 'And, um, I wish you well.'

'Yes. Thanks. You too.' She moved inside, grateful for his help, feeling better about leaving the boys now he was going to keep an eye on them.

But she hadn't changed her mind about having nothing more to do with him and she'd refused to give him her address in England, or even the number of her new mobile phone.

Suddenly, it seemed, the last paper had been signed, the money deposited in the bank and the house handed over to its new owners.

The finality of it all took Nell's breath away. She felt exhausted, and no wonder.

She spent the last night with Robbie and Linda, and the others came round to share a final meal.

In the early morning Robbie drove her to the airport. 'Well done for getting those two out, Ma.'

'Your brothers?'

'Yes. Linda and I were discussing it and we think they needed shock treatment to wake them up to reality.'

'Yes. Let's hope it works. And at last I'm totally disconnected from your father.'

'You've never forgiven him, have you?'

'No.' She made a dismissive gesture with one hand. 'Let's not spoil this by talking about him. I don't know why I even mentioned him.'

'What do you want to talk about?'

'You and Linda. You're still not helping her enough in the house, though you're way ahead of your brothers.'

He didn't answer but she noticed him wriggle uncomfortably.

'A pregnant woman gets tired more easily. She needs extra help, Robbie love.'

'I've tried, Ma, but she always complains about how badly I've done things. It's got to be done her way or not at all.'

'Cut her a little slack. Just persevere and try to do things the way she wants. After all, you're not the world's best housekeeper, are you? And being pregnant isn't fun.'

'Having a pregnant wife isn't much fun, either.'

'I know. But the result makes it worth it. I've always been glad my marriage gave me you three.'

He patted her hand briefly then turned his attention back to the busy traffic.

When she stole a glance sideways, she thought he looked thoughtful. Maybe her advice would sink in.

At the airport she said, 'Don't come and see me off. Just drop me near the departure area.'

'Are you sure? I can easily park and—'

'I'll only cry and I don't want to go on board with red eyes.'

'You can sound really fierce but you're a softie underneath it.'

'Sometimes. Not always.'

'No. At the moment you're being very tough and brave. I admire that, Ma.'

He stopped the car, helped her get her luggage out and on to a trolley, then gave her a bone-cracking hug and got back in.

It warmed her heart. He didn't often hug her now he was grown up. The other two had hugged her yesterday as well, when they moved the final bits of crockery and other items she'd given them out of the house and into their flat.

As she watched Robbie drive away, tears welled in her eyes. She hadn't realised how alone she'd feel or how nervous. This was going to be a shock to her system as well as to her sons. Taking a couple of deep breaths, she walked briskly into the airport.

She hadn't told anyone that she'd booked a business class seat, thanks to her aunt's money. Just this once. That entitled her to take extra luggage, as well as promising a far more comfortable flight. It had surprised her that Robbie hadn't commented on how much luggage she had.

It was a rather special occasion, in so many ways. The first day of her new untrammelled life.

At Heathrow Nell retrieved her luggage then followed the signs towards the exit. In spite of the excellent service and comfortable lie-down seat, the flight had seemed to go on for ever. She wasn't used to being penned up inside a tin box for most of a day.

Most of the other passengers were met by friends and family, and kept hugging one another, beaming with joy, some crying happy tears. That made her feel even more alone.

She found her way to the counter of her hire car company. After she'd finished the preliminary paperwork she was directed to a small courtesy bus, which chugged slowly and with frequent stops through acres of car parks to where the hire vehicles were parked.

England in the middle of April was cool and felt alien after her decades in Australia. Grey seemed to be the predominant colour, even though it was officially spring here now. Rain spattered suddenly against the windows of the bus and Nell shivered, wishing she'd put on warmer clothes.

She didn't actually own many warm clothes and was planning to buy more here. West Australian winters were like cool, rainy English springs, and anyway, Nell went everywhere by car in Australia, so hadn't needed a really warm coat.

At last they arrived but even though the paperwork was got through quickly, it took a while for someone to bring her hire car to reception. A polite young man helped carry her luggage out to the car. He showed her how to use the satnav and checked that she understood the controls, then stood back.

'There you are, then, ma'am. Enjoy your holiday.' And he was gone.

She checked the satnav again, putting in the town of Sexton Bassett and then Peppercorn Street. The screen rippled and a map came up with arrows. The voice giving instructions sounded very upper-class English to her Aussie-tuned ears, so she christened the speaker 'Felicity' after her aunt, who had also spoken like that.

You can do it, Nell told herself but she felt nervous as she put the car into drive and set off on her first journey across England, because she hadn't driven a manual change car for many years. But the automatic cars were much more expensive and it had seemed a waste of money.

Vehicles seemed to whiz along more quickly here, but she prided herself on being a competent driver, so eased into the traffic and concentrated hard, following the clear instructions 'Felicity' gave her about where to go.

Almost before she knew it, she was on the M4 heading west. She breathed a sigh of relief and settled down to drive to Wiltshire.

After a few miles the traffic in all three lanes slowed down to a crawl and it was twenty minutes before it speeded up again. By that time she judged it wise to turn off at a services and visit the Ladies before she continued.

While she was there, she bought a few bits and pieces to eat, just in case there were further delays and she couldn't find a shop that was open. Then she launched herself into the traffic again, feeling a little more confident now.

It seemed like an anticlimax when there were no more hold-ups. The miles ticked by and she saw a sign to Swindon, which she knew was a big town near Sexton Bassett. But Felicity hadn't told her to turn off the motorway so she carried on, praying she was doing the right thing.

'Take the next exit,' the voice commanded gently a few minutes later at a second Swindon turn-off. So she did and was then directed to Sexton Bassett.

She slowed down as she got to the main street of the small town, expecting to remember it from her childhood visits, but she didn't. It had changed beyond recognition and there were shops all along it with garish signs. Even the library wasn't the library any more, it seemed, but part of a heritage centre.

It wasn't until she turned into Peppercorn Street that things began to look vaguely familiar. To her surprise, the house the satnav directed her to on the long uphill street was the same one she'd visited as a child.

She hadn't remembered the house number from her childhood and had just accepted the one the lawyer gave her, assuming Fliss had moved into a smaller house on the same street, as she'd talked of doing. But when Nell stopped at number 95, it was the house she remembered. So her great-aunt hadn't moved at all. Well, why shouldn't Fliss stay in her own home if it had good memories for her?

Things had changed near the house, though. There was a new cul-de-sac a little further down the same side of the street called Sunset Close. Tiny new one-storey dwellings huddled together in three clusters.

The two houses between these and Fliss's looked unoccupied, as did the house on the uphill side of her new home. Beyond that were two large dwellings, which looked new and were ultramodern in style.

She stopped to shove open the double gates, which were old, wooden and very stiff. There was no carport or garage, just a paved space to one side for a vehicle to stand on, so she drove the car into it and closed the gates again.

The keys the lawyers had sent her were clearly labelled, one saying 'Front door' in tiny script, the other 'Back door'.

As the new owner, she decided to go in by the front door, so followed the paved path to the front of the house. The outside paintwork was shabby and peeling in parts. She inserted the key, surprised when the door opened easily, because it looked old-fashioned and it hadn't been used for a while, so she'd expected it to be stiff.

It was dusk now and the hall was dim. She fumbled for the light switch and let out a long exhalation of relief as the hall light came on. Thank goodness! She'd asked the lawyers to arrange for the electricity to be connected but no one had confirmed that it had been.

If it hadn't been on, she'd have had to find somewhere to stay for the night. She wasn't into roughing it without any amenities.

At last she truly recognised something from her childhood: the interior of the house. Indeed, at first glance it didn't seem to have changed a bit since her family had emigrated. Nearly four decades that was now.

She remembered the stained glass window in the wall halfway up the stairs, the mahogany banisters and the pattern of old-fashioned tiles on the hall floor.

She almost expected to see Fliss coming out of the living room to greet her and felt sad as she remembered her great-aunt. Her father had cut off communications with everyone in the family, but Nell had tentatively contacted Fliss years ago and they'd been emailing each other ever since. Fliss had, it seemed, been taught by a young neighbour how to use the Internet.

Not quite in my dotage, eh? she had said in her first email. This is a lot easier than posting a letter, isn't it?

Propping open the front door, Nell lugged in her two

suitcases, the backpack she'd used for cabin luggage and the two plastic carrier bags of food she'd bought on the motorway.

Locking the car, she went back into the house, her footsteps echoing on the Victorian tiles of the hall floor. She shivered. The inside felt damp and distinctly chilly, and there was a faint, musty smell. Well, more than faint, actually. Rather unpleasant. She'd have to air the house out thoroughly to get rid of that.

She checked the rooms on the ground floor, leaving lights on here and there to make the place feel more cheerful. A very old computer stood on a pad on the dining-room table. She wondered if it still worked.

Last of all she went into the kitchen at the rear, which had always been her favourite room, warm and full of delightful smells of cakes baking.

Here things had changed drastically and the image she'd carried in her heart of a cosy, old-fashioned kitchen was gone. There were new appliances and new cupboards along one wall, but the kitchen as a whole hadn't been modernised.

It looked bare and unloved. No plants on the window sill now, no bunches of dried herbs hanging on a line. Fliss had been a great one for drying her own herbs.

However when Nell looked more closely there were signs of live occupants: mouse droppings on the counters and floor, and shredded paper in one corner. Ugh! She'd have to get someone in to rid the house of them ASAP. She hated the horrid creatures.

She plugged in the fridge, which was fairly new, and put the perishable food inside. It might be dusty on the outside but it was clean inside and no mice would be able to get into it.

She lugged one of the suitcases upstairs and checked out the bedrooms. She'd asked the lawyers to leave things as they were inside the house, except for clearing out perishables.

There were six bedrooms. Fliss's old room was as her great-aunt had left it, with clothes still hanging in the wardrobe and filling the drawers. She didn't fancy sleeping in there.

After checking out the other bedrooms, she decided to use the one her parents had always slept in on visits. Like her aunt's room, it was at the front of the house. Another point in its favour was that it had a bolt on the inside of the door. She wasn't paranoid about intruders, but she was careful and in strange territory, so it'd be good to lock the bedroom door.

Her childhood bedroom was up on the top floor and, if she remembered correctly, had been rather small. She was feeling tired so didn't go up to check it.

It pleased her how much she remembered about the house. It made it seem like a home, rather than just a house, even if it did need a lot of attention.

She didn't know how long she'd stay away from Australia, probably not permanently. But even if she sold this house eventually, she could make a big difference to the price she got by doing it up. It certainly needed attention. Fliss had let things slip badly.

There! She'd found herself something to do with her new life already. She quite enjoyed decorating but had always had to do it on the cheap before. Now she had enough money to indulge in any reasonable whim that took her fancy.

A sudden yawn made her realise how tired she was, so she decided to have a quick snack then go to bed.

'Jet lag rules,' she muttered as a second yawn followed the first. It wasn't bedtime yet, still only early evening, but she could hardly keep her eyes open.

Chapter Four

Winifred Parfitt walked slowly up Peppercorn Street after taking tea with a young friend near the bottom end of the street. She'd never had grandchildren, but if she had, she'd have wanted a granddaughter like Janey Dobson, who at eighteen was coping with being a single mother to a delightful baby, as well as going to college. And yet the dear girl still made time to befriend an old lady.

Winifred and her friend Dan were acting as unofficial older relatives to Janey, whose family had disowned her when she got pregnant. Her father in particular had first not believed her when she said his friend had raped her. Then he'd said she must have led him on. That friend, an ex-policeman, had later been found guilty of raping the poor girl.

Strange that from such a terrible act could come that wonderful baby.

Lights were shining from what had been Felicity Chaytor's house. Winifred stopped in surprise, leaning on her father's silver-headed walking stick for a moment to catch her breath, as she often did part way up the hill.

Her long-time neighbour Fliss had died a few months ago and rumour had it that she'd left everything to an Australian niece, though where the rumours came from, Winifred couldn't think. She'd heard them from her friend Dawn, whose daughter had told her.

Perhaps the lights meant that Fliss's heir had arrived at last, and about time too. The house had been standing empty for too long and was in desperate need of maintenance work if anyone was to live there.

Everything was changing in the street and even Winifred was wondering whether she should change her mind, sell her overlarge house and move somewhere smaller. But the bungalows that she'd just passed, advertised as suitable retirement homes for over 50s, were too small and too close together for her taste. She didn't want to live in her neighbours' pockets.

Why did people assume that just because you were old, you'd want such cramped accommodation? What most older people wanted was to stay in their own homes and have help with the cleaning and gardening. She sighed and forced her stiff limbs to move on.

Suddenly, something hit her from behind and she cried out as she started to fall. A young man in a hoodie loomed over her and bent to yank her handbag off her arm before taking off running.

As a second person pounded towards her, she let out an involuntary cry of panic and huddled closer to the wall. What now? Were they going to beat her up?

But this man ran straight past her and tackled the

mugger, who had tripped on the uneven pavement and lost his momentum. The pursuer brought him down in a flurry of fists, kicking feet and yelling.

The hood came off and in the light from a street lamp she saw a brutal young face with a shaven head. The young man rolled suddenly to one side and was up and away before the second man could stop him.

Her rescuer got up and walked back to Winifred, who had pulled herself painfully to her feet. 'Are you all right, Miss Parfitt?'

She recognised him at once: Angus Denning from the big old house behind hers. She wanted to thank him, but couldn't string the words together. She had to clutch the wall because she wasn't all right; she was feeling extremely dizzy.

Before he could say anything else, more footsteps made them both turn round. This time it was a woman hurrying out of the gate of Fliss's house.

'I saw what happened from my bedroom window. Are you all right?'

Winifred had always scorned women who fainted in a crisis, but when she felt the world turning black around her, she could do nothing about it.

Nell saw the old lady's eyes roll up and her body start to crumple. She managed to grab her before she hit the ground and the rescuer moved quickly to help.

'Let me take her.' He picked up the poor woman quite easily.

Nell gestured to the house. 'Take her into my place. We can't see how badly she's hurt in this light.'

'Thanks. If you'll bring her handbag and stick, I'll carry her. She's so thin, she doesn't weigh much.'

Nell led the way inside, locking the door behind them, then taking them through to the kitchen at the rear. 'Who is she? Do you know her?'

'Yes. Miss Winifred Parfitt. She lives at number 5, one of the grand old houses at the very top of the street.'

'Put her into this armchair.'

As he did that, the old lady moaned and he asked, 'Do you have any brandy?'

'I don't know. I only arrived here an hour or so ago and I haven't explored the cupboards yet. Anyway, I don't think they recommend brandy for shock nowadays. A cup of sweet tea, perhaps?'

'Good idea. Is that an Australian accent?'

'Yes. Is it so obvious? In Australia, they think I sound like a Pom.'

'I've worked with Aussies several times. I'm Angus Denning, by the way.'

'Nell Chaytor.'

The old lady moaned again, opening her eyes and looking round as if she didn't know where she was. She tried to brush away the wisps of silver hair that had come loose from the bun at the back, but gave up the attempt.

Angus crouched beside her and took her hand. 'You were mugged, Miss Parfitt. When you fainted, we brought you into Ms Chaytor's house. How are you feeling?'

'Dizzy. So silly to faint.'

As she struggled to sit up properly, Nell helped her. 'It's the shock. It's perfectly normal to have a reaction like that if you're attacked.'

'He took my handbag.'

'No, he didn't. I couldn't manage to keep hold of him but I did get your handbag back. Here,' Angus held it out, but when Miss Parfitt tried to take it, her hand was shaking so badly, she drew back.

'Did he get my purse?'

'Shall I look in the bag?' Nell asked.

'Please.'

She opened it and found a shabby leather purse. 'Is this it?'

'Yes. Thank goodness!' Miss Parfitt looked back at the man, her eyes focusing properly now. 'I didn't know you were a hero, Angus.'

He grinned. 'Neither did I. You're getting a bit of colour back, Miss Parfitt, but I think we should take you to the hospital and get you checked by a doctor.'

'Certainly not. Once they get old people into those places, they never let them out again. I'll be perfectly all right in a minute or two, especially if you'd kindly make me a cup of tea, dear. There's nothing like tea to buck you up.'

'Of course. I'll put the kettle on.' Nell was relieved to hear the old lady's voice sounding less quavery.

'I would appreciate you escorting me home afterwards, though, Angus, if you don't mind.'

'I'll be happy to.'

Winifred turned to her hostess. 'Are you a relative of Fliss's?'

'Yes. I'm Nell Chaytor. She was my father's aunt. I used to stay with her when I was a child. She kindly left me her house.'

'I remember a little girl coming here for the summer

holidays two or three times. That must have been you.'
She looked round the dusty kitchen. 'This house used to
be beautiful, but even the new part of the kitchen looks
unloved. Felicity was rather frail towards the end and
didn't keep up with things, I'm afraid.'

'Didn't any of her other relatives help her? I know there
used to be some cousins. Mona? Would that be the name
of one?'

'Yes, but Fliss quarrelled with Mona and her husband
because they kept trying to persuade her to go into a care
home and wouldn't stop nagging about it. I don't blame
Fliss. One clings to one's own home, even when it gets too
much to manage. I'm in much the same boat myself.'

She looked round again. 'Oh, good! They didn't take
my walking stick. I'm so glad. It belonged to my father and
it's just the right size for me. I'm very fond of it.' She began
to tidy her hair, this time succeeding in setting it to rights.

Nell investigated the cupboards and set out three delicate
china cups and a teapot, because there weren't any mugs.
'If care homes are like the ones in Australia, I don't blame
Fliss for refusing to go into one. I'd not like to lose all my
possessions and be shut up in a small room surrounded by
strangers.'

'Nor would I. Fliss was really happy when you got
back in touch with her. She said your father had sworn
to have nothing to do with anyone in his family after the
big quarrel. I thought she said you were married, though.
Didn't you take your husband's surname? I know some
women don't these days.'

'I did at first but then I got divorced so I reverted to my
maiden name.'

68

'Well, if you didn't love him any more, why should you keep his name?'

Nell wanted to ask about the big quarrel, but this didn't seem the right time. She made a mental note to call on Miss Parfitt another time and ask what had caused it.

The old lady seemed more alert now, too alert if she could ask questions about Nell's marriage, something Nell didn't want to discuss with strangers. She contented herself with a brief answer: 'I hated my husband in the end. Good riddance as far as I was concerned. Sugar and milk?'

'Milk but no sugar, thank you.'

'It's supposed to be good for shock to have something sweet.'

'I'm getting over the shock now and I detest tea with sugar in it. But I would love a warm drink. Ah, thank you.' She took a sip then set the teacup back on its saucer and clasped her hands round it.

'What were you doing out so late, Miss Parfitt?' Angus asked.

'I'd been having tea with my young friend who lives in a flat near the lower end of the street and we got talking. Janey's baby is growing so fast. Millie's six months old already. I can't remember when I enjoyed an evening so much. We didn't realise how late it was. Janey wanted to walk back with me but that would have meant taking Millie out of her cot.'

She sighed. 'I've always felt safe on Peppercorn Street before.'

'I don't think anywhere's safe after dark these days,' he said.

When she'd drunk the rest of the tea in delicate, bird-like

sips, Winifred looked from Nell to Angus. 'I'd like to go home now, if you don't mind. There's nowhere as comforting as your own home in times of trouble, is there?'

As she got to her feet, Angus passed her the stick and handbag. She smiled at him and reached up to touch his face gently. 'I'm afraid you're going to have a black eye, dear boy. Thank you for helping me.'

'I hope that young sod has one as well! I got in a few telling punches.'

'Good for you.'

'I'll come with you so that I'll know where you live, Miss Parfitt,' Nell said. 'I'll pop in tomorrow, if you don't mind, to check that you're all right.'

'Very kind of you. I suppose someone had better do it in case I die in my sleep. I'm getting a bit old for shocks like that.'

Angus offered Winifred his arm and she took it. He let her set the pace and the three of them walked slowly up the quiet street to the top of the hill. Her house was only a couple of hundred yards away and they took her right to the front door.

She insisted she'd be all right from then on because she had good locks and bolts on the insides of all the outer doors, but Angus waited to see the lights go on in the house, then the hall light go off again.

When they came out of the garden on to the street, he turned to Nell. 'I think I'd better escort you back home as well in case that damned mugger is still around. I'll report the incident to the police in the morning, though I doubt they'll be able to do anything. But they ought to know about it, at least.'

'Do you get a lot of muggings round here?'

'It's the first I've heard of. This is quite a peaceful little town, usually. I don't think they'll catch the mugger because they won't have any idea where to start looking. I didn't see his face clearly as I was struggling with him, so I doubt even I could recognise him again, except that he had a shaved head.'

'Miss Parfitt might have seen him more clearly.'

'And he might come after her if she identified him. I'd rather not encourage that with her living on her own. I keep a bit of an eye on her, but obviously I need to do something about her security.'

He gave Nell a rueful smile. 'What a dreadful welcome to Wiltshire for you.'

'Never mind me. I'll be fine. I'm just glad we were able to help her. She reminded me of my Aunt Fliss.'

'They were acquaintances, but I'd not say they were close friends. Towards the end, your aunt kept herself to herself, though I did help her set up a computer a few years ago, and found her a student to help her learn to use it. It was very interesting watching her come to grips with a new range of skills.'

After a few more paces, he added, thoughtfully, 'I think Miss Parfitt is in better health than your aunt was during the past year or two, even though she must be in her mid eighties now. She's a feisty old lady.'

'Goodness! She doesn't look that old. Do you live near here?'

'At number 1.'

'Oh, then I'll probably see you around. Here we are.'

'Will you be all right?'

'Yes. I'm not the fearful sort and I've been on my own for long enough not to jump at every shadow. Besides, there's a bolt on the inside of my bedroom door. I may put another bolt on it as well if I stay in that room.'

'So you're a handywoman as well as independent.'

'I've had to be. Small jobs, anyway. I didn't have a man to do such things for me even when I was with Craig. He didn't like to get his hands dirty.'

She held out her hand. 'Good night, Mr Denning.'

He took it, holding it in both his for a moment. 'Thank you for coming out to help Miss Parfitt.'

'I was happy to.'

As he strolled home, keeping a careful eye out for anyone lurking nearby, Angus became angry all over again at the cowardly attack on an old lady. The irony was, the mugger would have been disappointed even if he had got away with the handbag because although Miss Parfitt had inherited a friend's house and possessions recently, there hadn't been time for probate to go through. He knew what a struggle she'd had to make ends meet, so he'd bet she hadn't been carrying a lot of money.

His thoughts turned back to Nell Chaytor and he smiled. She was very Australian, frank and open about her circumstances, and in the light from her hall, he'd seen that she was still sporting a golden suntan. She was about his age, he'd guess, but to his relief she'd made no attempt to flirt with him or find out whether he had a wife. That always put him off a woman.

Indeed, from the expression on her face when Miss Parfitt asked if she was married, she wasn't enamoured of the institution, so he doubted she'd be hunting for another husband.

He particularly liked the way she hadn't hesitated to help the old lady. She'd make a good neighbour. Well, she wouldn't exactly be a neighbour of his because, although technically he lived on Peppercorn Street, his house and land were half-hidden behind the top few houses.

He didn't know many people at the upper end of the street these days, because several of the houses had changed hands in the past few years, some being knocked down and replaced by modern monstrosities. Anyway, he was too busy to do much socialising.

But Miss Parfitt was a friend of his family from way back and he felt guilty that he hadn't kept a closer eye on her. He'd do so from now on.

When he let himself into Dennings he checked the security system and looked at it thoughtfully. She'd had a security system fitted in her house, but he knew of a gadget she could carry with her that screamed for help. Maybe he could find one for Miss Parfitt and persuade her to use it?

He stopped dead as that gave him an idea, then popped into his office, noted it down and answered a couple of urgent emails.

He didn't linger to work on into the night, as sometimes happened. In spite of tonight's incident, he felt relaxed and tired after eating a delicious lamb shank with all the trimmings, followed by apple pie and ice cream at the pub. The evenings with his friends were always pleasant.

He went into his bedroom, converted from one of the ground-floor reception rooms for convenience, yawning as he took off his jacket. When he looked in the mirror he grimaced. Miss Parfitt was right: he was definitely going to have a black eye, and a big one too. He also found a couple of large bruises on his body as he got ready for bed.

After switching on the security system to cover the rest of the house, he lay down, expecting to fall straight asleep. But it took a while.

He couldn't get the mugging out of his mind, or his pleasant new neighbour. She was an attractive woman for her age, very natural-looking. He'd never been attracted to glossy, stylish females. Horrible to kiss a cheek covered in what he thought of as gunk.

He turned over and eventually felt sleep beginning to take over his body. What a strange end to his evening out with the lads!

Chapter Five

When Nell woke it was fully light. She glanced at her wristwatch, amazed to find she'd slept for a solid ten hours. She smiled when she realised she hadn't even bothered to take off her clothes the previous night, had just flung herself on the bed 'for a moment or two'.

Humming, she showered by standing in an ancient bathtub in a huge bathroom with old-fashioned fittings. The green shower curtain clung to her body and she almost had to fight her way out of it.

Feeling comfortable in clean jeans and a casual top, she went down to the kitchen and put the kettle on. She stood stock-still with a piece of warm toast in her hand as it occurred to her that she hadn't worried at all about the possibility of intruders after she got back last night. Strange, that.

She'd taken self-defence classes as part of her recovery from Craig. It would have been hard to defend herself against him, though, whatever she'd learnt, because he was so much bigger than her. But at least the classes had made her feel pretty sure she could give a good account of herself if she was attacked in the street.

She buttered the toast and ate it quickly, finishing with a nice crisp apple.

Now, decision time. Should she go and see Miss Parfitt first or should she go shopping?

She decided to check on her elderly neighbour first and at the same time ask her advice about where to do the shopping.

After that she had to get the telephone here connected again so that she could get online. She'd check the old computer, but even if it still worked, it was so out of date compared to modern technology, she doubted it'd be much use. Anyway, she'd brought her laptop.

There were all sorts of things that needed doing.

She wrinkled her nose in disgust at the sight of fresh mouse droppings in the empty pantry. She'd have to get some mousetraps. And that smell was still hanging around, though she'd opened her bedroom windows, as well as the front and back doors.

It was ten o'clock before she was ready to go out. Before she left, she walked round the house to study it – her house now. It didn't feel at all like home after such a short time.

It was very shabby and there were a couple of tiles missing from the roof at the back, while others looked slightly misplaced. Storm damage, perhaps? She'd better go up to the attic later and check that the roof hadn't been leaking. Perhaps dampness might be causing the smell.

The nearby houses on the upper side of the street were all well maintained, but the two houses between hers and the retirement development downhill looked ready to blow down in the first puff of wind. There was a big sign saying 'New Houses for Sale, Over 50s'. More like horseboxes, she thought scornfully.

Peppercorn Street was quite long, and though it hadn't occurred to her as a child, she realised now that this was the posh end. So in spite of its condition her house would probably be worth good money if only for block value, should she choose to sell it. She peered down to the left, but beyond Sunset Close, the street curved round slightly so she couldn't see the next stretch clearly.

There were no pedestrians around. It was the same in Australian suburbs during the daytime. The families were probably all at work or school.

She strolled up the slope, found number 5 and rang the doorbell.

She heard footsteps inside almost immediately, and when Miss Parfitt opened the door, she smiled to see the old lady looking neat and tidy again. More than that, distinctly elegant, even if her clothes were old-fashioned.

'You can't be too bad today if you can answer the door so quickly, Miss Parfitt. But shouldn't you take more care who is outside?' Nell was going to miss the Australian security mesh doors; she hadn't seen one 'guarding' the front door of any houses she'd passed.

'I have a peephole,' Miss Parfitt pointed to it. 'Ironically, my nephew fitted it when he was trying to cheat me out of this house. He was protecting the house, not me, but when I forbade him to come here any longer, he couldn't take the peephole with him, could he? I do find it useful, I must admit.'

She stepped back. 'I'm chattering on again. Blame it on living alone. Do come in, Nell. Can I offer you a cup of tea?'

'Another time I'd love it. Today I wanted to check that you were all right, which I can see for myself, and also ask your advice about shopping. Is there a big shopping centre somewhere with easy parking? I have a lot to buy.'

'There's one on the outskirts of town.' She gave Nell an assessing look. 'I wonder . . . No, not today. You must be very busy settling in.'

'What were you going to ask?'

'Would it be possible for me to come with you to the shops? I find it hard to carry the heavy items back, even with my shopping bag on wheels. My friend's daughter takes us sometimes but one doesn't like to impose on the same person all the time. Don't worry if it's inconvenient today. I always keep good stocks, so I'm not desperate for anything.'

'I'd be happy to take you with me sometimes and especially this morning because you can show me the way. You and Angus are the only people I know in England.'

'Well, he won't be much use to you socially, I'm afraid. Since his wife was killed, he's turned into a near recluse, though I do see him going out sometimes on Friday evenings. I think he meets some friends at the pub.' She frowned. 'Aren't there any other Chaytors left?'

'Fliss always said there were some in Wiltshire, but she didn't have much to do with them, except for one great-niece, who kept an eye on her. I wonder why Fliss didn't leave her anything?'

'Who can tell? Old people can get . . . stubborn. Besides,

you kept in touch with her as well. Her choice, my dear, her choice.'

'My father wouldn't even talk about his family. I must see if I can find them sometime. But they might be resentful at me being left the house.'

'They might or might not. It'd be worth giving them a try, don't you think?'

'Sure, but it's not a priority at the moment and the shopping is. I'll come back for you with the car in about ten minutes, if that's all right?'

'That'd be fine. Thank you, dear. It'll be such a big help.'

Miss Parfitt directed her to the shopping centre, offered advice on which brands to buy and why, and explained a few things about shopping in the UK that were not immediately obvious to Nell.

In her turn, the old lady listened with alert interest when Nell mentioned the differences in Australian superstores.

As the shopping went on for a couple of hours, Nell kept an eye on Miss Parfitt and when her companion started looking tired, took her to a café and bought them a pot of tea and some scones. She noticed a nasty bruise on Miss Parfitt's hand, presumably where she'd tried to keep hold of her handbag, but didn't comment on it.

'I must admit I was ready for a rest, dear. I'm not usually so feeble, I promise you.'

Nell smiled. 'You don't usually get mugged, either. Will you be all right to sit here on your own for a while? There are just a few other things I want.'

'Of course I will.'

Nell continued shopping, buying a few expensive treats

that she wouldn't have to guard from her permanently hungry sons. Most food was much cheaper here, though meat was more expensive. To her surprise there were more varieties of fruit available, whether they were 'in season' or not.

She had to ask for help, because they weren't prominently displayed, but eventually managed to find some mousetraps. She hated dealing with vermin, but she couldn't let them run riot in her kitchen.

When she got back to Peppercorn Street, she carried Miss Parfitt's things into number 5: bottles of bleach, lemonade, wine, heavy jars and tins of food. She again refused an offer of refreshments, but did accept half of a home-made cake before she went home.

Home?

She got out of the car and stared at the old house. No, this wasn't home to her and for some reason, now that she'd had a good look at it in daylight, she didn't think it ever would be. It was such a tired old house, sagging here and there.

'Hi, Nell. Did you go and check on Miss Parfitt?'

She swung round and saw Angus standing at the entrance to her drive. 'Yes. She's fine, just a couple of grazes on her legs and a big bruise on one hand. We went shopping together. Not having a car, she has trouble carrying heavy things back.'

He looked guilty. 'I should have thought of that and offered to take her occasionally. Kind of you to do it.'

'I enjoyed her company, and anyway, I learnt a lot from her about shopping in England.'

He started to turn away. 'I'll leave you to it, then.'

'Just a minute. You mentioned something about working in the IT industry. I wonder if you can give me some advice about getting online. I'm already missing my access to the world. Which Internet service provider would you recommend?'

He turned back with obvious reluctance. 'I'll contact a friend, then come round and set you up, if you like. Otherwise you'll have to wait a few days for them to do it.'

She drew herself up. 'I wasn't trying to get you to do it. I wouldn't be so cheeky as to ask. I just need the name of a reliable ISP. I'm perfectly capable of—'

He held up one hand. 'Sorry. I must have sounded grudging. It's not much trouble, really it isn't. Maybe one day you can cook me a meal in return. I can cook adequately but only quick, easy stuff.'

'Do you mean that or are you just being polite?'

He looked at her in surprise, then grinned. 'I'd forgotten how blunt you Aussies can be sometimes. I really do mean it. Think how virtuous I shall feel about helping one of our colonial cousins.'

'Am I a colonial?' She stared blindly at the garden. 'I don't actually know where I belong at the moment. I was born here and was old enough when we emigrated to remember England clearly . . . and to remember Fliss. I've only been back once before and that was on a whistle-stop tour round Europe with my husband. I didn't get a chance to revisit my past and look round the country where I was born.'

She sighed. 'Not long after our third son was born, I became a sole parent, to all intents and purposes. Craig was not into the practical aspects of fatherhood. Goodness, it must be twenty-two years since I've been free of the main responsibility for my children.'

'It must have been traumatic leaving your sons.'

She chuckled. 'More for them than for me. I had to chuck them out of home or they'd have stayed on for ever. I'm very excited about my freedom, actually. Do you have children? Miss Parfitt said you'd lost your wife. I was sorry to hear that.'

'Yes. Joanna was killed in a road accident a few years ago and that took some adjusting to. We were very happy together. We had two children. My son has got his first degree and is currently overseas backpacking round the world. My daughter's married with one son and another due to arrive any day.'

'So you're a grandfather. My eldest is expecting, so I'm a grandmother-to-be. I don't feel old enough. Did you stay in the same house?'

'Yes, but it still feels strange to be completely on my own. I didn't have to chuck my children out, though; they left of their own accord. I still miss having them around, and I confess to being concerned about Oliver's safety. He's travelling where the whim takes him in the Far East, and I can't help worrying about where he'll go next.'

'You can't help worrying about them whatever they do, can you? My two youngest won't be looking after themselves properly, but if they get into trouble their father can deal with it, for once. Or they can just flounder their way out of it.'

He gave her a sympathetic smile, then glanced at his wristwatch. 'I'd better get back. I'm working for myself and I'm at an interesting stage. How long do you want your online connection for? I'm assuming you're staying in England for a while?'

'I am, yes. At least a year, possibly longer. I don't have the faintest idea about anything, except that I don't want to be tied down till I know exactly what I want to do with the rest of my life.'

'What was your job?'

'Office manager.' She grimaced at the memory. 'I've had enough of that.' Then she grinned. 'I was very efficient, though. I treated them all like naughty schoolchildren, even the lawyers, and they were all terrified of upsetting me. But they didn't want me to leave. I did think ahead and train up a good replacement, though.'

'You even sound efficient. I'll do some research and then get back to you later today.' He raised his hand in farewell and carried on walking towards the town centre.

She watched him go, still feeling guilty for taking advantage of him. But she would invite him round to a meal as a thank you.

Then she shrugged. Better to think of it as helping one another than taking advantage. Miss Parfitt had helped her and it'd been fun. She hadn't had much to do with people who were that old and had been fascinated by some of her companion's reminiscences.

She unpacked a dozen bags of 'stuff', set a couple of mousetraps with bacon rind, not cheese, as advised by the man who'd found them for her. Then she settled down in the kitchen to enjoy a cup of really good coffee. She'd bought a drip cone, but not a grinder, so put the unused ground coffee into the ancient freezer.

As she drank her coffee, she opened up the free local

newspaper she'd picked up at the shopping centre and checked through the services offered in the classifieds. She tore those pages out for future use.

Around two o'clock she began to feel sleepy and it was an effort to stay awake. It must be because of the time differences, but she'd read that it was better to fit in with local time from the start, so she made a start on clearing out Fliss's bedroom. It was sad how many worn, old clothes there were, neatly packed in drawers. Had her aunt ever thrown anything away?

She thought she might sleep in there when it was clean. She loved the elegant, old-fashioned furniture, which had pretty inlay work.

When she got fed up of clearing things out and realised she couldn't possibly finish even that room today, she remembered that she hadn't looked in the attic, so went up the narrow stairs. To her surprise, newspaper was stuffed all around the door, old yellowed pieces, which didn't look to have been moved for a long time.

When she opened it, the smell became suddenly much worse. Had some small animal died up here?

She stayed by the door, studying the top floor. It was divided into three smallish bedrooms to one side, one of which she'd slept in as a child. The rest was an open space. She remembered it being full of fascinating junk, but now it was clear, thank goodness, just an expanse of dusty bare boards.

She guessed the horrible smell was mould, so the roof must have been leaking, but she couldn't see anything in the big open area.

She hunted through each of the rooms but could find nothing. The bed frames and furniture might be worth something, but the mattresses were only fit to throw away.

She walked the perimeter of the attic and the floor felt spongy under her feet. The smell grew much worse as she reached the rear, but it was dusk now and she couldn't see the details as clearly as she'd have liked.

Dirty streaks marred the white walls in several places and there was something pale in one corner. The smell was worst of all there.

When she tried to switch on the only light to see more clearly, nothing happened and she squinted up at the dirty bowl-shaped shade, which seemed to contain a thick layer of dead insects. Maybe the bulb had gone. But since the fitting looked old-fashioned and the wire was frayed, she decided not to try putting a light bulb in till an electrician had checked it out.

She crouched down, squinting to get a closer look at the corner and realised the pale stuff was some sort of fungus growing on the damp, cracked plaster. The smell made her feel nauseous. 'Ugh!' She backed away, worried about how the floor seemed to ease up and down beneath her feet in this corner.

Things would have to be seen to quickly before more water leaked into the house. It rained all year round in England, unlike Western Australia, where the summers were hot and dry.

How much would it cost to fix this? Did the place need a whole new roof? She hoped not.

She'd been feeling happy about doing up the old place!

Now, she felt uncertain of her immediate future again because it might not be worth doing up.

* * *

Nell managed to stay awake until eight o'clock that evening only by an act of will.

The strange dream replayed itself. She was in the same pretty garden but what surrounded it was no clearer than before.

Once again, women were talking softly somewhere close by, but when she tried to find them, she got lost in a tangle of greenery, ending up in a small clearing dotted with clumps of daffodils.

It was most annoying to see only parts of the garden and not know how they fitted together. She was sure they did, which would mean it was quite a large garden.

She didn't know why, but she was equally sure the place she kept visiting in her dreams was real.

But though she called out to the women who were chatting, this time they didn't answer her.

She woke to a tangle of sheets and was annoyed with herself for having such persistent dreams.

And even more annoyed to realise it was still only the middle of the night. She tossed and turned for over an hour before she could get to sleep again.

The next time she opened her eyes it was light and once again she'd slept later than she'd meant to.

She had a faint memory of sounds during the night, sirens perhaps. She'd thought it was part of her dream, but now she wondered. She'd slept very heavily, once she had got back to sleep. She lay for a few moments, then remembered the roof leak and groaned. That had to take priority today.

Winifred woke up to the smell of burning. The moonlight was bright tonight. No, it wasn't moonlight, it was flickering, like flames.

She snatched up her dressing gown, dragging it on as she rushed to the window to find out what was on fire. She didn't need to look inside the house, because she slept downstairs and one glance out of the window showed her that the summer house in the back garden was on fire, its old, dry timber burning brightly.

'Oh, no!' She clapped one hand to her mouth, feeling like weeping. The summer house had not only been her mother's favourite place to sit, it held sweet memories for her too.

Everything was so brightly lit by the conflagration she could see that someone had trampled on the nearby plants and several shrubs had been pulled up and tossed onto the paths.

So the fire must have been set deliberately!

She should have heard them doing it, she really should, but she had to admit that her hearing wasn't as good as it used to be. Well, this settled one thing, at least. She'd have to get a hearing aid and hang the expense and (worse, to her) the sheer indignity of wearing one.

In the meantime she dialled 999 and asked for the fire brigade, explaining what had happened.

When she opened the back door, things got worse, because she found a note nailed to it.

YOU NEXT YOU OLD BITCH
WE MISSED GETTING YOUR BAG LAST TIME
WE WON'T MISS IT NEXT TIME
YOU WON'T EVER FEEL SAFE IN PEPPERCORN STREET

She didn't touch the note, feeling her heart thumping in anxiety as she slammed the door shut and locked it.

She couldn't see anyone outside but she wasn't taking any risks; she shouldn't have opened the door in the first place without checking.

Was it . . . could the arsonist be the young chap who'd tried to mug her? Why would he pursue her? Or give her warning of his intentions? It didn't make sense.

She forced herself to breathe slowly and deeply as she waited for the fire brigade, and her heart began to calm down.

Thanks to the flames she could see anything that happened at the back quite clearly and when a section of the rickety wooden fence began to shake and then fell inwards, she cried out, 'No!' Someone else was breaking in.

But the person who'd pushed it down was Angus. He had entered her garden from his own, which adjoined the rear of the top few houses. He stood for a minute studying what was happening, then ran to get her hosepipe, playing it first on the wooden bench near the summer house, then on the fire itself.

She should have done that, wet down the surrounding area, but she'd panicked, hadn't she, afraid of being knocked about again?

'Stupid old woman!' she muttered. 'What good does it do to panic . . . or talk to yourself?'

She heard a siren in the distance, coming gradually closer, and then it sounded like a large vehicle had stopped at the front of the house. Before she could check it out from the front sitting room, two people in firefighters' clothing ran round the corner of the building and took charge of the back garden.

'Thank goodness!' she muttered.

At their gesture, Angus moved away from the blaze and when one of them asked him something, he shook his head and pointed towards the house.

She was already opening the back door and going outside to join them.

'Did you leave anything burning in the garden, madam?' one firefighter asked.

'No. I haven't gone near that area for days. Anyway, I think the fire must have been deliberately lit because some of the bushes nearby have been uprooted and the plants trampled – and there's a threatening message pinned to my back door.'

'You haven't touched it?'

'No. I knew not to do that.'

'Show me.' Angus left the officers to deal with the blaze and read the message, letting out a choking sound, as if disgusted. 'Must be that nasty little sod who tried to mug you. But why's he coming after you again?'

'That's what I was wondering. And why is he warning me? That's stupid if he's intending to try to break in. Unless . . . do you think someone is trying to drive me away from here? I've had a few other things happen lately.'

'What?'

'Noises in the night. Stones thrown at the windows. I threw away the first message they left, which just said, "Get out or else!" I didn't realise then what was going on.'

'Have you had offers to buy your house?'

'Yes. Several. Estate agent people have come to the door, but I didn't even let them in, just told them I wasn't interested in selling.'

He looked at her thoughtfully. 'I've had a few offers to

buy my place, too. Pushy devils, a couple of them. Dennings would be a developer's delight, with two acres of land. I haven't heard of any other cases of people being harassed into selling their houses, but I'll ask around. Now, how about a cup of tea? Shall I put the kettle on?'

'I can do that. I'm not going to faint on you again, Angus.'

He gave her an unexpected hug, which pleased her greatly. So few people touched you when you were older. She'd read about how people missed being touched. They called it 'skin hunger'.

She put the kettle on, pleased that her hands weren't shaking, though she still felt shuddery inside.

'Do you want to sit down?'

'I'd rather stay by the window and keep an eye on what's happening, if you don't mind.'

'You do that. I'll just nip into my bedroom and put some clothes on while the kettle's boiling. I don't like meeting officials in my night gear.'

He grinned. 'You always look elegant, whatever you're wearing, and I like the plait. I didn't realise your hair was that long.'

That remark pleased her. When she got into her bedroom, she stared in the mirror at her pale face and the plait she wore her hair in every night, as she had from childhood. Such a nice compliment, but she looked a mess.

The two firefighters soon had the blaze under control. One of them turned out to be a woman when she took off her helmet. How interesting! Winifred wished sometimes that she'd been born in the twenty-first century. She might have had a more interesting life, and with the better welfare services they had now, she'd not have been so tied to being the only one available to look after her mother. But it was what unmarried daughters did in those days, stayed at home and cared for their ageing parents.

She would have no one to care for her if she became too feeble to look after herself. It was quite a dilemma to decide how to deal with that, which was why she had briefly considered selling her house and putting the money in the bank.

Only she didn't want to leave. Oh, she definitely didn't! This was her home, the only one she'd ever known. And she'd found out that the price she'd been offered was well under the market value. Did they think she was so stupid, she'd not check that?

So unless she got dementia, she intended to stay here and continue managing her own life as she saw fit. When she received the money from her friend's will, she'd husband it carefully, so that she could pay for a little help with the housework.

Another friend was about to move into a retirement housing complex, into a brand-new home about the same size as the ones in Sunset Close. Hazel was urging her to buy a house in the same complex, but Winifred had never wanted to live in a group situation. And Hazel's complex was even worse than the houses down the road because it was a block of flats, rather small to her. She was used to big rooms in a large house.

Winifred would hate to live in a flat for other reasons. She still enjoyed a stroll round her garden, even if she couldn't keep it tidy. She watched the plants come to life in spring and parade their flowers. She really missed the borders of annuals there used to be.

Growing old presented one with a series of dilemmas. Thank goodness she'd been blessed with good health.

She smiled. And stubbornness!

Chapter Six

As it was starting to get properly light, there was a hammering on the front door and Angus came to the back door to ask, 'Shall I answer it for you?'

'No. I can do it.'

He stayed nearby in case it was someone with trouble in mind, but heard her say in a pleased tone, 'Janey! Come in, dear.'

'Are you all right, Miss Parfitt? Have you had a fire?'

'It was in the back garden, not the house.'

'Thank goodness!'

'You're up early, dear.'

'Millie's teething again. She was crying half the night. I felt so guilty because she must have disturbed people in the other flats. Nothing settles her down like going for a walk, so as soon as it got light I brought her out. Then I saw the fire engine outside your house and came to check you were all right.'

'I'm fine, dear. Look at her now, cheerful as you please, the little minx.'

Angus heard the sound of something bumping on the hall floor and saw a young woman bring in an infant in a buggy. He hadn't met her before, so he went in to join them. The more people who were linked in protecting Miss Parfitt, the better.

'Do you two know one another? No? Janey Dobson meet Angus Denning. Janey lives near the bottom of the street and Angus is at the very top, number 1, no less.'

He gave a friendly nod to the newcomer. 'We haven't spoken to one another, but I've seen you going up and down the street, Janey. And this young lady with you.' He smiled down at her daughter.

'Yes, I've seen you too. This is my naughty little daughter, Millie, who kept me awake half the night.'

The rosy infant in the buggy held her arms out to Winifred, who bent down to kiss her and kept hold of one plump little hand.

The tender smile on her wrinkled old face touched Angus's heart and he had to swallow hard.

When Janey heard details of what had happened, she looked even more shocked. 'If I'd walked you back the night you got mugged, all this would probably never have started.'

'No, but you could have been mugged on the way back, instead,' Winifred retorted. 'And then Millie might have been hurt. Better that it happened to me.'

'It shouldn't happen to anyone. I do worry about you living here on your own.'

'So do I,' Angus said.

'Well, I'm not moving into one of those retirement places. I'd go mad with claustrophobia,' Winifred said defiantly.

'Perhaps you should get someone to live here with you, then?' Angus suggested. 'Rent out a room.'

'Who would want to put up with an elderly woman's fussy ways?'

'I think I'd be fussy about things if I had a lovely house like this one,' Janey said.

Winifred stared at her thoughtfully for a few seconds, then changed the subject and began pouring cups of tea and cutting slices of her latest cake.

Angus answered the back door when one of the firefighters knocked.

'The fire's out now, Miss Parfitt, but we've called the police because it was definitely a case of arson.'

She looked sad. 'I feared so. But I can't understand why they'd do it.'

'Who knows what gets into some of them? The police will be here in about fifteen minutes and, unless we get another emergency call, we'll stay to speak to them about what we found.'

'In that case, you must have a cup of tea and a piece of cake while you wait.'

'That's very kind of you. I won't say no and I'm sure my colleague feels the same.'

When the police arrived, Angus heard Janey whisper to Miss Parfitt, 'Do you want me to leave you to it?'

'No, stay please. I'd like to ask you about something.'

'I'd prefer to stay for a while, too,' Angus said. 'I want to see if there's anything I can do about that back fence of yours. I damaged one section to get into your garden to the fire, so the least I can do is repair it. I can perhaps prop it up till I can buy what I need, so that it looks solid on first glance, but I'll be able to open it and get to you more quickly.'

'That's very kind of you, Angus.'

'The rest of the fence is in a pretty bad state, Miss Parfitt. I'll see what I can do to strengthen it.'

'I can't ask you to do that.'

'You didn't ask, and as your garden backs on to mine the fence is my responsibility as well as yours, so I'll benefit too.'

'How kind of you to put it that way!'

He could see he hadn't fooled her.

She sighed and he saw her eyes go towards the window and the smoking, blackened mess that had once been a pretty white summer house.

'I used to sit there on sunny days, chatting to my young man. Poor Jack was killed in 1944.'

Janey patted her arm and Winifred gave her a sad smile, repeating, 'I don't understand why people vandalise things.'

'No sane person can figure it out,' Angus agreed.

When the police arrived, they asked Winifred if they could examine the site of the fire before they talked to her, so she went to join Angus and Janey by the window and watch what they did.

They consulted the firefighters, pointing and nodding to one another, then discussing something earnestly, with long pauses and more pointing.

After the fire engine had driven away, the police came to examine the threatening note. They donned rubber gloves to take it down from the door, putting it and even the nail that had been used to hold it into a protective plastic bag.

Only then did they come inside to talk to Winifred.

She was glad to have Angus and Janey with her, because the thought of being targeted by arsonists was still making her feel a bit shaky. What if they came back and set her house on fire while she was asleep? Would she be able to get out in time? And where would she go?

Sometimes she felt every one of her eighty-four years sitting heavily on her shoulders. At other times she felt as young as Janey – inside her head, anyway.

Once they'd gone through all the questions twice, one of the officers asked Winifred if she'd come to the police station and look at photos of local youths who had been in trouble with the police for break-ins and vandalising property.

'You might recognise one of them. You said you got a good look at your attacker.'

'Yes, I did. I'm sure I'd recognise him again if I saw him. I'll book a taxi and come tomorrow, if that's all right. I feel rather tired today after all the upset.'

He patted her arm. 'You take it easy till you've recovered. We'll send a police car for you tomorrow afternoon, if you like, though we can always postpone it if you still don't feel up to it.'

Angus intervened. 'I think it'd be better if I brought Miss Parfitt to see you, then it won't be obvious that she's trying to identify her mugger.'

'Good thinking. Very kind of you, sir.'

When the two officers finally left, Angus said, 'Don't hesitate to call me if you need help, Miss Parfitt. I mean it. Any time, day or night. Promise you'll do that.'

'I promise.'

But he wondered if she would. She was so fiercely independent.

Once he'd gone, Winifred turned to Janey, who was collecting the dirty plates and teacups. Millie was now sleeping soundly in her buggy.

'Never mind clearing up now, dear. I want to talk to you about something important. Please sit down.'

Janey looked at her in surprise, wondering what she could want. She took the seat indicated opposite her companion.

'Before I start, I want you to promise me that you'll answer truthfully. I don't want pity to make you do something you don't really want.'

'OK. I promise.'

'Then here we go.' She took a deep breath and said hesitantly, 'I've been wondering if you'd consider coming to live here instead of in that flat.'

Janey gaped at her. This was the last thing she'd expected to hear. 'But—'

'No, let me finish. I have a lot of rooms that I never use and you'd have your own bathroom, but you'd have to share the kitchen and washing machine with me. You could stay rent-free and just share the costs.'

Janey could see how nervous the old lady was, so spoke gently. 'Why?'

'So that I won't be on my own.'

'Are you sure it's not because you're feeling sorry for me and trying to help me?'

'No. It's because I think we can help one another. I hate

to admit it but I believe I've reached a stage in life where someone ought to be around in case I need help. I don't need a personal carer – I'd absolutely hate that – but if I fell, no one would know, or hear me, even if I called out for help.'

Janey looked round the kitchen, feeling as if she was seeing the place for the first time. 'It is a very big house for one person.'

'Yes and . . . it can get lonely, so it'd be good to have some company now and then. Not that I'd expect you to spend all your time with me.'

Her voice came out a bit husky as she admitted, 'I get lonely too.'

'I thought you did. The house isn't centrally heated, but I'm thinking of putting it in. I inherited some money and when I get it, well, I can make things a bit more comfortable.'

'It's pretty comfortable now.'

'It's not bad, but if you choose to come here, I'll do something about the upstairs before next winter. I live down here during the cooler months, in what used to be the housekeeper's room, and I'm thinking of staying down here permanently because of the stairs. Come and see.' She took Janey into the rooms that led off the kitchen, a large bedsitter with a neat little shower room.

'You have a nice outlook over the back garden from here,' Janey said as they went back into the kitchen. She was glad Auntie Winnie wasn't pressing for a decision immediately, because she wouldn't have known what to say. It had come as such a surprise.

'Before you decide anything, let's go upstairs and I'll show you the bedrooms.'

'Good idea. We can leave the kitchen door open, then I'll hear Millie if she wakes.'

Auntie Winnie walked up the stairs slowly but steadily, Janey noted, but she did hold on to the rail. And she wasn't out of breath when she got to the landing. She did really well for her age, better than Mr Shackleton, who must be ten years younger than her.

'There are six bedrooms, two dressing rooms and one bathroom on this floor and more bedrooms in the attics.' She opened each door as they came to it. 'You could have your choice, except for this room at the front, which I used to occupy in the summer and in which I keep my spare clothes.'

She threw open the door next to it. 'There are two bigger bedrooms besides mine. This one might suit you, because it has a dressing room next to it where you could do your studying or put Millie to sleep while she's so little. Or you could take a nearby bedroom for Millie. I know you're sharing a bedroom with her in the flat but it isn't very big, is it? As she gets older, you might both find it easier if she has her own place to sleep.'

Janey went across to the window and looked out on to the street. The 'small' dressing room was the same size as their shared bedroom at the flat. The bedroom was as big as the whole flat. She went back to join the old lady on the landing. 'It's a lovely big room.'

'You could have a room on the ground floor as well for your personal sitting room. You may want to invite friends in or just be on your own in the evening. There's a room with a TV point in it, but no television. But you'd also be welcome to join me in my sitting room any evening. I have a brand-new TV.'

Janey was tempted. Very. But would it be the right thing to do?

Winifred looked anxiously at her. 'I shan't be in the least offended if you don't like the idea. But I thought, well, it won't cost me anything and it'll save you quite a bit of money and . . . I'll feel safer.' She waited, not pushing for an immediate answer.

'I do like the idea, but it's taken me by surprise, so I need to think it through, if you don't mind.'

'I'd prefer you to do that. This is too important to rush into. Look, I'll go downstairs and sit with Millie. You have another walk round the whole house and think about it. You can go up and look at the attics as well, if you like. You could store things up there.'

'No, wait! I've changed my mind.'

Winifred went very still, then inclined her head. 'As I said, it's up to you and if you don't want to—'

Janey felt emotion well up inside her. 'I don't need to think about it because, if you're quite sure, I'd love to come here.' Suddenly she was crying, reaching out blindly for Winifred and weeping in the old lady's arms.

'It's been so lonely living on my own. And Mr Jones is moving out of the ground-floor flat when he marries Mrs Gainsford. He's offered it to me, but I can't afford it, and anyway, people walk past in the parking area so close to the windows that I'd feel nervous living there without him nearby.'

She let Winifred draw her across to sit down on a dusty old couch on the landing and was surprised to find the old lady crying silently beside her.

'I can't think of anything nicer than having you here,

Janey. I'm on my own for day after day, unless I walk into town or see Hazel, and I can't even do that in bad weather. Oh dear, I never let myself weep, but now look at me.'

They both laughed through their tears, then hugged one another again.

'So you'll come to live here?'

'I'd love to. If you're really sure.'

'Very sure.' Winifred hesitated. 'At least . . . you don't think those hooligans will come back again, do you? I wouldn't want to put you and Millie in danger.'

'We could get a couple of those false CCTV cameras. Mr Denning might put them up for us where people can see them. They're quite cheap and no one will ever know they're not real. I'm sure that'd help keep burglars away. I was going to suggest it, anyway.'

'What a good idea!'

She hesitated. 'I've been feeling as if you're a relative for a while.'

Winifred smiled at her. 'Dan and I did say to consider us honorary grandparents.'

'It might sound better to other people if I called you Auntie Winnie from now on? They know you're not my grandmother, but people can have all sorts of aunts and uncles. It'll seem more natural me coming here if I pretend you're a relative, and anyway, you feel like one.'

To her embarrassment, Winifred couldn't stop herself from bursting into tears all over again, this time sobbing loudly.

Janey put both arms round her. 'What have I said? What's wrong?'

She clutched the girl's hand. 'There's nothing wrong,

nothing at all wrong. You've just given me a very wonderful gift, my dear girl. I feel close to you, too, and I wish we really were related. We'll have to say I'm a great-aunt, though. I'm much too old for anything else.'

So they had another hug and mopped their eyes, after which Winifred said, 'I'll go down and keep an eye on Millie while you choose which bedrooms you want.'

'If she wakes and seems upset, call me. She's getting quite heavy so I don't think you should try to pick her up.'

'I know. I daren't even offer to babysit for you. But I can keep an eye on her while you're busy, then call you if you're needed.'

'I can't ask you to do that.'

'My dear, I'd love it and she seems to enjoy me playing with her nearly as much as I do.'

Janey didn't come down for a while, which Winifred thought was a good sign.

When she came into the kitchen, she smiled and twirled Winifred round the table in a gentle, joyful dance. 'I think this is going to work out brilliantly.'

'So do I.'

'I have to go now because I've got classes at tech this afternoon, but I'll come back later and we'll work out how to do it. I think I ought to tell Dawn about it, as well. She's been so kind and likes me to keep in touch. I'm sure she'll approve, though.'

Winifred wasn't as sure about that, but surely Dawn wouldn't say it was a stupid thing to do? After all, her friend's daughter was a very capable woman, who understood the world and its vagaries. The charity she ran for young girls who got pregnant was highly respected.

She hesitated, then got out her bottle of Christmas sherry, which she hadn't felt like opening on her own last Christmas. The sun was shining brightly outside and her mother would have been horrified at her drinking in the morning, but this was such a wonderful day, in spite of the burning of the summer house, that she felt like celebrating. People were so much more important than objects.

She got out one of her mother's best crystal sherry glasses, washed it carefully, then poured herself a half glass of dry sherry. As she raised the glass, she said quietly, 'To a better life.'

She sat down, thinking hard. She really must do more to bring herself up to date. Especially learning to deal with computers. The classes she'd gone to with Hazel hadn't been very good, but there must be others. Or she could afford to hire a private tutor.

She smiled. Hazel had a daughter to help her and until now Winifred had had no one from the family to keep in touch with except a cheating nephew who was only after her money. Now she'd have Janey.

And how wonderful it would be not to be always on her own, to have other people around!

As she took another sip, another idea came to her, a very good idea, and she smiled as she drank a second toast to it.

The following morning Janey telephoned Dawn, who had stressed that if ever she needed to talk about anything, she could come to her.

She went to the headquarters of the charity, an old house that had been gifted to Just Girls. Here the organisers had offices and held meetings for the girls they helped. The conference room was also rented out to other groups who needed a meeting place, which helped pay the running expenses of the house.

She stopped outside to look at the small sign by the door. Just Girls. If she ever got any spare money, she would make regular donations to this wonderful group of women. The refuge they'd created had made all the difference to her at a very traumatic time in her life. Her attacker was now behind bars, but she still had nightmares about him pursuing her. Here was where she had first found sanctuary.

Dawn welcomed her with a hug. 'Do sit down. You look solemn. Is there a problem?'

'No, but I do want to run something past you.' She explained about Miss Parfitt's offer.

Dawn looked thoughtful and it was a minute or two before she spoke. 'Miss Parfitt is a dear, but she's very old. What would you do if she dropped dead suddenly, or developed Alzheimer's? You might have to move out quickly when the new owner took over. I'm assuming she'll leave the house to someone in her family.'

'I didn't think of that.'

She looked so upset, Dawn said quickly, 'I'm not saying don't do it, but there are ways of dealing with such situations. They need to be faced before you move in, not after. You should have a proper lease, for a start, one giving you at least a month to move out if anything happens to her. I'm sure Miss Parfitt won't object to that.'

Janey nodded. She was sure of that, too.

'And it wouldn't hurt for you to learn something about first aid, in case she has a medical crisis and needs your help.'

105

'I'd like to do that anyway – well, if I can find someone to babysit Millie. I once thought of training as a doctor, but I knew my father would never let me do that, however good my school results were. He doesn't believe in female doctors. I'm not at all frightened of blood or human bodies, you know. Dead people can't harm you like the living ones do.'

Dawn patted her hand, understanding that sentiment. 'We'll find you a first-aid class, then, and a babysitter, if necessary, because I think Miss Parfitt is too old to leave in charge of Millie.'

'I know – and she admits that. But she says she can keep an eye on Millie while I'm in another part of the house studying or cleaning, and I'd trust her to do that. Millie already recognises her and they love one another.'

'Then let me go over a few things with Miss Parfitt and make arrangements for a rental lease before you do anything. I could phone her now and then take you home on my way there, if she's free. I know you've walked a good way to come here.'

Janey smiled. 'Thanks, but no need. I enjoy walking and it's a cheap way of keeping fit. I have some shopping to do in town, anyway. But perhaps you could phone me after you've spoken to Miss – no, she wants me to call her Auntie Winnie! Isn't that wonderful? Neither of us have relatives, so we're making our own family together.'

'That's an excellent idea. More people should do it.'

Dawn watched her go with tears in her eyes at this last statement. She hoped Janey hadn't noticed. Social workers weren't supposed to get personally involved with their clients, but there was something special about that young woman.

She wondered if there was some way she and her co-workers could help Janey become a doctor. She'd have to look into it. What an achievement that would be, for them as well as for Janey!

She sat for a while, still slightly worried about whether this move was a good idea. She liked both of them but Winifred was eighty-four and Janey only eighteen. That was a huge disparity in age. And as she'd tried to point out, the risks of living with an elderly person were considerable.

Her supervisor, when she'd worked for a local council, would have vetoed this proposal very firmly, but Dawn wasn't going to do that.

Sometimes you had to take a chance and hope for the best, because if things went well, if Winifred continued to be in such good health for a woman of her age, even if that only lasted a year or two, there would be a lot of benefits for both her and Janey.

Not just financial benefits, but emotional ones too. She knew from her own mother's situation since she'd been widowed how lonely older people could get. And from her work with the charity she knew how lonely the young mothers could feel.

In the end Dawn decided that if ever there was a time to take a chance, this was it. After all, she'd be around to keep an eye on things and help if needed. She picked up the phone. She'd check things out with Winifred and, subject to a proper lease being drawn up for Janey, she'd tell them both to go for it.

If only all her girls could have such help with their new

lives. Some of the ones Just Girls helped had had a very hard time and were still having it tough. She stretched the money and help as far as she could, but it was never enough.

Later that day, Angus came to pick Winifred up and take her to the police station to look at photos of young men. She recognised the one who'd attacked her at once.

The policeman seemed doubtful. 'Are you sure, Miss Parfitt?'

'Very sure. He has a sort of twist to one eyebrow. Very distinctive. And his face was quite close to me.'

He peered at the photo again. 'Well, if you'll sign a statement to that effect, we'll investigate further.'

As Angus drove her home, she relaxed, feeling she'd done a good thing in identifying her attacker.

Tomorrow, she promised herself, she'd make an appointment for a hearing test. The community nurse at her doctor's would know who she should see, and if it was on the other side of town, she could get a taxi there. After all, the money her friend had left her should be coming through soon.

How rich she'd feel! She'd be able to buy some new clothes. She did love nice things to wear. And she'd give presents to her friends. She could buy something for Janey and Dan Shackleton, and perhaps a small thank you gift for Angus.

Life was still good and getting better. Or it would be, if these vandals would just leave her alone.

On Saturday morning, Nick sorted out his clothes and sighed. The day had come when he'd have to do some washing.

He went into his brother's bedroom. 'Do you remember what Ma told us about how to do the washing?'

'Nah. I'll think about that later.' Steve put his headphones back on.

Nick shook his shoulder.

'What?'

'We need to buy some food and some detergent to do our washing.'

'I'm not into cooking. I'll get takeaways if I get hungry. And I'm not interested in washing. I'm not out of clothes yet, so I'm not wasting my money on detergent.' Back went the headphones.

Nick decided to go shopping on his own and, if possible, to keep what he'd bought for himself. Steve had been mooching off him for long enough. Nick had done a few sums today. He had some savings he hadn't told anyone about, but he didn't want to touch that money. He couldn't afford to keep buying meals out and if he couldn't get the hang of cooking, well, he could always buy bread and make sandwiches.

The trouble was, if he got some food in, Steve would 'borrow' it. And not put anything back in its place.

His younger brother wasn't the ideal flatmate and Nick had quickly started wishing he'd gone in with someone else or rented a bedsit on his own.

But Ma had paid their deposit for this place as a farewell present, and paid the first two weeks' rent as well, so that they could move out several days before she left for England. She had wanted him to keep an eye on Steve, he knew, but that was harder than she realised.

He had a sudden idea and studied the door of his

bedroom. It was old-fashioned, like the whole building, a solid core door. It'd be easy to put a lock on it, and if he always wore the key on a chain round his neck he'd not lock himself out. He ought to ask the owner's permission but that'd take time, so he was just going to chance it.

He had a few tools that had belonged to his grandfather and he'd brought them with him. If he could just remember where he'd put them . . . He got his boxes out from under the ancient single bed and five minutes later let out a yell of triumph. There the tools were.

So he went out, the first time he'd done any serious shopping on his own. In the supermarket he put some bananas in his trolley. Fruit was good for you, right? He grabbed a bag of apples as well, then went to the frozen foods section, where he studied the ready meals.

'They're cheats,' a voice said next to him.

He turned to see a girl, not beautiful, but easy on the eye with nice brown shoulder-length hair. 'What do you mean?'

'I tried the ready meals when I first got my own flat. They look good on the box, but they're tiny portions when you open them up. You'd be better buying a steak or chop, a roll and some salad. Anyone can cook a steak and butter a roll.'

'Thanks. Good idea.' He wanted to keep talking to her, so he added, 'This is my first time shopping for myself.'

'I guessed from the expression on your face. Did your parents chuck you out of the nest or did you fly of your own accord?'

He could feel himself flushing in embarrassment. 'Ma pushed us out.'

She patted his arm. 'Sorry. I didn't mean to upset you.

My mum was the opposite. She didn't want me to leave. Your mother was probably being cruel to be kind. Guys are harder to dislodge.'

'It's cruel, all right. I'm hopeless at looking after myself and I don't know where to begin with food. You wouldn't . . . help me do some basic shopping, would you? I'll buy you a coffee afterwards as a thank you.'

She studied him, head on one side. He must have passed some sort of test because she nodded. 'OK. I'm Carla Baldino, by the way.'

'Nick Vincent.' He offered his hand and she shook it. Her skin felt nice, soft and warm against his. He didn't want to let go.

She flushed slightly and tugged her hand away, pointing to the fresh stuff. 'This is not only good for you, it's cheap and easy to deal with.'

He didn't tell her he wasn't into vegetables, because he didn't want to upset her. She pointed and he obediently loaded his trolley. Then something occurred to him. 'Oh, no. I can't take this much home, or my brother will pinch it out of the fridge. He's a lazy slob.'

She looked thoughtful. 'Well . . . My flatmate has just chucked out an old booze fridge. It's sitting on the kerb waiting for the council pickup. It works OK, but it looks a real mess, with dents and rusty patches. If no one's taken it, you could grab it and keep it in your room. Well, you could if you fitted a lock on the door.'

'Brill! I owe you a pastry with your coffee for that. Let's go and check out the fridge.'

'We need to pay for this food. And didn't you say something about doing the washing?'

'Oh. Yes.'

'You'll need detergent, then.'

It astounded him how much the bill came to, even though he'd not bought anything extravagant.

'Shall we go in my car?' he asked.

'No. I'll follow you.'

It was sensible really. He could be a serial killer for all she knew. But he hoped he wouldn't lose sight of her in the traffic. He should have got her address.

He didn't lose her and she didn't try to get away from him, either. That was hopeful. Wasn't it? He hadn't met a girl he liked this much in ages . . . well, actually, never before. She seemed a bit special.

He hoped she liked the look of him.

The fridge was still there, looking about a million years old, but if it worked what did that matter? Carla helped him lift it into his car. She was fit and toned, moving easily.

'Would you trust me enough to come in my car and help me carry it into my place? Then I'll buy you that coffee. I'll drive you back here afterwards, I promise.'

Another long scrutiny, then, 'OK.'

He felt as if he'd passed some sort of test again. He beamed at her.

She smiled back. Lovely smile, she had.

To Nick's relief, Steve wasn't at home. The kitchen looked like a whirlwind had hit it. 'I'm sorry. I did tidy it up a bit this morning and I was going to do the washing-up after I got back, only my brother must have been on the hunt for food.' Spilt milk, flakes of cereal, crumbs, an open jar of jam. Didn't Steve ever pick anything up or put it away?

When Nick opened the door to his bedroom, it looked

a mess, but it wasn't half as bad as the rest of the flat, and at least his dirty clothes were neatly piled on the end of the bed. 'I'd got as far as sorting stuff out to wash when I realised we didn't have any detergent,' he explained.

Carla leant against the door frame, arms folded, looking disapproving. 'Well, you're not a total pig, at least.'

She helped him get the fridge inside, then grinned. 'I bet you've never washed clothes before.'

'You'd win the bet. Um, you couldn't . . .'

'Help you do the washing? No. Give you instructions, yes. But you will be doing it. I don't do washing for guys. Your mother should have given you lessons before she chucked you out.'

'Ma tried. We didn't listen. I wish I had now.'

'Can't you go back to her for advice?'

'She's gone off to England.'

'With your dad?'

'They're divorced. Have been since I was little.'

'Ah. Well, I'll take pity on you, then. We'll get the food into the fridge first, then you can start on the washing.'

It turned out to be fun and afterwards the coffee turned into them making lunch at his flat from some of the stuff he'd bought. Another lesson. She was right. Salads were easy.

When she looked at her watch, he screwed up his courage to ask, 'Are you seeing anyone?'

'No. But I've got a weekend job in a bar and I don't want to be late.'

'Would you . . . come out with me sometime?'

'Yes.' She grinned. 'You sounded nervous then. Am I so frightening?'

'No. But it was important.'

'Oh.'

She looked pleased, then she frowned and waggled one finger at him. 'I'm still not cooking or washing for you. I'm not your mummy. I will help you shop, though, and give you advice. You're a grown-up. You ought to be able to look after yourself.'

Put like that, it seemed ridiculous that a grown man couldn't see to his own needs. The idea had never struck him so strongly.

Nick drove her back to her flat and when he came home he finished washing his clothes and used the dryer because it was raining. Then he laboriously ironed his shirts and folded up his t-shirts and other tops. As Carla had pointed out, you'd be stupid to let them get crumpled when you'd just washed them.

After that he nipped out to the hardware store and bought a lock for his bedroom door. Made a good job of fitting it too, if he said so himself. He liked doing little jobs around the house.

Which proved he wasn't completely helpless.

He stared at himself in the mirror. His hair needed cutting and unshaven wasn't the best look for his face.

He hadn't realised how much there was to sort out if you lived on your own. And he was only one person.

For the first time it occurred to him to wonder how the hell his mother had coped all those years with three children and no practical help from their father?

Why hadn't they helped her more?

Even his father helped his second wife around the house these days. Well, Jenny was much stronger than

Ma and didn't let him get away with a thing.

There was still no sign of Steve coming home. What would he say to the lock and eating separately? Nick looked at the clock. He was getting a bit worried about his brother's new friends.

More important, would his brother have the rent money this week? It'd be the first time they had to pay it themselves.

Nick decided to get it out of him before the idiot spent it on booze. Or worse.

Chapter Seven

Nell parked her new car next to the house, got out and studied the vehicle approvingly. Bright yellow wasn't her favourite colour for a car, but it was supposed to be the safest colour of car to drive. Or so Nick had once told her. She'd bought it because of its reasonable price and modest size, not because of the colour, and because it was an automatic.

She'd not enjoyed changing gear manually on her hire car and was glad the company would be picking it up this afternoon. Well worth the extra money not to have to drive it somewhere and then get herself back here somehow.

She kept wondering how her sons were going on. They'd probably have turned the flat into a pigsty by now, knowing them.

Wait till they ran out of clothes! She wished she could be a fly on the wall when they did their first load of washing. She'd tried to teach them how to sort and wash things before she left, but they'd only said, 'Yeah, yeah!' and gone glassy-eyed, so she'd dropped the subject.

She'd sent all three sons an email yesterday from the local library, telling them she'd arrived safely and promising more information when she got online again. She'd ended with an outright lie: 'I'm loving it here in my tiny cottage.' She didn't want them to think she had any spare bedrooms.

Thank goodness she didn't need to worry about Robbie. He'd always been the sensible one and Linda didn't put up with any laziness from him.

Nell had only given her new street address to him with strict instructions to keep it to himself.

The other two hadn't even asked her for it.

When Steve had suggested coming to England with her, she'd been horrified. If either of them dared follow her there, she'd run for the hills. Once they'd learnt to stand on their own feet, it'd be different, but she wasn't funding a long holiday for them.

Anyway, she was pretty sure they didn't have any money saved for the airfare, so she ought to be safe in her new domain for a good while.

She hadn't mentioned their father in her emails and had cut all connections with him. She'd put him on the 'block senders' list when she got her own email again. The only ties left between them now were their sons – and the invisible scars from their unhappy marriage.

Well, enough of that. She had to look forward now, not backward.

In a few minutes Angus was coming to help her set up her new computer system and Internet connection. She'd asked him to get her a screen to which she could attach her laptop for the time being. Using a laptop for long gave her a crick in the neck.

She could probably have managed to set things up on her own, because she was reasonably capable with technology, but she'd rather have help getting connected in a different country. Just in case.

Anyway, he seemed a nice guy and she needed to make friends here. It was good that he, too, was taking an interest in helping Winifred. She hated the thought of a woman in her eighties first being mugged then having her summer house deliberately burnt down, with threats made of further attacks.

A car stopped in the street and she looked down the drive. Not Angus. He drove an old rattletrap and this was a recent model, large and luxurious.

The man who got out of it stood for a moment studying her house, looking at it so intently she continued to keep a surreptitious eye on him. He was showily dressed and she quickly decided he must be trying to sell something.

Seeing her at the side of the house, he turned away from the front gate and came along the drive. 'Miss Chaytor?'

'Ms Chaytor,' she corrected.

'I'm Grant Jeffries.' He held out a business card.

He hadn't corrected the way he'd addressed her, which was a strike against him as far as she was concerned. She glanced at the card he'd shoved into her hand and saw it was from an estate agent's and his name had the title 'Manager' after it.

She thrust the card back at him but he didn't take it. She'd have tossed it on the ground, only she'd have been the one who had to pick it up again. 'I don't want to sell my house, thank you.' She said it firmly and turned to go indoors.

'Could I beg the favour of a few minutes of your time, Miss, er Ms Chaytor? I'm sure you'll be pleased with what I have to tell you.'

She sighed and turned round, thinking 'persistent toad'!

'I'm here to present an excellent offer from a client who wishes to buy your house.'

'Why would anyone make me an offer when I haven't put it on the market?'

'My client knew the former owner had died and asked me to keep an eye on it. When I heard you'd moved in, I came to see you on his behalf.'

She did not, she decided, like Jeffries' smarmy smile. Her guess had been correct: he was a salesman. 'I've already told you that I do *not* wish to sell my house. What part of that statement did you not understand?'

He blinked in surprise at her sharp tone and a scowl replaced the practised smile for a few seconds. 'You haven't even heard the offer, my dear lady. And this house is, if I may say so, in need of a great many expensive repairs. You can save yourself a lot of trouble by selling it as is.'

'Who's made the offer? Perhaps they understand English better than you do.' She spoke more loudly. 'I do not – wish – to sell my house.'

He winced and pressed on. 'The offer is from the developer of the over-50s housing project just down the street from you.'

'Ah. I see.' Angus's car drew up outside her house and when he sat waiting for her to finish dealing with her visitor, she beckoned to him.

Jeffries carried on speaking in a soft, earnest voice. 'The two houses next to yours on the downhill side have just been sold to the same developer, as well as the house uphill from yours. He also owns the nearby plots in the next street behind your back gardens. Your property would neatly round off what my client needs to add another short street to his over-50s project.'

When she said nothing, he continued speaking. 'The developer has even had the street's name approved in theory by the council: Cinnamon Gardens. Pretty name, isn't it? The planning department is very much in favour of this development. Why don't I come in and discuss the matter with you?'

'Because I'm not interested. Please leave my property and don't come back.'

'But—'

'Damned well go away!'

Her words must have carried clearly, because Angus was grinning as he joined them. 'Is this fellow giving you trouble, Nell?'

'Nothing I can't handle. He wants to sell my house and his English is so poor, he doesn't understand me when I say I have no desire to sell it at this point.' She turned and made a sudden shooing gesture towards Jeffries, who took a couple of hasty steps backwards. 'Let's try some other words . . . Scram! Vamoose! Get lost! Rack off! Am I making myself clear yet or do we need an interpreter?'

When she paused, Jeffries opened his mouth as if to say something else, so she turned her back on him and said loudly, 'Come inside, Angus. If that nong wants to stand there all day talking to himself, he can.'

Keeping his face turned away from the angry man and looking as if he was dying to laugh, Angus hurried towards the kitchen door. 'Nong?' he queried once they were out of earshot.

'An old Aussie word for a fool. I've always liked it.'

Jeffries bellowed after them, 'You will be hearing from me again, Ms Chaytor! The council is very eager to encourage more housing suitable for the elderly in this town. You should strike while the iron is hot. A good offer doesn't last for ever, you know, and there are such things as compulsory purchases.'

A minute later they heard a car door slam then the engine start up.

'Just out of curiosity, how much was he offering?' Angus asked.

'Haven't the faintest. I don't want to sell, so I didn't ask.'

'Wouldn't have hurt to find out, though. Always gather information about your opponent.'

She gave him a rueful smile. 'I suppose you're right, but he approached me at a time when I was enjoying a quiet moment in my new home. And he got right up my nose with his patronising tone. Maybe I'll call him in a week or two and find out what his client is offering. Even if I decide to live permanently in England, this house is too big for me.'

'You should call him sooner than that. As I said, it pays to know your enemy.'

'He isn't my enemy, not exactly. He said he was acting for the developer of those retirement villas in Sunset Close, who has apparently bought the nearby houses on the next street as well.'

'That'd be Gus Nolan. Not my favourite person on this

planet – but don't let me prejudice you against him. He's perfectly capable of doing that himself.'

'OK.'

'But if what your visitor said was right, Nolan's well on his way to putting together another stage to this development. You can be sure he has a couple of people on the town council in his pocket, so if you're the last one to hold out, there may indeed be pressure put on you officially not to stand in the way of the project.'

'In which case, maybe I can get them to up their price. But I don't want to move anywhere yet. I've just done one house clearance and move, the first for twenty-five years, and it wasn't fun.'

'Are you really thinking of staying in England permanently?'

She shrugged. 'Probably not permanently. I want to keep in touch with my sons, and there's a grandchild on the way.'

He grinned at her. 'Well, mine just arrived early. It was supposed to be a boy, but it turned out to be a girl. It happens sometimes, apparently. Ashleigh is very annoyed. She'd bought boys' things for it.'

'Congratulations on becoming a double granddad.'

He shrugged. 'I don't get to see them very often. She's a two-hour drive away, and you have to book weeks in advance to hit a gap in her social life.'

'Yes. I have to bear in mind that my sons may move away from Western Australia. It's like a juggling act these days, isn't it, keeping up with your children? Anyway, I've only just arrived in England and all I'm planning at the moment is to enjoy having a house and life to myself. Fliss's house came at the perfect time.' Then she remembered something.

He picked up her change in mood instantly. She'd never met a guy as sensitive to other people's moods as he was.

'What's wrong, Nell?'

'The roof has been leaking at the back and there's fungus growing in one corner of the top floor. I have to do something about that.'

'If you like, I'll have a look at it once we've sorted out your Internet connection.'

'I can't keep taking advantage of you.'

'I offered. You didn't ask.'

She gave him a puzzled look. 'You're being extraordinarily kind to a stranger.'

'I am, aren't I? I haven't quite figured out why myself.'

He reached out to tuck a wayward strand of her hair behind her ear and she sucked in her breath involuntarily because even that light touch got to her.

She edged away from him, unnerved by her own reaction. It had been so long since she'd responded to a man's touch. 'Do you, um, know much about house repairs?'

He looked down at his hand as if it had acted of its own accord, then stuffed it into his pocket and took a deep breath. 'I know a fair bit because I have a large old house to take care of too.'

'Ah. Well. All right, then. But I'd better invite you round twice to meals as a thank you.' He could easily say no if she was misreading the situation and he wasn't interested in her.

'I won't say no. You don't know how to make chocolate mousse, do you?'

'Yes, of course.'

'It's my favourite dessert.'

'Mine too, actually. I'll make you one.' She gestured to the vehicle. 'Before we go inside, how do you like my new car? Do you know about cars as well?'

'I know far less about cars. That one isn't new but the bodywork looks in good nick. Come to think of it, I've read some excellent reviews of that model.'

'I thought you said you weren't into cars?'

'I may have to buy a newish one for myself soon, so I've started gathering information. Mine is wearing out fast. Well, it is twelve years old. I only need that police harridan to find something wrong with it and I'm in trouble.'

'Police harridan?'

'Long story.'

'I'm not in a hurry.'

He flushed slightly. 'I suppose you're bound to find out so I might as well tell you. As it happens I'm related to an earl and that makes me an honourable. A certain police constable, Edwina Richards by name, is from a family which hates the aristocracy with a passion. She's carrying on her father's tradition of picking on the Dennings. And I'm the only Denning left round here.'

Nell smiled. 'I don't care either way, so I promise to forget about your title.'

'It's not really a title and I don't usually mention it.'

'I read a novel once with an "honourable" in it. If I remember correctly, you only write it, not use it when speaking to the person.'

'Yes. Um, how did you decide on this car?'

He was clearly trying to change the subject and looked so embarrassed she followed his lead.

'I went to the car yard in town and thought this one looked about the right size and price for me. It felt right when I sat in it, so I told them it was too expensive.'

'A demon bargainer, are you?'

'I've had to be. Craig might have paid the basic maintenance for the boys on time, but he was never generous about anything else they needed.'

She could have kicked herself for bad-mouthing her ex, so went on hastily, 'When the salesman tried to persuade me to consider buying that car, I said I'd think about it but wanted to check other car yards out. Then I left.'

Angus grinned. 'Definitely a demon bargainer. Good for you.'

'I went to a couple of other places to compare prices, then to the library, where I got online to research this model. The price seemed fair and the reviews said it was a reliable car with low running costs, so I went back two hours after my first visit and allowed the guy to persuade me to buy. I managed to knock him down a bit first, though.'

'Well done, you. Now, let's get this computer fixed up. I'll just fetch the various pieces of hardware in from my car.'

'I'll help you carry the boxes.'

'I can—'

But she'd already gone down the drive.

He caught up with her and pinged to unlock the car. 'Are you always so ferociously independent, Nell?'

'Yep.'

He put on a mock Aussie accent. 'Good on yer, lady.'

They both chuckled and she thought how pleasant it was to joke with him. She'd been avoiding men of her own age socially for years, not only because of Craig, but because she'd worked with some selfish masculine prats, even if they did have legal degrees.

'Just a minute. Let me jiggle with my car lock. It's a bit wonky.'

Her thoughts continued to wander as he fiddled with the old vehicle. Her life in Australia had been quite pleasant, if busy, but oh, it had been so very tame! There was no other word for it. Tame. Motherhood, her day job, an occasional coffee or meal out with her women friends, and always something needing doing in the house or garden.

No real excitement, certainly no towering joy. She was fed up of that sameness.

She didn't want to marry again – no way! – but she'd not say no to a relationship. She wasn't very experienced with men, though, because she'd married young, so she was going to tread warily.

She stole a glance at Angus. He was rather nice, in a nerdish sort of way. She loved the way his spectacles magnified his eyes – pale-blue eyes, the colour of winter skies. He must have gone grey early because his hair was pure silver now, even though his face looked young still. In her experience, people turned old inside their heads much more than on the outside. It wasn't grey hair but facial expressions that betrayed whether they considered themselves old.

Why was she thinking about Angus like that? Because he'd touched her, that's why. One damned touch and her whole body had reacted to it. He was dangerously attractive.

She nodded her head. Good! About time her emotions had an outing.

'There you are. I think the catch needs oiling again. Or something.'

She grabbed a couple of the boxes and led the way inside the house. 'I'm going to keep the computer in the dining room. It can sit on the table for the moment. Fliss had her connection there, so there's a connection point. See.'

He got her online quickly, which was great, but then his phone rang and when he looked at the message, he sighed. 'I'll have to come back another time to look at your attic. I need to deal with this straight away.'

And he was gone without another word.

Saved by the bell! she thought. She'd actually been thinking of inviting him to stay to tea.

And was disappointed that he'd had to leave.

Oh, she was a fool! She hardly knew the man. But she wanted to.

Dan Shackleton had been out of circulation for a few days, having a minor procedure done at the hospital. The doctors had expected it to be a day surgery only, but his stupid elderly heart had chucked a wobbly and they'd kept him in for a couple of nights.

How he hated being shut indoors! Hated hospitals, too. He'd spent too much time in them in recent years, watching his wife's health follow her mind downhill.

When he got home, he obeyed instructions and didn't do anything strenuous, just pottered round the house and leafed through his latest gardening catalogues. But he could look out of the window and watch the birds in his garden. A cheeky little robin soon had him smiling.

Well, he didn't feel up to doing much, he admitted to

himself, but he might sit outside in his garden once he'd made himself a decent cup of tea. He had a table and chairs in a nice sunny spot.

The next day Dan felt much more lively and since the weather was fine again, he strolled across to see how his allotment was going on. He wasn't going to do anything to it, except maybe a bit of watering. The doctor had told him short walks were good for him and it was only three streets away, after all.

To his relief, someone had watered his seedlings. It'd be young Janey. She loved gardening nearly as much as he did.

There was no one else at the allotments and he admitted to himself that even the short walk had tired him more than usual, so he sat outside his hut, enjoying more of the mild sunshine on his face.

The sound of a squeaky wheel made him open his eyes, and to his delight, it was Janey with little Millie sitting in the buggy, watching the world with a big wide smile.

'That wheel needs oiling again,' he said.

'You stay where you are, Mr S and I'll get the oilcan. I came to check whether the seedlings needed watering. I thought you'd be resting at home today.'

'I am resting. But it's nicer to rest here.'

'I bet you walked here.'

'Well, yes. But it's not far and they said to do some gentle exercise.'

She parked the buggy where Millie could see what was going on around her, then studied him. 'How are you really, Mr Shackleton? I rang your neighbour and she told me you'd been kept in the hospital, but I couldn't visit you there because it's a bit too far out of town. I didn't dare miss my classes at tech after starting the course late.'

'I'm fine. They had to put in a pacemaker as well as a stent, so they kept me in prison for an extra day or two.'

'Prison! That's a bit unfair to hospitals, isn't it?'

'It's what it felt like. Those nurses were so bossy. Anyway, never mind them. What's been going on round here? Did I miss any excitement?'

'You did. I'll put the kettle on, then tell you about all the goings-on.'

'Good goings-on or bad?'

'Both.' She came out of the hut and sat beside him, bringing him up to date on what had been happening to Winifred.

'Well, I never! You're sure she's all right?'

'Yes. And you'll never guess what's happened!'

He saw tears fill Janey's eyes, but she was smiling so that was all right. 'Go on. Tell me.'

'She's invited me and Millie to go and live with her. Isn't that wonderful, Mr S? She needs to have someone around and I've been feeling so lonely in that flat. And it'll save me money as well.'

He fumbled for his handkerchief and passed it to her, so that she could mop her eyes. 'I'm glad for both of you, lass. If Winifred's been having trouble, she definitely shouldn't be living on her own. She's ten years older than me, you know. She's wonderful for her age. She'll see me out, that's for sure.'

'Don't talk like that!'

He laughed softly. 'By my age most people have faced the fact that life doesn't go on for ever. The important thing is to enjoy what life you do get.'

'Well, I hope yours goes on for a long time yet. Anyway, there's something else wonderful. I know we said you two were like honorary grandparents, but people know you aren't. She's asked me to call her Auntie Winnie instead. People can't tell immediately whether that's right or not. Neither of us has any actual family. Not now.'

'Eh, that's really good.' He hesitated, then said, 'You could, um, call me Uncle Dan if you wanted. I'd like that. I never see my grandchildren and I enjoy young company.'

'Really? Oh, I'd love to.'

He reached out to take hold of her hand. 'That's good, lass.'

She patted his leathery old hand. 'Won't your sons mind? You do have relatives.'

He snorted in disgust. 'I don't see much of my sons. Terry lives in Reading. Simon's wife left me some food in the fridge and they rang up last night to check that I'd got home safely, but they didn't come near me.

'They left a message that they'd come round to see me at the weekend. I could die and they'd not know it.'

He shrugged but she could see he was upset about that.

To take his mind off it, she said, 'You know how we were talking about setting up a garden-share scheme at Auntie Winnie's?'

'Yes.'

'Well, once I've settled in and you've recovered properly, will you help us plan and organise it? You could be the expert adviser, no hard digging but helping folk get going. You know so much about plants. It's far too big a garden for me to look after and it frets Auntie Winnie to see it looking such a mess.'

To her relief he brightened up at once.

'Well, if Winifred's still OK with the idea, I'm in for it too. It'll give us both something to do and it makes sense for folk with too much garden to share it with those who don't have one. Think of the good vegetables we can grow for you and young Millie once we've got the soil up to scratch, and without all those nasty chemicals. I shall start making plans and checking my catalogues when I get home. That's something I can do without tiring myself out.'

He'd have liked to go and visit Winifred today, but the extra walking would have been too much for him, he knew, so he contented himself with phoning her later on and having a good long chat.

He saw his smiling face in the mirror as he put down the phone. Well, he should be happy: he had friends now, an adopted niece and something to look forward to.

He missed his wife, always would. Alzheimer's was a dreadful thing to happen to anyone. But Peggy had passed on and that was that, so very final.

You had to make a new life for yourself when you lost someone or you'd just moulder away.

But it would be good if he could still be a useful member of the community. He didn't like to sit around watching TV all day like some retired people he knew. He liked to do things.

In Australia, Steve was woken by the alarm clock his mother had bought him ringing loudly in his ear. He hadn't set the stupid thing, so why was it going off?

Cursing, he fumbled for it and knocked it off the cardboard box he was using as a bedside table in the new flat. Only it carried on ringing, out of reach now.

He groaned as he sat up. His head was thumping and his mouth tasted foul. He tried to remember the previous night and couldn't work out what he'd been drinking. No, it hadn't been booze. His friend Nate had scored some pills that were supposed to make you feel good. Only Steve couldn't remember a thing, good or bad, after taking one, and he felt awful now.

He'd tried a few things to get high, but they didn't always work.

He struggled to his feet and found the alarm clock, fumbling till he'd stopped it making that awful racket.

As he turned to get back into bed and continue sleeping, the door of his room opened and his brother Nick yelled, 'Don't go back to bed, you dill! It's Monday. Good thing I set your alarm clock. Hurry up or you'll be late for work.'

Steve gave him a rude sign, but on consideration he decided Nick was right. He'd better not be late again or his supervisor would go ape.

His brother was already dressed and ready for work, but Steve couldn't find any clean clothes.

'Can you lend me a clean shirt, Nick?'

'No way. You spilt coffee down the last one I lent you, then left it on the floor. I washed and ironed all mine and I told you to do yours but then your so-called friend rang and you went rushing off to meet him.'

'What do you mean by "so-called friend"?'

'He's bad news, that one is. The word is he's dealing.'

'No way. Nate just uses a bit of the good stuff occasionally for recreation. Everyone does these days. He didn't sell it me, he gave it me to try.'

'And look what it did to you.' Nick stared at him. 'You've got a really dopey look on your face.' He hesitated, then added, 'We both promised Ma we wouldn't do drugs. If I find you getting into them again, I'm out of here, and then how will you pay the rent? You owe me for the next two weeks, by the way.'

'Yeah, yeah.'

When Nick had left for work, Steve went to raid his brother's room for clean clothes, but found a brand-new lock on the door.

For two pins he'd break it down.

He raised one fist, then let it drop again. No, better not. He might damage the door, then he'd have to buy a new one.

He fumbled through the clothes scattered around his bedroom floor and found a shirt that didn't look too bad. He'd have to do some washing tonight.

It was all his mother's fault for abandoning them so suddenly. She should have been here, helping them get used to it.

What the hell was she doing in England that was more important than looking after her sons, anyway?

He agreed with his dad that she was hiding something from them. But what?

Chapter Eight

Her landlord lived in the ground-floor flat, but he was away so Janey rang the company that managed the flats to say she wanted to give notice.

Kieran himself rang her back within the hour, instead of letting his property manager deal with it.

'Just out of interest, where are you going, Janey?'

She explained about Winifred.

'That's great. Look, there's no need to give notice. Just pay until the day you leave.'

'That doesn't sound fair to you.'

He laughed. 'I'm not short of money and I'll easily find another tenant, I promise you. Oh, and you might like to congratulate me. Nicole and I got married last week.'

'Never! I didn't see any announcements.'

'We didn't tell anyone except her younger son and my brother and his family. Given the circumstances, it seemed better to do it quietly. Which didn't make it any less joyful an event.'

His voice had grown all soft and she smiled in sympathy. 'Well, I certainly do congratulate you. I'm sure you'll be very happy together. Are you going to move out of the flats as you said you might after you got married?'

'Yes. We'll need a bigger house because Paul will be living with us. We've bought a house, but we need to put in a new kitchen and bathroom, and buy some furniture, then we'll reveal all by throwing a party, to which you and young Millie will be invited.'

Janey had been worried about Nicole, who was a local librarian and had been kind to her, so she was glad the two of them had got married.

Nicole's house had been burnt down by her older son in a drug craze. Dawn had told her Nicole would be able to sell the plot for land value and the insurance company would no doubt pay for the house and contents, but still she'd worried. She knew what it was like to suddenly lose your home and possessions from when her father threw her out for being pregnant.

Smiling, Janey put down the phone. She had fallen lucky with her landlord. Kieran had been recovering from a serious road accident and had bought a small block of flats with his compensation money. He had been generous with his tenants, each of whom seemed to have some sort of problem, not charging top rent.

He'd even helped Janey trap her rapist and get him arrested. Well, Kieran had been a famous investigative journalist before his accident, hadn't he? So he knew how to do that sort of thing.

If anyone deserved to be happy it was those two.

Janey sighed wistfully. Perhaps one day she'd meet

someone she could love, too. Good things seemed to happen on Peppercorn Street – well, most of the time, anyway. She was so glad she'd come to live here.

She looked round her small furnished flat: one bedroom, a tiny shower room and a living room/kitchen. It wouldn't take long to pack her possessions, then she'd contact a company doing small removals. The sooner she moved in with Auntie Winnie the better, as far as she was concerned.

That thought made her realise that whatever Dawn said about the risks, she was going to move to Number 5.

Dawn went to see Winifred about a rental lease for Janey, showing her the standard form.

'Does she really need a lease? I'm not likely to throw her out.'

'Yes, but if anything happened to you, your heir might throw her out.'

'Ah. I see.' Winifred looked at her thoughtfully. 'You're right, then. I'll sign this straight away. She'll be quite secure here while I'm alive and I'm thinking of changing my will and leaving her a little something, so that she'll have money behind her. What do you think?'

'That'd be very kind of you.'

'I shan't say anything to her, so please keep this to yourself, Dawn.'

'Of course. Besides, Janey would be happiest of all if you managed to stay alive. She's very fond of you and she's absolutely thrilled to have an adopted family. That poor girl has been dreadfully lonely. She didn't even have a computer or TV at first.'

'I'm thrilled too. I understand loneliness. Don't worry.

137

I'm not sick or anything. I've been very lucky in my health, but at my age you have to plan for the inevitable. Now, how about a cup of tea and a piece of cake?'

'Sounds good. You bake the best cakes of anyone I know.'

Winifred went pink with pleasure at this compliment.

The doorbell rang as Janey was about to start sorting out her kitchen equipment. She went to the intercom and heard Dawn's voice, so pressed the button to let her visitor in.

'Would you like a cup of tea?'

Dawn shook her head. 'No, thanks. I'm full of tea and cake after visiting Miss Parfitt.'

Janey laughed. 'I'm going to put on weight living with her. She does love making cakes.'

'That wouldn't be a bad thing. You're far too thin. Anyway, I came to tell you that she's happy to give you an official lease and here it is. Check it through, then you can sign it too.'

'I'm sure it'll be all right if you've arranged it.'

'Wrong thing to say.' She slapped the paper down on the table, one hand on it to prevent Janey simply signing it.

Janey looked at her in puzzlement.

'Never, ever sign a contract without reading every word. It doesn't matter who tells you it's OK, always check for yourself.'

'Oh. Sorry. I suppose you're right.'

'I am right and don't you ever forget to do that.' Dawn looked round, then asked in a gentler voice, 'When are you planning to move?'

'Tomorrow, if possible. I was grateful for this flat, but I've had some unhappy times here.'

'You got through them, though. You're a capable young woman. How are you going to move your stuff?'

'There are companies doing small removals.'

'Waste of money. We have a van at Just Girls. You don't have any big pieces of furniture, apart from Millie's playpen, so you and I can easily move your things in the van. I'll nip down to the supermarket and get some empty boxes for you. You won't have any way of carrying enough of them home.'

'You're wonderful, Dawn. I thought I'd have to go to and fro to get what I need. You always understand the practical side of things.'

'I try to.' She patted Janey's shoulder. 'I've dealt with a few girls in your position.'

She was back half an hour later with the van this time, and it was full of empty boxes and some extra cleaning materials. 'They're a lot more generous with boxes if you buy something,' she said airily.

'Thank you.' Janey knew this was a small way of helping her and since she had to count every penny and knew Dawn loved to help people, she didn't let on. She helped carry the boxes up to the flat, excitement rising in her at this tangible sign of the changes to come.

Once Dawn had left, Janey picked up Millie, who was getting restless in her playpen, then rang Winifred. 'Can I move in tomorrow, Auntie Winnie?'

'Of course you can, dear. But I'll have to leave you to sort out the bedrooms to your liking. I'm not up to moving furniture about these days.'

'I'm happy to do that myself.'

When she put the phone down, Janey danced Millie

round the flat. 'We're going to live in a proper house with a garden, yes we are, yes we are! And we're going to have an adopted family. They want us, oh they diddly, diddly do.'

She tickled her daughter's tummy, which made her give one of her fat chuckles. 'Isn't that wonderful, my little darling?'

Millie let out another gurgle of laughter then began to suck hard on her thumb.

'Sorry. You're hungry and I'm nattering on. I can't help being excited. We'll have something to eat, then I'll do a big clean of this place. I don't want to leave a mess for Kieran.'

Angus came back to see Nell the next afternoon. 'I'm sorry I had to duck out on you yesterday. Crisis with one of my customers. Is it convenient now to check the attic? Perhaps there's a cracked tile leaking up there.'

'Yes. But I had another look and it's more than a leak.' Since she didn't dare use the ceiling light fitting, she'd bought a torch and some batteries, and had checked out all the dark corners of the top floor more carefully.

Someone might have modernised the kitchen but she'd bet no one had touched the top floor of the house since she'd stayed there herself as a child. Only it hadn't been mouldy then.

She took Angus upstairs and stopped in the doorway. 'It looks all right at this side, but the rear wall feels damp to the touch and some parts are squishy. I found several other patches of fungus, though none as big as the first one.'

When Nell showed him the problem area, he whistled softly. 'You were right not to risk using that old light fitting.' He took out a torch of his own, a far more powerful one than hers, and it showed the damage all too clearly. 'Oh, hell!'

Her heart sank. 'It's bad, isn't it?'

'Not good at all. Let's see if it's affected the nearby floor.' As he took a few steps it shook visibly under him. 'Stay back!'

'I've been walking on it.'

'You've been lucky, then.' Taking out a penknife, he jabbed it into the planks on the floor near the biggest patch of livid white fungus. The stuff looked so horrible, like a rotting fish's underbelly, that she hadn't wanted even to touch it.

She watched in dismay as the knife blade went straight into the floorboard as if it was cutting butter.

'Damn!' He pulled out the knife and jabbed it into a few other places nearby with the same result, before checking the rest of the rear wall.

Then he took her arm and pulled her to the doorway. 'Don't come up here again without a mask. Some sorts of mould are toxic. And don't walk near that back wall again, whatever you do. Some of those floorboards are rotten and might not bear your weight. If it's got into the joists, the whole floor might crumble suddenly under you.'

'You walked there.'

'I walked on where it'd been nailed to cross-beams and even then I didn't like the feel of it.'

She didn't speak till they were downstairs, then she sat down at the kitchen table, feeling upset. 'It's going to be expensive to fix, isn't it, Angus?'

'Won't be cheap. Could even mean replacing the whole roof as well as some of the joists.'

Silence, then she faced it because she never pretended to herself, well, almost never. 'It's not worth repairing, is it? I mean, you can see from outside that the place has been neglected for a long time.'

'No, I don't think it's worth it. But you should get it checked, in case I'm wrong.'

'Once I got up there in full daylight, I could see for myself how bad it was. I wish I hadn't been so rude to that estate agent. You were right. I should have found out what his client was willing to pay.'

Angus didn't say anything, but he took her hand and gave it a comforting squeeze.

She sniffed, but one tear wouldn't be held back and he wiped it away with the tip of his forefinger, sending more of those delightful shivers round her body.

'I did so want a home of my own here, not a rented place,' she confessed.

'Life's like that. As John Lennon said . . .'

She repeated the rest of the line with him, '"Life is what happens to you when you're making other plans".'

It had happened two or three times now that one of them had started a quotation and they'd finished chanting it together. They seemed to be on a very similar wavelength, for all the differences in their backgrounds.

She sighed. 'I suppose I'll have to go crawling back to that horrible Jeffries man and find out what his client is offering.'

'Pity you were quite rude to him.' He thought for a moment, then said, 'Hey! How about I go and see him, pretend you and I are together and tell him you were having a bad day when you spoke to him? I'll say I'm trying to make you see sense about the house. He and I can have a man-to-man chat about how best to make you consider an offer.'

'Would you really do that for me?'

Silence hung like a fragile gossamer curtain between them, then he nodded. 'Yes. I would. And before you ask, I'm not saying that to get into your knickers.' He twirled an imaginary villain's moustache.

She chuckled but then she had to ask, 'Why are you saying it, then?'

'Damned if I know. Because I want us to be friends, I suppose, and friends help one another.'

'I'd like to be friends. I don't know why I feel so comfortable with you, but I do. And I gratefully accept your offer of contacting Jeffries. Here's his business card.' She handed it to him, then looked out of the window. 'Do you think the sun is over the yardarm yet?'

'Definitely.'

'I haven't bought any wine yet but I'll buy a couple of bottles. Then we could drink to Mr Whatsit paying me a fortune for this sad wreck of a house. We could either walk into town to buy the wine or you could have a ride in my new car.'

'I have a better idea. I've got plenty of wine at my place. Why don't you come and visit me? I'll show you round and then stand you a comforting glass or two.'

'All right. You're on.' She felt happier at his kindness. Younger inside, too.

He joined her, looking up at the sky. 'It's going to be a fine evening. How about I drive you to my place in my car and then I'll walk you home later? I don't care to drink and drive.'

'Sounds good. I'll lock up this house.'

'I'll nip upstairs first and open all the attic windows. It won't hurt to start drying it out.'

She didn't say, 'Why bother?' but she thought it. She always tried to be honest with herself, even when it hurt.

'I must start going for walks,' she said when he rejoined her. 'I've not done any real exercise since I got here.'

'Don't tell me you like walking.'

'Yes, I do.'

'So do I.'

'One of the things I've been planning to do here is to go for long walks in the countryside. I've looked online at this part of England and seen photos of it in the spring and summer. It's so pretty.'

'Yes, it is. You can get booklets showing where to walk locally. And . . . if you like, I could show you some of my favourite walks. I've been neglecting exercising, too, except for moving about to stop my body seizing up from too much work at the computer.'

'I'd like that very much.' She looked back at the house and wrinkled her nose. 'Ugh. I can still smell that horrid mould.'

'It was pretty bad up there. I shut the door from the house into the attic again but you should sleep with your bedroom windows open.'

'Good idea. You're being kind and thoughtful towards me again.'

'Yes. And I'm enjoying it . . . again.'

They stared at one another for a moment, then he opened the car door for her and drove off.

* * *

Angus stopped at the top of Peppercorn Street, which was a dead end with a circular turning circle for vehicles. He gestured to a drive with high hedges on either side and a rather uneven surface. A big sign said: PRIVATE. KEEP OUT.

'That leads to my place. But first, it's time for another confession. Nell, my house is quite big and it's been here for more than two centuries. I have a couple of acres of land with it as well. The developers have been trying to get hold of it for years.'

'Wow.'

'My official address is number 1 Peppercorn Street, but the house was here long before the street was extended so far up the hill. I think the numbering was just done as a convenience for the postal services.'

She was startled. 'What? You live in a stately home?'

'Hardly. The house is called Dennings and it's larger than average, yes, but nowhere near a stately home. It's just . . . well, a gentleman's residence. I wish I could afford to keep it up properly because it could be a little gem. However, unlike your late aunt, I do keep the roof and basic structure in good repair. Inside, though, most of the rooms are dusty and unused because I work long hours. Don't expect me to entertain you in grand style tonight. I live in three rooms downstairs, four if you count the kitchen.'

He stopped the car for a second time at the end of a drive about fifty yards long and gestured to a square stone building at the end of an even longer stretch of drive that curved to the right. 'There you are. A neat little Georgian residence. *Mi casa es su casa.*'

She recognised the Spanish phrase and repeated it in English: 'My house is your house. It's a nice way of saying welcome, isn't it? I may take you up on that literally if my house falls down on me.'

He stared at her solemnly. 'Any time you need a place to stay, you can come to me. I mean that. I have lots of spare rooms.'

She felt flustered by the way he was staring at her. She didn't know what had made her say that. 'Oh. Well, it's very kind of you, but I'm not without money, so I can afford to rent a place, even if I don't sell my house quickly. If the musty smell gets any worse, I may have to do that quite soon. Once I'd opened up the attic, it felt as if I'd let the genie out of the bottle. What's the rental market like in Sexton Bassett?'

'Mostly it's flats. Houses get snapped up quickly and seem to me to be rather expensive to rent. But what do I know? I'm into computers, not property.'

'Well, let's hope the fungus is manageable, so that I can at least spend a couple of months in Fliss's house before I hand it over.' She looked at Dennings again, sighing with envy. It was such a pretty building, but the garden was a mess. There was a gravelled circle for cars to turn round in and another gravelled track led round to the rear. Something about the place seemed familiar, she couldn't work out why.

Angus offered her his arm in an old-fashioned gesture and led her to the front door. 'I usually go in by the servants' entrance at the other side, but since I want to impress you, we'll use the front door today.'

He unlocked it, then held up a hand to stop her going inside. 'Wait there till I come back for you. I have to disarm the security system.'

The minute he stepped inside something began beeping. It grew louder, sounding quite frantic for a moment, then stopped abruptly. He came back and offered her his arm again. 'Won't you walk into my parlour, madame?'

'I'd love to.'

'Oh!' She stopped a couple of paces inside to take in the hall. As he had said, the house wasn't grand and this part did feel dusty and unused. But the hall was completely panelled in honey-coloured oak and had a pretty staircase rising on the left with elegant wrought-iron banisters. There was an elaborately moulded plaster ceiling and the floor was tiled in what looked like marble.

The late evening sun was shining through the stained glass panels on either side of the front door, splashing patches of vivid colour here and there across the floor and walls.

'It's beautiful, Angus. I can imagine why your family has never sold it. I've visited one or two grand houses – and, yes, we do have some in Australia – but I could never imagine living in them.'

'And you could imagine living here?'

She surprised herself by saying 'Definitely!' without hesitation. She thought she heard a sound of distant laughter, as she had done in her dreams, but told herself she was imagining it. That dream certainly had lingered in her memory. Ridiculous, really.

Angus let her peer into the ground-floor rooms from the doorways, but refused to allow her to spend long exploring. 'We're here for a glass of wine, not a guided tour or a historical lecture. You can look round at your leisure another time. It's easier in full daylight, anyway. White or red wine?'

'Either.'

He took her into the kitchen, got out some wine glasses and opened a door at one side to reveal steps leading down, presumably to a cellar. While he was gone, she found a tea towel, and rinsed and polished the two wine glasses.

He came back and caught her finishing that task. She was betrayed into laughter as he shook his head in mock sadness.

'They had been washed, you know, Nell.'

'I can't help it. I like to drink my wine out of sparkling glasses. And these are so pretty they deserve better treatment from you.'

'I don't even notice that sort of thing usually, I must admit. Well, I don't drink much. I'm too busy and I need my brain clear to work with, since it's the main tool of my trade.'

'Absent-minded professor type?'

'Something like that when I'm creating something.' He began to open the bottle.

'Can I ask what exactly you do for a living?'

'Computer stuff. I invented a specialist app and it's made me some money, so when I got offered voluntary redundancy, I didn't look for another job. I'm working on a suite of apps that might make even more money. Or might not, but I hope they will. More than that I won't say, because I don't tell anyone the details. I'm getting there, though.'

He looked at her very seriously and added, 'Since I already have one app doing quite well for me, certain people have been trying to find out what I'm doing. Someone's tried to hack into my computer a couple of times. They didn't succeed. I'm well protected.'

'Very wise. Give that to me.' She took the bottle and wiped round the top of it, then sniffed it. 'Smells good. Needs to breathe a bit, don't you think? There isn't a label. What exactly is it?'

'I guess you could call this *un petit vin de Bourgogne*. A cousin of my father's had a small vineyard in the Burgundy region of France. Dad used to buy his wines from them by the barrel, then bottle them himself. When the cousin died, his son sold the vineyard to a big wine company. Pity. I'm fortunate my father bought more than he consumed, so I still have a fair few bottles left.'

'Is your father dead?'

'Yes. He was a good guy but quite old to be a father. I was a late-life surprise to my parents.'

'And your mother?'

'She was younger than him. Now she lives in Spain and has a very jolly life there. I can't keep up with what she's doing. She used to descend on me sometimes, bringing her latest lover or friends, showing off the house. When I closed most of it up, she started to go to a cousin in Kent instead.'

'She sounds fun.'

'She is. In fact she and the cousin are an amazing pair, lively and outgoing. Both of them love partying, so I'm a disappointment to my mother. I spent a couple of days there with them at Christmas and they exhausted me.'

'I envy you having relatives. My father quarrelled with his, emigrated and refused to communicate with any of them again. I still don't know what they quarrelled about.

Something and nothing, knowing his chancy temper.'

'Are you going to try to trace the relatives?'

'It's on the list of things to do. I have to deal with the house first, though.'

He put one finger on her lips. 'We're not going to talk about that, remember? We're just going to have a few drinks and chill out.'

He stared at her, then said, 'Oh, hell!' in quite a different tone and pulled her into his arms.

The kiss began gently, but it didn't stay gentle and before she could think about it, she was kissing him back just as hungrily.

When he pulled away, he looked at her very seriously. 'Something keeps happening between us, doesn't it?'

'Yes. Chemistry. It's taken me by surprise. After my troubles with Craig, I never seemed to fancy anyone.'

'He must have done a right old job on you.'

'Oh, yes. Wife-beating was alive and well in our house. I still hate him.'

'He beat you?'

She shrugged.

'I don't blame you for hating him so thoroughly then. Joanna and I had eighteen glorious years together. You're the first woman I've wanted since she was killed.'

'Oh.' Nell's breath caught in her throat and a trace of fear crept in as well as desire.

He studied her as if he understood how she was feeling. 'I don't think it'd be good for me to try to rush you into anything, but I do think we should let things unfold and see if we keep feeling good together. Will you do that? It's worth a try, surely? Chemistry like ours doesn't happen very often.'

She felt shy, swallowed hard and managed to nod. It was as if she'd taken a step forward in her new life and it felt . . . right. Very right.

'I'm a pretty civilised guy, even though I do fancy you like crazy. I've never hit a woman in anger in my life.' He grinned briefly and looked down at his thin, wiry body. 'I've never hit a man, either. I'm not the macho type.'

She was silent for a moment or two, wondering how frank she dared be, then thought what the hell. Angus had been open with her from the start. 'I didn't think I was able to, um, inspire desire in anyone.'

'Well, you were wrong.'

'Good. But after three children, my body isn't . . . all that trim.'

'Ah. He made you ashamed of your own body, didn't he?'

She nodded.

'What is he, Mr Perfect? Joanna had to have a Caesarean when Oliver was born. I used to kiss her scar. It was a badge of honour as far as I was concerned. It gave me my son.'

'Would she approve of you finding someone else?'

'Oh, yes. We discussed it once or twice. As you do. When you're happy with someone you want them to be happy again if the worst happens. I mourned good and hard for a while, but I'm over that now. I'll show you her photo next time. I think you'd have liked each other.'

With a complete change of tone, he added, 'Now, drink your wine, woman.'

Nell felt so relaxed with him that after a mere two glasses she fell asleep and didn't wake until he shook her gently.

'It's getting late. Want to spend the night here,

sleepyhead?' he asked softly. 'No strings attached. I have plenty of spare bedrooms.'

'I don't think so. Sorry to fall asleep on you. I'm still getting over jet lag.'

'I'd better walk you home, then.'

When they got outside, she stopped. Something about the garden once again seemed familiar. It was nearly dark now so she couldn't see it clearly enough to be sure but it reminded her of the dreams. No, why was she thinking about those? And how could it possibly remind her of anything? She'd never been here before today.

'Was it a pretty garden once, Angus?'

'It used to be. The other side's in better nick than this one. I go out and pull up weeds sometimes when I'm thinking about a problem. Never fails to get the old creative juices flowing. I'll show you round the grounds next time.'

At her house she took the initiative, twining her arms round his neck and kissing him thoroughly.

'Ooh, you are so masterful,' he teased.

She smiled as she went inside, but wrinkled her nose at the smell of mould. It seemed worse than before, as if they'd stirred it up with their investigations.

She went straight to bed and lay for a few moments, going over the evening. Life could surprise you. She hadn't had any surprises as nice as this one for a long time, though.

Yeah, right! she thought as she slid into sleep.

She dreamt of the garden again. Only the voices this time promised her she'd find true love on Peppercorn Street.

Only . . . in the morning she wished that dream really could come true. Imagine finding happiness and safety with a man who was a friend as well as a lover.

She wasn't greedy, didn't desire a fortune, just kindness, love and companionship.

She dozed off again briefly and Angus appeared in another dream, holding out his hand and dancing her up and down his hall. It felt as if she was floating on a cloud of happiness and sunlight.

It was one of the nicest dreams she'd ever had in her life and when she woke up properly an hour or so later, she was smiling.

Chapter Nine

Janey was up early on moving day, getting dressed and finishing off packing her clothes quietly as she waited for Millie to stir. She'd felt so excited last night she'd not expected to sleep, but she'd slept as soundly as her daughter, for once. Life was so much easier now Millie slept right through the night.

By nine o'clock she had fed and dressed Millie and was ready to leave, which was stupid because Dawn wasn't coming to pick her up until ten.

When the reconditioned mobile phone supplied by Just Girls rang, she jumped in shock, she got so few calls. For a few seconds she could only stare at it. Who could be ringing her at this hour?

'Janey?'

Her breath caught in her throat. 'Mum?'

'Yes. Please don't put the phone down on me. I . . . this phone call is very important. I need to say something to you.'

'Oh. All right. I wasn't going to put the phone down, though.' She hadn't tried to get back in touch with her mother, who had taken her father's side in bullying her for most of her life. If it hadn't been for her granddad, Janey would have had no one to stand up for her and show her unconditional love as a child. She still missed him.

She realised her mother was weeping and found it in herself to ask gently, 'What do you want to say, Mum?'

'I need to . . . to apologise to you.'

'What for?'

'Everything. Not taking your side. Letting him, your father . . . be unkind.'

It was the last thing Janey had expected to hear. But the apology came too late. The harm had been done. She couldn't think what to say.

'You knew I'd left your father?'

'Yes. I'd heard.'

'I'm still at a women's refuge. I daren't go home. He'd kill me. He hasn't . . . come near you?'

'No. I've not seen him once.' And she'd kept her eyes open.

'His second court case comes up soon, I think.'

Janey was puzzled. 'What second court case?'

There was silence for a few seconds, then her mother said, 'For hurting me quite badly after the first court case. He was furious about being given probation, furious that his friend was put into jail for raping you. The neighbours called the police. I think they saved my life.'

'I didn't know about that, just that you'd left him.' She'd kept away from her parents and would have had trouble getting to their house even if she'd wanted to visit them.

'I hope they lock him away for what he did to you . . . and to me.' Her mother's voice surprised her, it was much firmer than her usual soft, hesitant tone.

'Yes. He needs stopping.'

'Amen to that. Look, Janey, I've been going to counselling here at the refuge, as well as discussing what's happened with the other women and . . . Well, I'm starting to see things more clearly. My first step is to apologise to you. And I do. From the bottom of my heart. I was a coward and a very bad mother. I'm sorry.'

'Um . . . right.'

'And next I need to get my head together and make a new life. That's going to take some time.'

Janey didn't want to go on with this. She'd find it hard, if not impossible, to truly forgive her mother. 'I wish you luck.'

'But you don't want to see me. You're still bitter.'

'Yes.'

'I was terrified of him, Janey.'

'So was I. He used to thump me for nothing.'

'He hit me too. Often.'

How often? she wondered. She hadn't heard cries or shouts from their room, or seen any bruises on her mother.

'They said you'd be upset still. I don't blame you. I won't annoy you by calling again.'

Janey felt mean; she didn't want it to end like this. After all, her mother had apologised. That was something. 'No, wait! Give me your phone number. I'll call you . . . in a week or two. Just leave things for now, all right? I've a lot on at the moment. I'm moving house today.'

'You will call? Really?'

'Yes.'

'Promise.' Her voice broke. 'Please promise.'

And Janey couldn't refuse, just . . . couldn't. 'I promise.'

'Thank you. You don't know how much this means to me. One more thing before you go . . . how is Millie? She looked so well cared for when I saw her. You must be a good mother. I'm sorry I haven't got to know her.'

'Millie's wonderful. She's a happy, healthy baby and I love her to pieces.'

'I'm glad.'

The line went dead. Janey swiped clumsily at the tears the call had brought. She wished she could wipe away the bad memories as easily. One thing she was determined about: Millie was going to have a happy life. No one was going to bash or bully her.

It was a relief when Dawn turned up, but of course she noticed at once that Janey was upset.

'What's the matter?'

After a moment's hesitation, she explained about the phone call.

'Hmm. Well, I'm pleased you were kind to her. Well done! Maybe, once you're settled in at Miss Parfitt's, you should get some counselling about how to handle this situation from now on. I can find someone who will be able to help you.'

'Oh. The problem is, I don't really want to get in touch with my mother again. Only, she was so upset, crying, that I couldn't refuse. It'd have been like treading on a kitten. And she knows I don't break my promises, so she'll be expecting me to call. I'll have to do it, but not yet. I'm relieved that I've never bumped into my father in town.'

'He's moved. Didn't anyone tell you? Apparently he beat up your mother so badly she had to go to hospital and the neighbours gave him the cold shoulder for how he'd treated you and her. Your mother didn't go back to the house. Then he lost his job because of his drinking and he was in trouble with the bank already because he'd lent his friend Gary money. So he put the house up for sale and left the district.'

'Do you know where he's gone?'

'To stay with some cousin or other who has a small farm. He couldn't go too far away, because he has to stay in touch with the police and his probation officer.'

'That'd be his cousin Wayne, who lives on the other side of Swindon on a smallholding. They grew up together. Wayne's a bully too. I'm glad my father's gone even further away.'

Dawn put her hands on Janey's shoulders and stared at her earnestly. 'I don't blame you. But I just want to say one thing more to you. You can afford to be generous to your mother. She was weak and cowardly but she wasn't the villain.'

'No. I suppose not.'

'You have a lot of good things going on in your life now. Your mother's lost everything, her home included, though I think the authorities will make sure she gets a share of the money when it's sold. If she really is trying to make amends, don't trample on her efforts, even if you're never able to feel close to her.'

Janey sighed. 'I'll try.'

'We all have to face dragons at times in our life, you know.' She patted her young companion's back, waited a moment then spoke more briskly, 'You've coped well with your problems so far. Very well. Now, come on. That's enough soul-searching. This is meant to be a happy day. Let's get your stuff loaded into the van. We'll take Millie and the playpen down last of all.'

When everything had been removed from the flat, Dawn picked Millie up. 'I'll give you a minute or two to say goodbye to your first home.'

Janey nodded but she didn't go back inside, didn't want to. She stared into the flat from the doorway. Kieran had decorated it nicely and provided decent basic furniture, but it had never felt like a home to her and now it looked bare and unwelcoming. She'd spent all too many lonely, unhappy hours here and was glad to leave.

She closed the door firmly. 'Onwards and upwards,' she murmured. It was a positive motto she'd found helpful in recent months. And perseverance had paid off. She was studying again, had her darling little daughter to love, and had begun making new friends. She even had an adopted family now.

It didn't take long for Dawn to drive them to the top of the street and Auntie Winnie opened the door of number 5, beaming a welcome.

She must have been watching out for us, Janey thought. She liked the thought of someone doing that.

Even the sun seemed to be shining more brightly on this part of the street as she got Millie out of the baby carrier and took her into the house, plonking a kiss on Auntie Winnie's wrinkled cheek as she passed.

Dawn helped her carry the things inside, then studied the bedroom. 'This old furniture is too heavy for you to move on your own. How about I round someone up to assist?'

'Later, perhaps, once I've decided what I want. I'll leave things as they are for now. There aren't that many choices about how you arrange a bedroom anyway, are there? Auntie Winnie said I could have another bedroom as well, for Millie, or for a study, and my own sitting room downstairs. I have to be able to hear Millie if she cries, though, so I'm not sure about sitting downstairs.'

'What you need in a big house like this is a baby monitor. I should have thought of that before. We have one or two second-hand ones at Just Girls. People donate all sorts of things to us. I'll bring one round and we'll see if we can fix it up here.'

Janey hugged her. 'You're wonderful, Dawn.'

She wanted to hug the whole world today.

With Millie making a mess of her face and bib as she sucked on a rusk in her high chair, and Auntie Winnie sitting nearby keeping an eye on her, Janey was able to go upstairs to her bedroom to unpack. Dawn had helped her erect Millie's cot next door in what had once been called a dressing room, but plastic carrier bags were still scattered everywhere.

She stood for a moment or two contemplating her new domain, enjoying the spacious feel to it, then began opening drawers. They were all empty, and some were so dusty she wondered how long they'd been unused. Well, she had a duster, but she might take a damp cloth to them first and leave them to dry. She rushed downstairs to get one, kissing Millie as she passed and daring to kiss Auntie Winnie too.

The drawers were dry by the time she'd hung up her clothes, taking up only half the big old wardrobe. Her other pieces of clothing didn't fill up even half the drawers, either. There was a chest of drawers in the small side room for Millie's things.

Janey decided to leave the single bed there pushed against one wall, ready for use later, because her daughter wouldn't be in the cot for ever. She smiled. Auntie Winnie might consider the baby's room to be small; in the flat, Janey and her daughter had shared one this size.

She left the doors open in case she was needed, but didn't get called down, so assumed Millie was all right. She felt sure Auntie Winnie would err on the side of being too careful, so didn't even go to check.

When she'd unpacked all the clothes, she sat for a moment on the bed, looking at a pretty painting on one wall and then she went to stare out of the window at the street and, beyond it, the roofs of the little town.

Unlike in the flat, she felt as if she'd come home here, she really did.

After doing some research online, Nell rang a company specialising in analysis and treatment of dry rot, which was what she suspected the problem was. Well, what else could it be?

'As it happens,' the man told her, 'we're doing a check on a house near you this afternoon. If you don't mind us coming at about five o'clock, we could take a preliminary look then and find out whether there's a need for anything more.'

'That'd be fine. The sooner it gets looked at, the better.'

The phone rang a minute after she'd put it down.

'Hello, sleepyhead.'

'Hello yourself, Angus.'

'Want me to go and see your estate agent today? I have a couple of errands to run in town.'

'Tomorrow would be better, if you don't mind. Someone's coming to look at the attic later this afternoon. I'd prefer to know exactly where I stand before you talk to that smarmy salesman.'

'OK. I'll see you this evening, then.'

'Oh?'

'Yes, we have a date.'

'We do?'

'I've decided to take you out for a pub meal. It's a very English tradition. It's not that I'd enjoy your company, perish the thought, but I feel it my duty to educate my colonial brethren.'

He hung up before she could reply and she laughed. She loved his light touch, the way he teased her.

She looked round the kitchen and frowned, wondering what to do with herself till inspection time.

In the end she decided that if she was going to have to sell this house, she'd better make a start on clearing its contents out. It'd help pass the time and divert her thoughts from her worries.

But oh, she was utterly fed up of clearing things out after spending weeks going through her Australian home and discarding her life and her sons' childhoods piece by piece. All she'd kept in the end had been some personal stuff she couldn't bear to part with, photos, some of her favourite books, a few ornaments and a few pieces of furniture she loved. They were in a hired storage locker, which was costing her an arm and a leg each month.

She looked at the mess and sighed. Since when did you only get to do the things you enjoyed? she told herself sternly. Just get on with it.

It took her the rest of the morning to sort out the contents of the kitchen cupboards, which were a jumbled mess. That made her feel sad, because she guessed Fliss hadn't cared towards the end, or perhaps not been able to do much. Beautiful fine china plates were stacked with chipped earthenware, delicate crystal glassware stood cheek by jowl with cheap, lumpy stuff.

And there was even a little silver box in among the cutlery. She'd have to check its hallmark date. She could no doubt find a list of them online. The box looked quite old and was pretty, with a delicate engraving of stylised flowers.

Once she'd removed everything from the cupboards, she sorted things into 'good', 'usable' and 'bad'. Some of the bad were so bad she tossed the chipped and cracked pieces into the dustbin without hesitation. Some of the good things were so delicately beautiful she decided to get them valued.

Thank goodness the lawyers had had the food cleared out or goodness knows what unsavoury messes she might have found in the cupboards. As it was she did come across traces of mice here and there, and a dead mouse in one of her traps. Ugh!

Her mobile phone rang as she was settling down to a late lunch. She glanced at it: Robbie. It'd be eight o'clock at night in Western Australia.

'Hi, Ma. Just wanted to check how you were.'

'I'm fine, love. How are you? And Linda?'

'She's fine. Only two months to go before we make you a grandmother.'

'I'm looking forward to it. Have you heard from the others?'

'I rang them before I called you. You'll never guess what: Nick – our playboy Nick – has fallen in love.'

'No! That's quick. Or did he know her before and not tell us? Who is she, anyway?'

'It's someone he met a few days ago at the supermarket. Her name's Carla Baldino and I think she does some sort of office work in the daytime and works in a bar at weekends. I've met her and I really liked her. The amazing thing is how together the two of them look already, as if they've been married for years. She's obviously fallen for my brother just as deeply.'

'I hope it lasts.'

'You know what, Mum, I think it might. I don't know why I'm so sure of that, but I am. Anyway, he sends his love to you.'

'Give him mine.' When Robbie didn't go on, she prompted, 'And Steve?'

'He's very angry with you at the moment because he had to do his washing all by himself at the weekend.' Robbie chuckled. 'It's not rocket science, but apparently he managed to mess up big time and dyed all his white shirts pink. And then – get this! – he had to iron them and it took him nearly three hours, when you could have done them for him in one.'

She chuckled. 'I wish I could have been a fly on the wall.'

'That ought to make him appreciate all you did for us,

something I realised after I got married because Linda says she didn't marry the house, so we share all the jobs.'

He was trying to distract her, she knew, so she asked bluntly, 'Steve didn't send any message at all?'

''Fraid not. I don't think he appreciates how good a mother you've been to us. He's a selfish sod, always has been. Even worse than Dad. Sorry, Ma, but he is.'

'Nothing to be sorry about. You're only telling the truth.' But whether it was true or not, her eyes had filled with tears.

'You are all right there, aren't you, Ma?'

'I'm fine. I've made friends with a couple of neighbours and I'm going out for my first English pub meal tonight.'

'That's good. Um . . .'

As the silence dragged on, she said, 'What else is there? Out with it.'

'Dad came round wanting to know where you were. He got really angry when I wouldn't give him your address or new phone number.'

'If you tell him anything, I'm never speaking to you again.'

'No need to be so sharp, Ma. I don't actually know anything except your phone number and I've not shared that with anyone, not even Steve and Nick. Why won't you give us your street address?'

'To save myself being put in prison. If your father turned up on my doorstep one day, I might have to murder him – and I'd definitely murder whoever gave the address to him.'

He laughed. 'Well, as long as we can phone or email you, we'll be able to keep in touch. It's not as if any of us will be able to visit the UK. You've earned your freedom, Ma. Go for it.'

'Thanks, love. Give my best to Linda.'

It was good that Robbie had cared enough to phone her, but even the mention of Craig was enough to irritate her. She really should be over getting annoyed by him, but somehow the memories of their time together still upset her.

She wasn't happy about Steve, either. Ungrateful brat! He needed to grow up. She should have been much stricter with him. But Craig had often undermined her authority with the boys so it had been hard going at times.

And Steve had always been the wayward one, in trouble at school, struggling at college.

Nick had been much easier to bring up, a gentle lad who took life as it came and often calmed his younger brother down.

Only, well, Steve was still her son and she worried about him. He was the one with the least common sense, even now. Surely he'd come round after a while, get his act together and get in touch with her?

She couldn't bear the thought of being estranged from him permanently.

Nell spent the afternoon clearing out the dining-room cupboards, which were in as chaotic a state as the kitchen ones had been, again with some beautiful pieces mixed in with rubbish.

Suddenly she realised it was half past four and she was filthy, so she rushed upstairs to shower quickly and change her clothes before the dry rot people arrived.

A tall, thin woman was nominally in charge, but the two seemed to be more of a team than a boss and subordinate. The minute they were inside the house, they stood and sniffed the air.

'You've definitely got dry rot somewhere, Ms Chaytor. You can't mistake that smell,' the man said.

They both took out face masks and at a nudge from the woman the man handed one to Nell.

'Better safe than sorry, eh?'

That didn't bode well, she thought as she put it on.

In the attic the woman held up one hand. 'Please stay by the door, Ms Chaytor.'

The man took a couple of steps forward, making hissing noises under his breath, then stopped and sniffed again, staring from one area to another.

'Lionel has one of the best noses in the business,' the woman said in a low voice. 'He could tell you'd got dry rot even from outside.' She moved to and fro, sketching a quick outline of the attic layout on the pad attached to her clipboard, then said, 'Ready.'

She watched her companion intently, making notes on the plan every time he spoke.

He held up one hand. 'Don't come any further, Meg. It feels spongy to me underfoot, so it's probably unsafe at this end.'

He came back to get a segmented rod out of his canvas bag and screwed it together. Then he moved cautiously towards the rear again, pausing well before he got there and poking the floorboards ahead of him.

'One of Lionel's little inventions,' Meg whispered to Nell.

After another of those hissing noises, he turned, shaking

his head. 'Not good, Ms Chaytor. Not good at all.'

They both took out powerful torches, and from a careful distance, surveyed the whole rear wall from one end to the other. Then Meg took out an electronic gadget and used it to measure something on the wall.

She put it away, scribbled more and looked across at Lionel. 'Got enough?'

'Yep.'

She turned to Nell. 'Can we talk downstairs, Ms Chaytor?'

'Yes, of course. Would you like a cup of tea?'

'No, thank you. We'll just have a quick chat, then get off home and leave you to decide what to do next.'

Nell took them into the kitchen and they all sat down.

'It's one of the worst cases of dry rot we've seen in a long time,' the woman said. 'Don't you agree, Lionel?'

'Yep.' He gave Nell a sympathetic look. 'Sorry to be the bearers of bad tidings, but that top storey should probably be knocked down and rebuilt. Or even the whole house. It's a good thing someone had already cleared out the attic or you'd be risking falling through the floor to do anything up there.'

'Oh, dear.'

'Family home, is it?'

'An elderly aunt used to live here. I inherited it but I lived in Australia, so until this week I hadn't seen it for nearly forty years.'

'Your aunt can't have looked after it or she'd have noticed the rot. They don't always keep up with things as they get older. I read somewhere that they lose some of their sense of smell.'

'Yes. It's very sad.' Fliss had been so lively in the old days.

'To be frank, Ms Chaytor, I doubt the house is worth repairing. It'd be cheaper to knock the whole thing down and build a new one. But get a surveyor in if you want to confirm that and do some costing of your own.'

'I'd already guessed it was in a bad way. And I'm not so attached to the house that I'm desperate to preserve it. Anyway, I have someone wanting to buy who intends to knock it down, so it seems the decision to sell has been made for me.'

She looked from one to the other. 'I'd be really grateful if you'd keep this news to yourselves or the buyer will probably try to knock the price down. I'll tell him about the problems in general, but I'm not going into details. I don't need a report from you other than this verbal one and I'll pay you in cash today if you'll tell me how much I owe you.'

When they'd gone, she sat staring into space, worrying about where she'd go until she was jerked out of her thoughts by someone knocking on the front door.

Angus took one look at Nell's expression and pulled her into his arms for a hug. 'Bad news, eh?'

'The mould is even worse than we'd thought. The house is only fit for knocking down. They even told me not to go into the attic at all from now on. So if you can see that Jeffries fellow tomorrow and get him onside about me selling the house, Angus, I'd be really grateful.'

'I'll have to spin some tale or other. Will you trust me to suss out what'll work best?'

'Yes, of course. I'll go along with whatever you say.'

170

'I'll call him tomorrow, then.' Angus sniffed the air and frowned. 'The smell seems to get stronger each time I come.'

'It's because we've had the attic door open, I suppose. I'd better check that it's closed now.'

'I'll do that. You grab your coat and handbag. We can walk into town from here.'

He took her to a pub on the main high street, a place where he was clearly a regular. She cheered up as they enjoyed a hearty meal, chatting as if they were old friends. She could feel herself relaxing.

When they got back to her house, Angus gave her another of his hugs. 'I have to get back and finish a job. I'll be in touch tomorrow, after I've seen Jeffries.'

'I feel guilty at taking up so much of your time when you're busy.'

He put one finger on her lips. 'Shh. Getting to know you and helping you is far more important than working non-stop.'

She stared, not knowing how to respond to that.

He changed the subject. 'Anyway, I'm still getting in a few hours' work every day.'

'You're so reasonable,' she said in wonderment. 'Does nothing ever faze you?'

'It used to when I was younger, but by the time the kids arrived, I'd sorted myself out. Losing Joanna hurt like hell, and for a while afterwards I wasn't all that reasonable about the world. But I still had the kids to care about, even though they were grown up, and they helped me get through the worst of my grief.

'Losing her emphasised what's important in life, and that's people and love and seizing the moment, not quarrels and avariciousness. It helped so much that she and I had been very happy together. I had nothing to regret about our relationship except losing her, you see.'

He hadn't tried to kiss her today, so Nell kissed him. It was a comforting kiss this time, not a passionate one, and he held her close afterwards, not speaking, just cuddling. It was what she had needed for years, to be held, cared about, really listened to.

She was getting addicted to Angus, to his warmth and kindness as much as to his masculine attractions, though those were definitely in the equation too.

He held her at arm's length. 'Get some sleep now, love. You look strained. I'll be in touch tomorrow.'

As she locked the door, she wondered whether he'd called her 'love' because some people in England did that to everyone . . . or because he was starting to care about her. Was she being a naïve old fool about him? She thought not, hoped not.

The old house creaked around her as she walked up the stairs to her bedroom. It no longer felt welcoming. Quite the opposite.

The sooner she was out of it the better.

But where could she go? She didn't want to leave Sexton Bassett, not now she was starting to make friends. Not now that she'd met Angus.

And she still wanted to find some of her relatives and was hoping they'd still be living nearby. They might have photos of their mutual ancestors to share. She'd love that.

Then there was Miss Parfitt, such a feisty old lady. Nell was sure she'd have some interesting tales to tell and wanted to get to know her better.

No, she was definitely going to stay in Sexton Bassett. Once she'd sold the house, she'd find somewhere to rent. She couldn't impose on Angus.

On that thought she snuggled down and fell asleep.

She dreamt again, walked round the garden, heard the woman's voice.

'You'll be happy in your new home, Nell. Don't hesitate. Seize the moment.'

She woke with the words still echoing in her mind. It was strange that the dream was ongoing, matching her new circumstances. Well, she wouldn't mind the new predictions coming true, as the one about selling her Australian home had done.

Oh, she was being silly again.

Well, why not? She'd had decades of being sensible and responsible. Time to enjoy a more relaxed life.

Chapter Ten

The following morning at the start of the working day, Angus rang the estate agent's office and asked to see Jeffries about selling a house. When he declined an offer for Jeffries to come to him and evaluate the house, he wasn't surprised to be given an appointment for that same morning.

He dressed smartly (for him), though not going as far as a suit. Hell, no! He'd worn those all too often when he worked for other people. They'd been hanging up in dust bags for years. As for ties, he'd cut all except two of his up when he 'retired' and burnt the pieces ceremonially in the garden incinerator. The two he kept were for 'emergencies' – one black, for funerals, and one which would go with anything – but he hadn't used either yet.

He studied himself in the mirror, something he didn't often bother to do. Yeah, he looked OK today, smart casual, wearing trousers instead of his usual jeans. He didn't want Nell to think him scruffy.

Oh dear, he thought as he walked out of the house. You've got it bad for her.

And did that worry him? Nope. He was old enough and experienced enough to know what he wanted and if this went further, he was OK with it because he missed being part of a couple.

He saw Jeffries from the reception area, sitting in a glass-walled office talking on the phone.

Angus didn't have to wait long before the office door opened and the manager surged out, smiling at him, holding out his hand. 'Grant Jeffries.'

'Angus Denning. I'm a close friend of Nell Chaytor,' He shook the other man's soft hand with its manicured nails as briefly as possible.

'Ah. Did she send you to see me?'

'On the contrary, I came of my own accord. You see, I heard her the other day when you were trying to tell her about an offer for that house of hers. She might love the place, but I think it's an eyesore and I'm damned if I'm going to live in it with her, even temporarily.'

'Ah. I thought I'd seen you somewhere. So may I ask what you're here for if you've not come from her?'

'To let you know you've an ally in her camp if you want one, though only because I think it's in her best interests, mind, not because I'm after her money or care about your sales. I've been working on her to give you a hearing and at least find out about the offer.'

'She seemed very certain she didn't want to sell.'

'Yes, well, you caught her when she'd just had bad news from her family in Australia, news which made her feel she wasn't going back there for a long time, so she figured she'd need the house. She wasn't all that polite, was she? I got my ears bitten off after you'd gone for trying to tell her she'd been too sharp with you.'

'Sharp is putting it mildly.'

'Yeah. But she really wasn't herself that day. So perhaps you could let me know more about this offer? I thought I'd tell her I bumped into you in town and we got talking. Is it a genuine offer for her house? If it's not, I'll let the matter drop.' He leant back in his chair and waited.

'Hmm. Will she listen to you? She seemed a very . . . well, stubborn sort of woman.'

Angus hoped he was managing to look smug. 'Yes, she will listen to me. We're . . . um, a newish couple and things are going well enough for us to discuss living together. The only problem is that damned house, which she loved as a child. She thinks it'd be romantic if I moved in with her for a while and we started our life together there. Hah! I already have a perfectly good house and moving into that one of hers would be a daft thing to do.'

The penny dropped quite visibly with Jeffries. 'You're that Denning, from the big house.'

'Yes.'

'No wonder you don't want to move into her place. You've had a few offers for your own property recently, I hear.'

'Yes, but when a house has been in the family for over two hundred years, one doesn't sell it, except *in extremis*. In fact, I'd rather sell my soul and keep the house.'

'You could make a fortune with all that land so close to the town centre. You'd never have to work again.'

How the hell had they got on to talking about this?

Angus wondered. 'It's a listed property, Grade I. Even if someone bought it, they couldn't demolish it or alter it. The wood panelling is thought to be rather special, and the early stained glass windows are of a rare type. Some of the garden features are listed, too, so it'd be no use for building land, either. It's not only the garden structures and statuary, but there are some rare old species of plants that conservationists are rather excited about.'

'Ah. Grade I listed can be tricky. And the conservationist lobby too! They're always pushing their noses in where they're not wanted. Pity.'

'Anyway, I'm here to talk about Nell's house, not mine. If you don't want me to try to persuade her to sell, I'll leave you in peace.'

Jeffries pretended to consider this. 'I suppose it'd be worth a try. Can you get her to listen to me if I call round again?'

'Might be able to if the offer's a good one.' He waited, frowning when he heard the amount. 'Not good enough. I'd advise her to refuse an offer like that. If it's all you have, I'll keep out of this.'

Jeffries lost his air of relaxed bonhomie. 'Her house is falling down, dammit. You only have to look at it. It's subsiding at the back and I'd guess it has dry rot.'

'But the block is the final piece of the jigsaw puzzle for Nolan, isn't it? Well worth paying a good price so that he can get started on the next stage of his development without any fuss and botheration.' Angus smiled and added gently, 'Ms Chaytor listens to my advice and I couldn't possibly recommend accepting that paltry offer.'

'I'll talk to my client and phone you later. I'm sure we can nudge the offer up a bit.'

'Nudge it up a lot and save us all a lot of toing and froing.' Angus handed over his business card. 'Don't waste my time, though. Remember, Nell is ridiculously attached to the house and if you don't have me on your side, you'll not even get to chat to her.'

'I'll do my best.'

Angus hummed happily as he drove back up Peppercorn Street. Now, if Nell would just play this his way they'd get her a good price from that rat Nolan.

As he pulled up at her house, he realised yet again how much he wanted to live with her and get to know her. And he already had a house where they could cohabit. He chuckled. He loved that word: cohabit.

It was the second time in his life he'd felt like this about a woman and you couldn't mistake that feeling. It had been quick to happen with Joanna, too. You just . . . knew someone was right for you. Well, he did.

His old aunt had told him once that his family had fey blood and could sometimes see the future or sense ghosts. Perhaps that explained it. Who knew?

His aunt had insisted that some of their ancestors were still keeping an eye on Dennings. A lovely idea. She'd said they talked to her sometimes, but he hadn't seen any ghosts.

He didn't want to see them, either. They might put Nell off living there.

When she opened the door, Nell let out a squeak of surprise as Angus grabbed her and demanded a kiss as his reward.

'What hap—'

He cut off the words with a searing kiss, which just

about melted her bones. She was breathless when he ended it, but so was he.

'Does that mean things went well?' She tried to speak calmly but failed.

'Yes. But I told him we're madly in love and about to start living together, so we need to practise kissing to make this convincing.'

He kissed her again, so of course she co-operated. Oh, his lips were so warm and soft.

Angus drew back, still holding her, and it was a few moments before she came down to earth enough to focus on his face and remember her question. 'So what did happen today?'

'I told him we were going to live together.'

'You did?'

'Jeffries knew who I was, so I said you'd gone all sentimental, wanting us to start our life together in your family home for a while.' He pulled her closer. 'You'll have to pretend to be madly in love with me when we talk to him. Can you do that?'

There was dead silence, then she said, 'Yes.'

'Because you're a good actress?'

She couldn't lie to him; she wasn't a good liar at the best of times. 'No. Because I do find you very . . . attractive.'

'Good. I find you luscious. Let your feelings show when he comes to see us, hold my hand, give me melting looks. I'll do the same.'

He gave her a mock soppy look that had her laughing. When had she last had so much fun with someone?

She ran her fingers down his cheek and pressed a slow gentle kiss on his lips.

He sucked in his breath quite audibly and muttered, 'Keep practising.'

'I will if you will.'

They stared at one another without speaking and she was aware that their relationship had just moved on a stage.

'I'll ring Jeffries tomorrow morning and ask him to come round in the afternoon. All right?'

She nodded. 'Mmm.' Then she realised they'd been standing in the doorway kissing in full view of any passer-by. Slamming the door shut, she pulled him closer. 'That's Jeffries dealt with, but I think you're right about the other matter. We do need a bit of practice at this . . . this smooching.'

'Smooching? That's an old-fashioned word.'

She was suddenly a little afraid. 'Maybe I'm old-fashioned. It's been a long time, Angus, since I've . . . felt that I wanted someone.' There. She'd said it.

His voice was gentle. 'I know, love. We can go at a pace you find comfortable.'

Then, as if he understood that this was enough high emotion for the moment, he put his arm round her shoulders and led her into the living room. He thumped one fist down on the sagging old sofa, and a cloud of dust rose. 'Ugh. I'm not sitting on that thing. Let's go and practise smooching at my place. I have food, wine and a very comfortable bed.'

She knew if she said no, he'd go along with what she wanted, but she was annoyed with herself for acting like a timid virgin. This was the twenty-first century, for heaven's sake. 'All right. I'll go and pack an overnight bag . . . if you want me to stay.'

'Oh yes, I do want. In fact, I want you very much.'

His smile was so warm, his expression so sunny and open, her doubts subsided. 'It'll only take me five minutes.'

'Good. I'll contain my impatience.'

Once again he twiddled that imaginary villain's moustache; once again the tension changed to laughter.

A short time later, as they stopped outside Angus's house, a police car followed them up the drive and came to a halt behind them.

A female officer got out. 'Mr Denning?'

'You don't have to ask; you already know my name.'

'Are you aware that one of your rear brake lights is not working, sir?'

'No. I'll get it fixed straight away, Officer.'

She walked round his car. 'I think there's more than the brake light to fix. The bodywork is rusty. I was worried about that last time we spoke. The whole car looks unsafe to me. In fact, Mr Honourable Denning, I don't think this vehicle should be on the road at all.'

Nell watched in surprise. The woman seemed to be enjoying her moment of power and was taunting Angus rather than speaking courteously. Her fellow officer was standing by the car, frowning as if he disapproved of how it was going, but he wasn't making any attempt to moderate the exchange.

She moved forward and linked her arm in Angus's; feeling so much tension radiating from him, she decided to step in and defuse the situation, much as she'd often stepped between her sons at times of crisis.

'It's very polite of you to try to use his title, Officer, but you don't call people "Honourable", you only write it. And anyway, Angus doesn't care to use it. So old-fashioned, don't you think?'

The basilisk stare was turned on her. 'And you are?'

'Nell Chaytor. I've moved into number 95 Peppercorn Street,' she gestured back towards the street and waited for an answer. She didn't get one for so long she wondered what was going on in her companion's head.

The woman was looking shocked rigid and her voice was barely above a whisper as she eventually asked, 'You're a Chaytor? Is that your married name?'

Nell was puzzled by the way she asked this. 'Yes, I'm a Chaytor. And it's my maiden name.'

'I've . . . er, not seen you around before, Ms Chaytor. Are you from Wiltshire?'

'No. I'm from Australia.'

'Ah. You're the one who inherited Felicity Chaytor's house.' This wasn't a question.

'Yes.'

The other officer moved forward to join them, as if realising his colleague was struggling for words. He gave Nell a professional smile. 'Edwina's mother's family name is Chaytor. It's not a common one, so if you had family round here, the two of you are probably related.'

'Goodness. We must go through our genealogy over coffee some day and see how we connect,' Nell said. 'And I agree absolutely with you about Angus's car. I've already told him we should use mine from now on.'

Edwina hesitated.

Angus opened his mouth but Nell dug her elbow into his side in a sign to leave it to her. 'Is that all or is there something else?'

The other officer took over. 'It'll be enough if you take that rattletrap off the road voluntarily, Denning.'

Angus shrugged. 'With you and my new partner nagging me, I have no choice but to give in.'

Edwina looked sharply at him as he said the word 'partner', so Nell cuddled up to him to back up his statement. She didn't mind doing that at all.

'Very well. We'll, um, catch up sometime, Ms Chaytor.' But Edwina didn't offer Nell a phone number or time.

'Good heavens!' Angus murmured in her ear as the police car drove off. 'You're related to one of my enemies. This is going to be interesting.'

'That woman didn't seem filled with joy at the prospect of being connected to me, but at least I got her off your back.'

'Yes. Thanks for that, love.'

'What's she got against you?'

'I'm related to nobility. She's Red Ed's daughter. He used to be the local police sergeant and he doesn't believe in a hereditary nobility. He thinks anyone connected to them should be stood against the nearest wall and shot. He's retiring and has left the area, but Edwina moved here recently and seems to have taken over the vendetta against the Dennings. Talk about a chip off the old block.'

'Sounds more like a chip on the shoulder to me. Anyway, she's right about the car. It's well past its use-by date.'

He patted it. 'I'm going to miss the old girl, though. We've been together a long time.'

'It's a heap of rusty tin and that woman's probably right about it being dangerous.'

'I don't think so. I do maintain the brakes and tyres. I'd not want to be involved in an accident.'

His expression was bleak now, and she suddenly remembered that his wife had been killed in a road accident, so she linked her arm in his. 'I'll drive you round the car yards tomorrow, shall I?'

'Is that what you call them in Australia? Car yards?'

'Yes. What do you call them?'

'We get them from dealers. Though there are other words, and there are a lot sold online these days.' He gave her a mock pitiful look. 'What have I got myself into? Are you going to henpeck me?'

'What do you mean by that?'

'When you move in here, after we've sold your house, are you going to boss me around?'

She gaped at him. 'Who said anything about me moving in with you?'

'You just did and I'm very happy about it.'

'That was only for your enemy's benefit. It's too soon to move in together. We've only just met, barely know one another.'

'Rubbish. We're old enough to know our own minds. Let's dive in at the deep end and see how well we can swim. It'd be daft for you to rent somewhere when I've got all those empty rooms – and an empty bed.'

'But Angus—'

He stopped her protests with a kiss. 'Mmm. Not your best attempt. You didn't put your heart into that one. Come inside and we'll try it again.'

Just like that, desire flared in her and her breath caught in her throat. How could this be happening so quickly?

He kissed her the minute the door was closed, then tugged her across the hall, kissing her every time she tried to protest, kissing her nearly senseless, so that in the end she quit fighting and kissed him back with equal enthusiasm.

'That was much better,' he said approvingly, kicking a door open. 'I don't want to rush you, but unless you object, I'm about to ravish you.'

He stopped the kissing, stopped everything, waiting for her to give permission.

'Who's objecting?' she asked. 'Not me.'

'Good. In fact, very good. *Mi casa es su casa*, Nell. In every way from now on.'

She forgot all her worries about an older body that wasn't as slim as it could have been, forgot too about being out of practice at making love, because it was Angus and he was so easy to be with, so kind and loving.

She thought she heard women's laughter in the distance, but then he kissed her again and she forgot about everything else.

When Nick met Carla after work on the Monday she was looking upset.

'What's wrong?'

She gave him a wobbly smile. 'Sorry, but I can't go out with you tonight.'

'Why not?'

'I've been given notice to get out of my flat. I've been living with my friend Kylie to save money. We were both keen to do that, so though it was a bit cramped, we managed. Only she's met this guy and she's going to move in with him, so she's given notice on the flat.'

'Can't you take it over and stay on there?'

'I asked the landlord but he said no. He's got a nephew who needs somewhere to live, you see, and family comes first. So I have to find somewhere else to live quickly.'

'How soon do you have to be out?'

'By the end of next week, if possible, then Kylie will get a rent rebate, which she'll share with me. Only . . . well, places that cheap don't come up very often and I can't afford to live on my own, so I'll have to look round for somewhere to share. Which can be chancy if you don't know the other people involved.'

'Move in with me, then. You know me. In fact, come and have another look at our flat now.'

'Do you mean that?'

'I wouldn't offer if I didn't.'

When they got there, she followed him round, then shook her head. 'I thought I'd remembered a third bedroom, but there isn't, is there?'

'No. But since you and I are together, I'd rather expected that we'd share a bedroom.'

She grew very still.

'Last night we admitted we'd fallen in love with each other. Didn't you mean it?'

'Of course I did. I'm crazy about you. Only . . . it's a big step to move in, especially with someone you've only just met. And what's more, it has implications.'

'I know. I like the idea of implications very much indeed. I fell for you that first day at the supermarket, Carla, and I can't imagine falling out of love – ever.'

'My family will go mad if I move in with a guy.'

'What about if we get engaged?'

'They'll still go mad if we try to live together. They're

Italian and very old-fashioned about things like that.'

'Then how about we get married?'

She gaped at him, her mouth falling open, her eyes wide with shock. 'Get married! We've only just met. People will think we've gone mad.'

'Let them. You're the one for me, Carla. I'm sure of that.' And he was. Utterly certain. It had surprised the hell out of him, but there you were.

'In just a few days?'

'Yep. How about you?'

She fiddled with her bracelet, then took a deep breath and smiled at him, that wonderful wide smile that curled his toes, and affected a few other parts of him as well.

'I'm crazy for you, too, Nick. You're definitely the one for me. I feel so comfortable with you, so right. But our families won't want us to marry this quickly. They won't believe we can know our own feelings yet.'

'I'm twenty-three; you're twenty-two. No need to ask anyone's permission. How about we just do it and then tell them afterwards?' He got down on one knee in front of her and took her hand, raising it to his lips. 'Carla, will you please marry me and make me the happiest man on earth?'

'You did that beautifully. Have you been practising?'

'No. I've never said it before and I never intend to say it to another woman again. So . . . will you?'

'Yes. But I'm not sure about doing it so quickly.'

He snapped his fingers. 'Of course. You'll want a fancy wedding with a big white cloud of a wedding dress and bridesmaids. Most girls do. OK. I'm prepared to wait to get married if I have to, but I would like to live with you in the meantime.'

'Actually, you're wrong about that. I don't want a big fuss. Well, it's silly spending so much money on one day's events when you're going to need as much as you can to set up a home and furniture. And my parents aren't rich, so I don't want them spending money they can ill afford on a wedding.'

'Very practical. But most people still seem to go for a big show. Are you sure?'

'Yes, I am. Last year I watched my cousin Mariana turn into bridezilla for six whole months. She was unbearable, expecting the whole world to revolve around her wedding. And then she cried three times that I saw on the wedding day itself, because the details didn't go exactly to her master plan. My aunt went equally silly about it all, getting into debt to buy clothes and pay for the fancy reception. All for one day. I vowed then that I'd not do it that way when my time came.'

'Where does that leave us?' He took her hands.

'Together. You're right. Let's just do it.'

'Don't you want to think about it?'

She put her head on one side and studied his face, caressing his cheek with one hand, then nodded. 'All right. I've thought about it. You'll do for me.'

As he pulled her close, her eyes filled with tears and she said in a husky voice, 'I do love you, Nick. I want to be with you for ever.'

Their kiss this time was gentle and sweet, full of unspoken promises.

Then she stiffened suddenly. 'Oh, no! You aren't a Catholic.'

'I'm not anything.'

'Then we'll definitely have to have a quick civil wedding and present them with a fait accompli or my mother will set the priest on us. She'll probably set Father Benedict on us anyway.'

'Won't the religious ceremony matter to you?'

She shook her head. 'No. I believe in a God, but not that there's only one way to reach him.'

'That's settled, then. Do you want to buy a bottle of champagne to celebrate? We ought to do something.'

'I'm not much of a drinker.'

'Actually, I'm not either. I used to pretend it made me sick to stop the guys trying to get me drunk, but I just don't care about booze. I'm hungry now, though. Let's get a celebratory takeaway from the Chinese restaurant down the road. Then we'll go online and find out what you need to do to get married quickly.'

When they went outside, he picked her up, making her squeak in shock as he spun her round.

An older man complained as they got in his way, but Nick smiled at him and said, 'She's just agreed to marry me. I had to do something with all these happy feelings inside me.'

The grey-haired woman who had her arm linked in the man's beamed back at them both. 'How sweet. Don't be so grumpy, John. I hope you two youngsters will be very happy together.'

As the older couple walked off down the street, Nick took Carla's hand again. 'I am so lucky to have met you.'

'We're lucky to have met each other,' she corrected. 'But I want to set one ground rule from the start: I'm not running round after you in the house. You'll take your share in everything there is to do and so will I. I'm quite good with cars, actually.'

'Sounds fine to me.'

'I won't have to nag you to do your share?'

'No. You said something to me the first time we met that struck home: a grown-up should be able to look after himself. I'd been lazy, taking advantage of Ma. But you'll have to teach me to do some jobs because I've still got my L-plates on about housework.'

'That's different.' She frowned. 'What about your brother?'

'Either he can find a place of his own or we will. Steve's a slob, and I don't enjoy living with him. Even before you and I decided to get married, I was going to tell him to get his act together or I'd move out. He'll create a stink about it, though. Maybe I'll see if I can get Dad onside about the arrangements. I know Steve hasn't got the money to live on his own.'

'Why did you move in with him if he's so bad?'

'I didn't realise quite how bad he was till it was just him and me, because Mum cleared up the kitchen after him when we lived at home, even though she grumbled. And I didn't go poking around in his bedroom.'

'I might have to live at home for a week or two after I move out of the flat. I'd better not stay over with you till we're married. I don't want to give my family anything to complain about afterwards. You don't know what they can be like.' She hesitated, then said quietly, 'Nick . . . you should know that you'll be the first man in my life.'

He caught his breath in wonder and pulled her close. 'I didn't think there were any virgins left these days.'

'There are in Italian families as watchful as mine, and probably in certain other ethnic groups, too. My dad created a big stink when I moved out, and for a while he kept turning up late at night to check that I wasn't sleeping with a guy.'

'I'm surprised a woman as gorgeous as you hasn't found someone before.'

'I'm a bit picky about men and I hadn't found someone who bowled me off my feet . . . till now. It's early days. I'm not exactly middle-aged, you know.'

'You will be middle-aged one day and you'll be as beautiful then as you are now.'

'You're not a tad biased?'

'Of course I am. Why would you marry someone if you weren't biased in their favour? Oh, what a wonderful evening! Wonderful world. Wonderful you.'

And he twirled her round again till they were both breathless and laughing.

When Steve came home, they'd finished the meal and were chatting quietly. He nodded when introduced to Carla, but his eyes were on the takeaway containers. 'Anything left?'

'Haven't you eaten tonight?' Nick asked.

'Didn't have time.'

'Or you were short of money?'

'Only temporarily.'

Nick exchanged glances with Carla and she nodded, so he pushed the containers towards his brother and they watched him gobble the food down like a man who'd not eaten for a long time.

When he'd finished, Steve leant back and patted his

belly. 'Thanks. That's better. Now if you were to offer me some beer out of your secret stash, it'd just round off the meal nicely.'

'I don't have a secret stash of booze and it'd do you good to have a few days without alcohol. I'll make us some cups of coffee. Want one, Carla?'

'Yes, please.'

Nick went into his bedroom and got out the makings, then took them back into the kitchen.

'What a tight-arse you are!' Steve muttered. 'Can't share anything.'

'And what a moocher you are, wanting me to support you.'

The air was charged with animosity for a few moments, then the kettle boiled and Nick turned to make the coffee. Afterwards he took the coffee jar and milk back into his room.

Steve's scowl grew heavier but he didn't refuse the mug of coffee his brother plonked in front of him.

Nick sat down again. 'We need to talk. I've got something to tell you, something important.'

'Oh? Can't it wait? I'm tired.'

'No. It's about Carla and me. We're getting married and—'

'Married!' Steve gaped at them. 'You have to be kidding.'

'No. I love Carla and we're getting married as soon as we can arrange it. So, naturally, we want our own place. You can either find somewhere of your own and move out, or you can take over this place and I'll move out. Your choice.'

'She's really done a job on you, hasn't she?'

Nick's voice grew sharp. 'Mind what you say!'

The air was heavy with anger now, from both brothers. Carla stood up. 'You'd better take me home, Nick. You two need to talk this out together.'

'Right. I apologise for my baby brother, who has the manners of a gutter rat.' He gave Steve a very firm look. 'I'm not having you talking to Carla like that. Not ever.'

When they'd gone Steve went into his bedroom, slammed the door and lay down on the bed, pulling out his last half spliff. How stupid could you get? You didn't need to marry a girl to get into her knickers.

He was shaken awake later when Nick returned. 'Go 'way.'

'No. We need to sort this out.' He pulled Steve upright.

'Nothing to sort, bro. I'm on the lease and I ain't moving. You may have gone crazy but I haven't. I'm not giving up my flat to that tart.'

Nick punched him in the jaw and he fell over backwards.

Normally Steve would have jumped up to do battle, but this time he got slowly to his feet and nearly stumbled.

Nick sniffed. 'You've been smoking weed.'

Steve shrugged. 'Not everyone's as old-fashioned as you.'

'Well, that settles it. I'll give notice to the agency and tell them you're taking over the lease. I'll move out as soon as I find somewhere else.'

Their glances locked and for a moment Nick was afraid his brother was going to attack him. What the hell had gotten into him lately?

'You'll regret it,' Steve said. 'She'll rule the roost, that one. You won't be able to breathe without her permission. But it's your funeral. Now, bugger off and let me sleep.' He turned his back and pulled the covers up.

Nick shrugged, visited the bathroom then went into his bedroom. He'd done his best to talk sense into Steve, but anything he said seemed to go into one ear and straight out of the other. In fact, he was getting worried because his brother seemed hell-bent on self-destruction.

He wished he could talk to his mother about it. His father was useless at that sort of thing, but he'd have to see him because he couldn't help worrying about what would happen to Steve once he left the flat. Anyway, he wanted to tell him about Carla and getting married.

But he wasn't putting his own life on hold. When something wonderful came into your world, you had to make the most of it.

And Carla was the best thing that had ever happened to him.

Chapter Eleven

On the Monday morning, there was no sign of Steve waking up, so Nick got his breakfast, locked up his room and went off to work.

When he came home, he found Steve sitting nursing a beer.

'You're starting in on the booze early, aren't you? I thought you had no money.'

Steve stared at him owlishly. 'I got fired today. My manager had a down on me and was just looking for an excuse. Bought this with my final pot of money.' He gestured to a slab of beer cans. 'I'm holding a wake. Come and join me.'

'Shit. What did you do to get fired?'

'Got in to work late. You should have woken me.'

'Every time I wake you, you curse me as if I've done something wrong. Anyway, why should I? You're a grown man. You should be able to get yourself up in time for work.' He put his things in his room, had a wash and changed into casual clothes.

When he came out, again locking the door carefully behind him, he found Steve still sitting in the eating area. 'Carla and I are going flat hunting. I won't be back till later.'

'Go on. Put your head in the noose. See if I care.'

Nick hesitated, shook his head in despair and left.

Carla was waiting for him at the rental agency. 'Oh, good, you're on time. As I said on the phone, I saw this flat advertised and made an appointment to view. It's a bit further out than we wanted, but it's a more reasonable rent.'

'Well done.'

The agent was waiting for them. She looked them up and down as if she knew every stitch they were wearing. This was a dragon lady, Nick decided within two minutes. He let Carla do the talking.

'We're getting married, so we're looking for a flat.'

'Do you have references?'

'I do,' Carla said.

Nick said, 'I can get a character reference from my employer, but I've only been in my present flat for a few weeks.'

'Why don't you set up house there, then? Did you get thrown out?'

'No, I didn't. I've been sharing with my brother and we don't get on. Besides, who wants to start married life with a threesome?'

Only then did she give a little nod, as if they'd passed a test, and gestured to some chairs at a table. 'Let me note down your particulars.'

She outlined the costs: bond money, rent in advance and insurance, then drove them out to view the flat, which had two bedrooms and was full of tired-looking furniture.

Carla checked the bed and looked in all the cupboards. 'Well, it's been properly cleaned, at least, but that mattress isn't nice.'

'You've just gone up in my estimation,' the woman said.

'My mother would kill me if I lived somewhere dirty. And I couldn't sleep on a mattress like that.' She shuddered.

'The owner will remove it. He always asks tenants to buy their own mattress, which they usually take with them when they leave. The last tenant had to be thrown out, so didn't take the mattress. And it cost a lot to clean the place up, so he didn't get his bond back, either.'

'Sounds like my brother,' Nick said gloomily.

The agent looked from one to the other. 'How about I wait in the car and you have a chat?' She looked at her watch. 'I can only give you ten minutes. If you don't take this one, I have places I could show you tomorrow, but the rents are higher. There are other people waiting to view this flat, but your fiancée was very persuasive, Mr Vincent.'

When she'd gone outside, Carla looked at Nick. 'If we have to buy a mattress, I don't have enough money to pay my share of the set-up costs till my friend gets the bond money back from our current place.'

'I can see to that.'

'Are you sure?'

'We're getting married, aren't we? We're putting our whole lives into each other's hands. The money is nothing compared to that. I have some savings. Not a lot, but enough. And my share of the furniture Mum gave us from the flat.'

She hugged him. 'We're going to be so happy together.

Look, this is the cheapest two-bedroom place I could find in a halfway decent area.'

Nick nodded. They'd already decided they needed two bedrooms, because Carla was planning to do some more studying if she didn't need to work in the bar at weekends, and he had some accountancy exams coming up. 'OK. Let's take it.'

They went out hand in hand to say they'd like to rent it.

The agent nodded but didn't crack a smile, just took them back to the office and filled in the paperwork, before taking a deposit from Nick. 'I'll get the mattress taken out and you can take over from Friday. Your rent payments will date from then.'

As they walked out holding the keys, Carla gave a little skip of pleasure and Nick smiled at her joy.

'Next step, we have to book the wedding. My boss says I can have some time off work tomorrow to do that, since you're free then as well.'

'And we have to tell our families about getting married.'

'Let's wait to do that.'

'Not too long, Carla. I'm not doing anything underhand because I'm proud to be marrying you.'

The following morning, Nick got online early to look up what they needed to do. He'd assumed they'd just register and then get married when it suited them, but was bitterly disappointed to find they had to wait a full month and a day after registering before the ceremony could take place. It wasn't cheap, either.

When he met Carla he found out that she'd been hunting online about regulations for getting married too.

'I daren't wait that long to move out,' he said glumly. 'Steve has just been sacked and goodness knows what he'll do if he's on his own in the flat all day.'

She sighed. 'I don't think we have much choice. It's more complicated than I'd expected and it costs more to get married, too. Look, I'll pay for that because you paid for the flat.'

'Can you afford it?'

She gave him a wry smile. 'Just. I'm pretty frugal because I've never had much money.'

'About getting married, do you think we could move into that flat first and get married afterwards? I'd like to move in on Friday.'

She sighed. 'Yes, let's. I'm being cowardly about my parents. You need to definitely get out of there quickly.'

'Yeah. I have a bad feeling about what Steve might get into.'

They went to the Perth Registry and filled in the forms, then arranged to have a civil ceremony at the Perth Marriage Office on the first possible day.

'We'll think about witnesses later,' Carla said.

After that, they both went back to work. But she was working in the bar that evening, so he decided to get on with his studying.

He arrived home at the usual time and to his relief Steve didn't answer when he called out from the front door that he was back. He could see why as soon as he saw his bedroom door. It had been jemmied open, causing considerable damage.

Inside his things were pulled out of drawers and scattered about the floor as if Steve had been searching for something.

Relief shuddered through Nick. He'd had all his papers and bank account details with him, and he didn't keep a stash of money.

Then he realised that his laptop was missing.

He went into Steve's room and found most of his brother's things missing, too.

He didn't know what to do but he needed that damned laptop for his studying.

In the end the only thing he could think of was to phone his father and ask his advice. He didn't want to call the police in, but he wasn't going to let his brother get away with this.

His father came round straight away, scowling as Nick showed him the mess and told him about the theft.

'Unless you can think of something, I'm going to have to go to the police, Dad. I need that laptop, it's got all sorts of stuff on it to do with my studies. Maybe they can retrieve it.'

His father walked round again, cursing under his breath, then sat down. 'Do you have some coffee?'

'Yes.'

'Black, no sugar.'

'Since when have you taken your coffee like that?'

Craig squirmed a little. 'Since Jenny decided I was putting on weight.'

Nick didn't let himself smile. Jenny was certainly the one in control of his father's second marriage. She was much harder than his mother. He'd rather have a gentler wife, like Carla.

He plonked a mug of coffee in front of his father, who

took a sip and then another, sighing with pleasure.

'Where do you think your brother went?'

'To his so-called friend's place. I only know his first name: Nate. Steve wasn't thinking straight, hasn't been for a while.' He took a deep breath. 'There's more, Dad. Steve's been playing around with drugs.'

'Oh, hell. That's all we need. You sure you don't know where his friend lives?'

'Not a clue. Not far out, though.'

'All right. Leave it with me. I know a private investigator. I'll put him on to the case. It won't do me any good to have a son who's into drugs. Can you hold back on the police until then?'

'I suppose so.' Nick looked at the damage. 'Who's going to pay for the door, though? I didn't bust it up and now that I'm getting married, I need all my money.'

His father gaped at him. 'Getting married? That's rather sudden, isn't it? Is she having a baby?'

'No, she isn't. I'm not stupid enough to have unprotected sex.' He told his father a few details about Carla.

In the end Craig held up his hand, grinning. 'Stop. I get the idea. You're madly in love and you've got it bad.'

'I fell for her just about on sight.'

'Yeah. It's how I was with Jenny.' He hesitated. 'She's been good for me. Your mother was too much into children, and I got . . . frustrated. I've kept my eye on her since, though. She's been a good mother.'

Silence fell and Nick sat waiting.

'My turn to get involved, I suppose. Look, I'll sort out this door and any other mess Steve's made for you,' his father said suddenly. 'Call it a wedding present. I'll also see if I can sort out your brother. If I can't, I'm done with him. You know what I think of drug-taking, and as a manager, I can't afford to have connections with druggies. It'd look bad. Um . . . have you heard from your mother?'

'Not for a day or two.'

'Can you let me have her phone number, at least?'

'I promised her I wouldn't.' He'd wormed the number out of Robbie on the firm promise that he'd never, under any circumstances, pass it to their father.

'What's wrong with the woman? Anybody would think she had something to hide.' He stood up. 'Get another key cut for this place and drop it in at my office. When's the wedding?'

'We have to wait a month and a day. We only just registered.'

'Jenny and I will be coming to the ceremony.'

'But Dad—'

'You'll need a witness and Jenny loves weddings. Besides, what does it say about the Vincent family if none of them are at your wedding?'

Nick was pretty sure this was a display of one-upmanship over his mother, who would not be able to attend. But as long as his father was dealing with Steve, that'd be OK.

When he was alone, he sat staring into space. He wasn't seeing Carla tonight and ought to be studying, but he didn't have his laptop. And anyway, Steve had upset him big time. He'd thought he knew his brother, thought they cared about one another, however much they quarrelled.

Now he wondered what the hell Steve had turned into and where he'd end up.

And he was desperate to get his laptop back. He had an

assignment on it that was nearly finished. Good thing he had backups. But he had no computer to put them on.

He had even more reason to improve his qualifications now.

Janey loved living with Auntie Winnie. The two of them could chat for hours, because the old lady had a brilliant memory for details and Janey found descriptions of life in the recent past fascinating, especially World War II because her mother's grandfather had fought in it and been killed at Tobruk in October 1941.

She'd never met her mother's mother, only seen photos of a plump smiling woman. Her grandfather had talked a lot about his wife, regretting her early death and missing her till the very day he died.

Had her mother managed to salvage those treasured photos when she ran away from home or had her father destroyed them? Probably the latter, knowing him. If he had, Janey could help her, because she'd scanned all the family photos secretly while her parents were out and they were safe on the computer she'd eventually managed to get back from her father.

Dawn had again offered to find someone to tell her how to deal with the relationship between herself and her mother, but after some thought, she'd decided to deal with it in her own way, one small step at a time. As Dawn said, Janey's life was settling down and she could afford to be generous. Her mother's future was uncertain and she was still living in the refuge. That must be terrible.

Winifred came into the kitchen as Janey was debating whether to phone her mother.

'Is something wrong, dear? You're looking worried.'

'I'm trying to gather the courage to phone my mother.' They'd already discussed the situation.

'Only you can decide whether you're ready or not. You know you can invite her to visit you here.'

'I know. But how would she get here? She doesn't have a car and she probably doesn't have much money, either, and she'll be worried about being seen. I don't even know where the refuge is.'

'An invitation to tea would please her, even if she couldn't come. It must be dreadful not to have met your own grandchild.' She cast a fond glance in Millie's direction.

'I'll think about it a while longer. I have some tests coming up at tech, so I need to concentrate on those for the moment.'

But she was making excuses, Janey admitted to herself later, anything to delay phoning her mother.

Who knew where getting together again would lead? Or not lead? Which might be worse.

The next day when she was walking home from tech, Janey began to feel uneasy, as if someone was staring at her. She stopped, pretending to adjust Millie's clothing and sneaking a glance or two round, but couldn't see anyone obvious.

She stopped again just before she turned into Peppercorn Street, but couldn't see anything. There was no one in the cars parked along the street, and other vehicles driving past didn't reappear. So she turned into the street.

The feeling of being followed grew so strong she didn't dare continue up the hill to her new home, because there was no one about. She hesitated, then turned into the car park of the building where she had lived before and rang her landlord's doorbell. She thought Kieran and Nicole were back from their honeymoon but wasn't sure.

It was Nicole's son Paul who answered.

'Is Kieran around?'

'They're not back yet, won't be till the weekend. There's just me at the moment.'

'Oh. Well I won't bother you, then.' But she couldn't help glancing over her shoulder.

'You look worried about something. Can I help?'

She hesitated, then explained the feeling she had.

'Why don't you come inside for a few moments? We can keep an eye on the street from the living room.'

She glanced at her watch. 'I need to get home so that I can put stuff in the freezer, not to mention feeding her little ladyship.'

'Well, how about I follow you and see if I can spot anyone?'

'I couldn't ask you to do that.'

'You didn't ask; I suggested it. Do you have any idea who it might be?'

'The only person I can think of is my father, only he has a court order saying not to come near me.'

Paul's expression was suddenly very sympathetic. 'Hard luck, isn't it, having a dodgy relative?'

He'd understand better than anyone because of his brother. 'Well . . . if you don't mind, perhaps you could follow me. But don't take any chances. My father can get violent. If you come to my house, I'll reward you with a piece of Auntie Winnie's cake. She makes the best cakes in town.'

'You're on. You're at number 5 now, aren't you?'

'Yes.' She set off again, and sure enough, she had a prickling sensation in her neck as soon as she turned onto the street again. That was so strange. How could you sense you were being followed? It was more than that: she felt threatened, as if whoever was following her didn't mean well, she really did.

She was sure it wasn't her imagination. Could her father really be coming after her again? Oh, she prayed not! He was so big and violent, and apart from being afraid for herself, she didn't want to draw the attention of a man like him to Auntie Winnie's house. Did he know exactly where she'd moved to? She hoped not.

If she had any sort of proof that he was following her, she'd report him to the police straight away.

She walked on up the street, moving slowly, as Paul had suggested, pushing the buggy, which held not only her daughter but some shopping.

When she got near the house, she slowed down, and since she still felt uneasy, she decided to turn down the narrow pedestrian passageway beside it. That led to the next street but she was able to stop where the path curved and look back at Peppercorn Street through the foliage of a bush that was about to come into flower.

She could see most of the turning circle at the top of the street and recognised the cars that were parked there. A woman she knew by sight passed the end of the passage. She'd be going into the house two doors away.

Was it safe to go back home or not?

Then Janey heard a car start up further down the street and she leant forward a little, keeping the buggy behind her. But she couldn't see anything and once it had driven away everything was silent again, except for the noise of distant traffic.

Millie made a fretful noise.

Janey knew she couldn't stay here all day: she had a baby to feed, but she still waited a few minutes before going back to the street. She stopped at the end of the path to stare round. There were only a few cars and commercial vehicles parked nearby at this time of day and none of them had people sitting in them. What's more, she no longer had that uneasy feeling.

Could you really tell if someone was following you and wanting to do you harm? Or was she imagining things?

Sighing, she went into the house.

She didn't say anything to Auntie Winnie about being followed, but started putting the shopping away, expecting Paul to knock on the door at any moment. Only he didn't.

Had he gone back home? Was he still following someone? She should have given him her mobile phone number.

It was nearly half an hour before the doorbell rang. 'I'll get that,' she called.

The minute she looked at Paul's face, she knew he'd seen something. 'Come in.'

She introduced him to Auntie Winnie, who produced the current cake and then winked at Janey and said she was going out to sit out in the garden, since it was such a lovely sunny evening.

The minute the old lady had left them alone, Paul said, 'There did seem to be someone following you. In a pale-blue van. What kind of car does your father have?'

'Not a van, an old red Ford.'

'There were two men inside this one. Do you have a photo of your father?'

'Yes. It'll take me a minute to find it, though. It's not something I keep on show. I'd have thrown it away but my granddad is in the photo too.'

'You go and look for it. I'll keep an eye on Miss Millie here.'

When Janey came back with the photo, she held it out to him and pointed out her father, standing with his belly hanging over his trousers as usual and his face unsmiling. Ugh, he was such an ugly man, as well as cruel.

How could she and her lovely Millie be descended from him? She hated the thought.

She couldn't imagine what her meek little mother could have done to make him violent towards his wife. And if he had been, he'd thumped her mother when Janey wasn't around. She knew from her own experience there was nothing you could do to stop him once he started to hit you or threaten you.

Something inside Janey eased at that realisation about her mother's situation. She had, she decided, been looking at the situation with a hurt child's eyes. Now, she too had experienced abuse and she could, she hoped, be more understanding. She looked at her companion. Had he seen her father or not?

Paul studied the photo, frowning. 'Your father could have been one of the men in the car, but I couldn't see them well enough to be certain. They kept the sun visors lowered and they were wearing baseball caps with the peaks pulled down. It's a definite possibility, though. The smaller guy took his cap off once to wipe his forehead so I saw him more clearly. He was a big man, bald with a little fringe of straggly grey hair and spectacles.'

'That could be my father's cousin. Only I don't have a photo of him.'

'The reason I was late was that they stopped down the street outside our block of flats and didn't move on for ages. I stayed further up the street watching them. I think they must have been waiting for you to come back. Perhaps they don't know you've moved. I certainly won't tell anyone where you live.'

Her stomach lurched as this information sank in. Surely it wasn't going to start all over again? Surely her father wasn't going to stalk her as his friend once had?

'I got the number on their licence plate and took a photo of the car, but I didn't dare get close enough to take a good photo of the men inside it, unfortunately.'

'I wouldn't have wanted you to risk anything. Thank you for helping me today.' She cut him a big slice of cake. 'Shall I make you some coffee? How do you like it?'

'White, no sugar, please. Why don't you phone me when you next start walking up the street? If I'm at home, I can let you into the flats and you can go out through the backyard and up the next street. So they'll still think you live there. I might even be able to get a photo of them, if it's the same two guys.'

'I can't ask you to do that.'

Paul grinned at her. 'Again, you didn't ask; I offered. I think Kieran and Mum will be happy to help you too, once they get back. You won't mind if I tell them?'

'No, of course not.'

He chewed his lip for a moment, then added, 'I do understand what it's like, Janey. We had trouble with my brother and he kept following my mother. He damaged the house and her car, and attacked other people too. He was on massive doses of steroids because he wanted big muscles, but the drugs made him go strange in the head as well as giving him bigger muscles. In the end he burned our house down and he's in a psychiatric hospital now.'

'I knew about that vaguely, but I was too wrapped up in my own troubles at the time to take in details of anyone else's problems.'

'And now your troubles have come back again.' His voice was warmly sympathetic. 'It's not fair, is it?'

'Or I could be mistaken.'

'Unfortunately I do think they were looking for you.'

She sighed, then changed the subject and they chatted for a while. Though Paul was a little younger than her, he seemed very mature for his age and he was easy to talk to. When he invited her to come down for a coffee one evening, she was tempted to say yes.

'I'd have liked to, but I have Millie to look after and . . . well, I don't like going out on my own at night. You could come round here again, though. I have my own sitting room. I don't have many friends nearby.'

'I don't, either. And some of the people from school stay clear of me since my brother was locked away. I'm not at all like him, but how do you prove it?'

'You just keep going as best you can.'

He smiled sympathetically. 'Like you did with Millie?'

'Yes. As I said before, one step at a time.'

When he left, she stood at the door for a few moments,

enjoying the evening sunlight on her face, then took Millie out into the back garden. She didn't know what she'd do without this buggy. It was so manoeuvrable. It was quite old and a bit battered, but she was hoping it would last through her daughter's toddler years.

She parked it on the garden path and sat on the grass next to Auntie Winnie for a few minutes, discussing the garden-sharing project, a sure way of bringing a smile to the old lady's face.

'Dan phoned while you were out, Janey. He's booked a room at the senior citizens' centre for a meeting and put up notices. And the local newspaper ran a story on it. I'm going to take a taxi to the meeting and talk to the people who turn up wanting to share, see if I like them.'

'It's such a good idea. And just think: you'll get a share of whatever they grow. Didn't Dawn say you'd get a quarter?'

'She did. And our family gardener used to say we had good soil. But we will use the vegetables, you and I, not just me.' She looked round at the untidy bushes and weed-filled garden beds. 'I must say, I'd be very glad to have this place tidied up. It's far too big for me, or for anyone in these busy modern times.'

'All the houses at this end of the street have bigger than average gardens, especially Mr Denning's.'

'Angus has about two acres, I think. He's let most of it get overgrown. His family used to have a full-time gardener when old Mr Jordan was there. Strange how the house has come back to a Denning, isn't it? They were the first family to live there.'

'It must be lovely to know about your ancestors. My parents wouldn't ever talk about theirs.'

'And when Mr Jordan's niece inherited Dennings, she had part-time help with the garden. The other side of the house always looked truly beautiful, with a fountain and statuary.'

'You can't see it from the road. I've walked past the perimeter wall a few times with this young lady and wondered what was on the other side of the wall.'

'I'll ask Angus if I can take you round the garden one day, if you like.'

'I can't poke my nose in like that!'

Winifred gave her a smug smile. 'One of the benefits of being very old is that you can do all sorts of things you'd not have dared to before. I'll ask him, of course, but I'm sure he won't mind.' She studied the bare earth area where the summer house had stood. 'The man Dan found me did a good job of clearing up the mess, didn't he?'

'Yes. You must miss the summer house.'

'I do. It had fond memories for me. But I've still got the memories, haven't I?' She tapped her forehead, then sighed. 'I do hope whoever it was won't try anything else nasty. I'm not going to sell this house, whatever they offer me. I want to stay here till I die.'

Janey shivered. 'Don't talk about dying.'

Winifred patted her hand. 'It's part of the cycle of life, dear. No one can avoid it, but your generation tries to pretend it doesn't exist. When I die, which I hope won't be for years, you must accept that this happens to everyone. I've already lived longer than my parents did, so I haven't done badly in the lottery of life, have I?'

Janey gave the old lady a hug. 'Don't die yet! I've only just found you. Now, I must get tea started. I hope you like my cooking.'

'My turn tomorrow. I enjoy cooking and it's wonderful to look forward to sharing a meal. What with you, and my friends Hazel and Dan, I'm never short of company for long these days.'

Cooking and eating tea was something to look forward to? Janey shook her head as she took Millie back into the house. How many years had poor Auntie Winnie been so achingly lonely? She'd had a few months of that herself and had missed having people to talk to. Even her mother had sometimes chatted when her father was out.

When she went into the house Janey saw something white on the hall floor. Someone must have pushed an envelope through the door. She picked it up and saw that it was addressed to 'Miss Parfitt'. She put it on the kitchen table.

When Auntie Winnie came in, she opened the envelope and sighed. 'They won't let up.'

'Who won't?'

'These people who want to buy my house. Look. It's from an estate agency.'

Janey took the letter and read it. 'It doesn't look like a mass mailing. It's addressed to you specifically and it mentions "other letters" and "sorry to hear you've been targeted by vandals, hope this doesn't go on". I think we should keep it. Perhaps show it to the police.'

Winifred took it from her and read it again. 'There's nothing one could object to.'

'No. But how do these people know what you're doing? It won't hurt to show it to the police, will it?'

'If you think it best.'

'I do. We can't be too careful after the scares you've had.'

Winifred looked at her in dismay. 'Do you think they'll come back and do something else?'

'I don't know. But we may as well take precautions.'

'I suppose so.'

Unfortunately the letter, innocuous as it seemed, had worried the old lady and it was a while before Janey managed to cheer her up.

Chapter Twelve

When Nell woke up, she couldn't for a moment think where she was, then it all came rushing back to her. She'd spent the night with Angus. He wasn't in the bed with her, but the pillow still held the indent of his head.

She got up and peered into the next room, which was his living room. He wasn't there, either.

Hearing sounds from beyond it, she followed them into his office. She had to call his name to get his attention, then he held up one hand, entered something on the computer and swung his chair round to smile at her.

'Hello, sleepyhead. Awake at last.'

'I've not slept so soundly since I arrived in England.'

He came across to give her a kiss on either cheek. 'Go and have a shower and I'll join you in about ten minutes. I just need to finish this bit.' He was back at work before she'd even left the room.

She took a quick shower, then went to make some coffee. He came into the kitchen just as she was sipping a beaker of instant and she couldn't help smiling at him. 'Nice coffee, for instant. My eldest son is a coffee aficionado and makes a big fuss about brewing his morning cup.'

'I couldn't be bothered with all that fuss.'

'Me neither. There's some hot water in the kettle if you're ready for a drink.'

She was surprised that she didn't feel at all awkward with him, kept being surprised by how easy he was to get on with. 'Perhaps I should go home and leave you to work. I have to arrange for that estate agent to come round.'

'I'd like to be there when he does to keep an eye on him.'

'Yes, please.'

He held out his mobile phone. 'Give him a ring now. His number's programmed in.'

She let him make the connection, then took over the call and arranged for Grant Jeffries to come round to see her that afternoon. 'Two o'clock?' She looked at Angus and he nodded.

When she'd ended the call, he said, 'I'm glad you're letting me help you. It's always good to have a witness to important transactions. And few things are more important than selling a house.'

'Yes. But we have another important transaction to conduct first.'

'Oh?'

'Yes. We need to go and look at cars. You know you can't manage without one.'

He gave her a resigned look. 'No. I suppose not.' Then he brightened up. 'But if you're moving in with me, you could lend me your car occasionally.'

'And what if I wanted to go away at the same time as

you wanted to use mine? I'm planning to see some of this country while I'm here and I'm also going to start hunting for my relatives.'

'You've already found one.'

'Who obviously didn't want to keep in touch and whom you dislike, which makes me wary of her.'

He considered this, head on one side. 'Actually, I don't know her well enough to dislike her personally, because she only moved back to the area recently. But I do dislike the way she's picking on me for no reason, I must admit.'

'Well, I'll be on my guard but I do want to talk to her if I can, so I'm going to get in touch once I've sorted the house stuff out. She may know what the big Chaytor family bust-up was about and why my parents emigrated so suddenly. Neither of them would ever talk about their families.' She waited a moment for an answer, then prompted, 'So we'll find you a new car this morning, shall we?'

'Oh, very well. But a cheap one and we won't spend a long time on the search. I don't give two hoots about the engine details or the colour, just that it's reliable, comfy to sit in and complies with safety regulations, so that I can keep that damned woman off my back.'

They found a car for Angus quite quickly, at the same place where Nell had bought hers, a modest little vehicle that was economical to run. The salesman promised to make sure there was nothing that could be faulted by a picky police officer and said it'd be ready to collect the following day.

'I need to buy some food on the way home – you're invited to tea, Angus.'

'Don't forget that we're both going to talk to Jeffries this afternoon.'

'Of course I won't forget. But I need to do a load of washing in Fliss's antique machine, so I can't come back to your place.'

'Are you sure about that?' Angus pulled her close. 'I can think of far better ways for us to spend the time than you doing your washing.'

She was tempted, she admitted to herself, feeling surprised. What was there about this man that made her feel like throwing herself into his arms any time he held them open?

'I'm not going to bed with you just before I confront someone who's going to try to get the better of me,' she managed, hoping she sounded firm and sensible, but not feeling it, not with his arms round her.

'Ah, you're such a spoilsport,' he teased. Pulling away, he glanced at his watch. 'I'll go home and do a few little jobs, then.'

'You won't be late?'

'No, love. I'll set the alarm on my mobile phone right now.'

She did the washing and pegged it out in the sunshine to dry, enjoying the brightness of the day. After that she forced herself to go inside and clear out another cupboard on the ground floor, then felt like a breath of fresh air, so went out into the garden.

As she walked round, she noticed one or two plants that might be worth saving and transferring to Angus's garden, but she didn't even recognise many of the plants.

There were times when she felt at home in England

and times when she felt like a foreign visitor, she thought ruefully. Today she felt to be see-sawing between the two states.

At five to two Angus strolled round to the back of the house and found Nell sitting on an old wooden bench, staring into space.

'That skirt is a lovely colour of blue.' He saw her jump in shock and realised she must have been lost in thought. 'Sorry. Didn't mean to startle you.'

'Oh. Is it time for our visitor?' she glanced at her watch.

'Yes. Are you ready to face the ogre?'

'As ready as I'll ever be.'

He pulled her to her feet and they started walking towards the house, hand in hand. 'Nell, you seem a bit nervous about dealing with this.' Her nod surprised him. 'How can you possibly be nervous of that buffoon, with his manicured hands and lacquered hairstyle?'

'I'm not nervous of him, but I'm on edge about selling the house, I must admit. It's such a lot of money, double what I got for my Australian house, and I had to share that with Craig.'

'Why don't you let me do the negotiating, then?'

'I don't like being the helpless female, that's why.'

'Well, I used to do a lot of negotiating for far bigger amounts, so I don't think this is about male versus female but about personal skills and experience. Why not use my expertise? I'd love to help you.'

She hesitated, then shrugged. 'Well, if you really are good at that sort of thing . . .'

'I am. Very. But you'll have to go along with what I say

or we'll not get the top price possible. It'd be best if you told Jeffries straight away that I'm acting on your behalf and then kept quiet. Make sure you look stern and unimpressed by his offers and refer him back to me if he asks for your opinion. Do you trust me enough to do that?'

'I'm not a very good actress but I'll try. And yes, I do trust you. It's just that selling this house will make a huge difference to the rest of my life, not to mention my retirement.'

'You hanker after security, don't you, love?'

'I guess so, though I think what I really hanker after is not to have to work so hard just to survive. I'd hate to have nothing to do with my time but I've always had so much on my plate that I sometimes felt like a spinning top. Craig paid maintenance money for the boys, but he didn't do much else.'

'Hmm. I don't know that I can promise you total security. My area of work is very up and down, and my house takes a lot of maintenance and keeps springing expensive surprises on me. If I can get this app suite finished – and I'm nearly there – maybe I'll take a leaf out of your book and set some money aside from what it earns to help provide for our old age.'

She stopped as they reached the back door, staring at him in shock. 'You're talking about *our* old age? Already?'

'Yes. Didn't last night mean anything to you?' He pretended to pout. 'Or were you just using my body?'

'You idiot! You know last night meant a lot to me.'

'But I made you smile again, didn't I? I love doing that. I don't think you've smiled nearly enough in your life.' He was about to kiss that soft curved mouth when the doorbell rang. 'Ach. Bad timing, that. Another black mark against the man.'

She went to open the front door and he heard her take a deep, steadying breath on the way.

'Mr Jeffries. Do come in. We'll sit in the front room, if you don't mind.'

Angus ambled in to join them, nodded a greeting and sat next to Nell on the sofa.

'You've already met Mr Denning. He's going to act for me with regard to the house sale, since he has considerable expertise in that area.'

Jeffries looked from one to the other, his expression growing tighter. Clearly he didn't welcome this news.

Angus leant forward and took the initiative. 'How about we cut to the chase and start considering sales figures, Jeffries? Since your client will be knocking the house down, you won't need to look round it or have a survey done.'

The agent opened his mouth to protest, then thought about it for a few seconds and shrugged. 'All right. My client has increased his offer.' He named the amount.

Angus laughed. 'Not enough. Not nearly enough. Stop fooling around.'

'The place isn't worth more.'

'Not to someone who needs a home to live in, I agree, but it's worth a great deal to your client. In fact, it's not only perfect for his needs, it's necessary: the final piece in the jigsaw puzzle, so to speak. Buying it so easily will save him a lot of trouble with the council and planners, so he must be prepared to save Ms Chaytor a lot of trouble in her turn. You surely know your client's top figure?'

Silence reigned until Jeffries suddenly said, 'OK. This is the top figure.'

Angus saw Nell's eyes light up as she heard it and poked her in the side. 'That's better. We're nearly there now.'

'I just told you it's the top figure.'

'And I told you, it's not quite good enough. If you need to get back to him about moving a little higher, we can meet another day.'

'You're a cool customer.'

'Yeah, well, I used to be a demon negotiator for one of the big international IT companies, dealing in millions, not paltry sums like this. Nowadays I help out my friends and work for myself. Life is much more enjoyable but I haven't forgotten how to talk money.'

'What do you think he should offer?'

Angus named a figure.

Jeffries didn't speak for a few moments, then said slowly, 'If we agree to that, you won't try to pull a fast one? It'll be a firm sale? No gazumping.'

'It will be absolutely firm.' Angus gestured towards Nell. 'My lovely friend here isn't the conniving sort. Surely you've summed her up by now?'

A reluctant smile crossed Jeffries' face. 'No offence, Ms Chaytor, but I agree with your, er, adviser. You were wise to get someone else to do your negotiating. So, we're agreed. Let's get the contracts signed.' He pulled a sheaf of papers out of his briefcase. 'I just have to add the figures to the offer.'

'I like people who come prepared to do business,' Angus said.

Nell leaned forward as if physically joining in. 'I have two small conditions.'

'Oh?' Jeffries paused, frowning at her.

Angus glanced sideways in surprise.

She took a deep breath. 'The sale won't include the contents of the house. They include a lot of rubbish but also things that belong to my family's history.'

Jeffries let out a snort of laughter. 'No one will worry about the contents. In fact, if you agree to remove some of the things, it'll probably save my client the cost of taking a load to the council tip. And the second condition?'

'I'd like to take some of the plants out of the garden, for sentimental reasons.'

'Fine by me. It's getting bulldozed, so take what you like.'

She nodded. 'That's all.'

Angus relaxed again. He'd been a bit concerned there.

'If you'll give me a few minutes, I'll fill in the necessary details on the offer.' Jeffries took out a flashy fountain pen and flourished it over the paper.

'After which you can give us a few minutes and we'll both read the offer through carefully,' Angus said.

Jeffries shrugged. 'It's a standard format.'

'Nonetheless.' Angus winked at Nell, who was sitting looking frozen, as if she couldn't quite believe what was happening. 'We'll start moving the things you want to keep into my house as soon as you like, love. I have plenty of storage space.'

She nodded and he could see her relaxing slightly.

He'd enjoyed the short joust with Jeffries. He'd never believed in posturing and pretending about sales. He could usually get most of what he wanted with a confident grin and a stubborn refusal to give way beyond a certain point.

Fifteen minutes later the offer had been sorted, the preliminary papers signed and Jeffries had driven off.

Nell turned to Angus, flung her arms round him and burst into tears. 'You're marvellous.'

'I am, rather.'

'I mean it. I shall be truly independent when the sale goes through.'

'No, you won't.'

'What do you mean by that, Angus?'

'I'm hoping you'll be permanently attached to me. Total independence is vastly overrated, believe me.'

'You certainly go straight for what you want, don't you?'

'Yes. And what I want is you, love. Never doubt that. Now, let's stroll up to my house and choose some rooms for you. It's a lovely sunny May day, birds are singing, butterflies are fluttering and I am hoping, in my artless little masculine way, that you'll share my bed from now onwards.'

'Do I have the choice?'

He looked at her very seriously. 'Yes, Nell, you do. It's not the price of your accommodation at Dennings. But you did give me hope yesterday that you'll consider building a life with me.'

She nodded.

'However, I think you should have your own rooms as well as those we share. The only thing is, they'll be dusty because I haven't touched the rest of the house for a long time. Perhaps I should get someone in to clean the rooms you choose, then I'll help you move furniture around or whatever else you need doing?'

'No, let me do the cleaning. I've had years of practice at

it. Just help me with moving the furniture afterwards.'

She beamed at him suddenly, her eyes sparkling with happiness. She looked younger than when he'd first seen her.

'I can't believe I'm moving in with you, Angus. I've never been an impulsive type.'

'Believe it. When you see a good thing, you have to grab it and hold on with both hands. Like this.' He drew her gently towards him and kissed her.

Nick's father rang him the day after their meeting. 'I'll be round tonight with a new door to that bedroom and a man to fit it. Make sure you're in.'

'OK. What time?'

But Craig had already ended the call.

Nick decided this would be a good time to introduce Carla to his father, so they bought some rolls and had a scratch meal as they waited.

The doorbell rang just as they were finishing.

She cleared the mess away quickly while he answered the door.

His father came in, carrying a bag of tools, but stopped to stare at Carla in an assessing way. He nodded and held out one hand. 'So you're the one.'

She gave him back stare for stare as she shook hands. 'Yes.'

There was the sound of footsteps on the stairs and another man appeared, carrying a door.

'Come in, Kev. This is my son Nick and his fiancée Carla. The door goes here.' He led the way to the short corridor that led to the bedrooms and bathroom, and came back shortly on his own.

'Got some coffee? I've had a bloody awful day.'

Carla stood up. 'I'll get it. How do you take it?'

'Black, no sugar.'

Since the kitchen was part of the living area, she continued to listen to the conversation as she waited for the kettle to boil.

'Did you get on to Steve?' Nick asked.

'Yep. Your brother's bringing the laptop back tomorrow night and while he's here, he'll clear out the rest of his stuff. He's staying with me for a couple of days.'

'Is Jenny OK with that? He's a real slob in the house.'

'He won't be with us for long and she'll make sure he doesn't mess her kitchen up, believe me. After that he'll be working for a friend of mine in the country as a farm labourer.'

'Steve? Labouring. He hates to exert himself, has trouble raising a mug of coffee to his lips. He won't stick with that.'

'I'm not interested in what he likes and he'll have no choice about sticking to the job. He needs to pay me back what he owes for this place, and for settling his debts. Jenny and I are driving him down to the farm at the weekend.'

'Can't he even drive himself?'

'I'm selling his car. He wouldn't be allowed to take it anyway, and he had a lot more debts than he admitted when your mother left, so the money can go towards paying them off. The friend who owns this farm lost a son to drugs. He helps young guys out from time to time because of that. Steve knows that if he leaves the farm, I'll wash my hands of him completely.'

'I still can't see him sticking at it.'

Craig hesitated, then added, 'Steve's had a bit of a scare.

His so-called friend put the hard word on him to pay his debts by dealing drugs.'

Nick let out a soft whistle of surprise. 'He was that far into it?'

'He was starting to get into it. So half his wages from the farm will be paid into a special charity commemorating my friend's son and the rest will be given to me. I'll save it for Steve. My friend will know when he's safe to let loose again.'

'And you feel that'll work?'

'Best chance I can think of for him. He knows I won't give him another.' Craig drew one finger across his throat in a cutting motion. 'I've helped with this charity from time to time, because I hate drugs. I never thought I'd need to put a son of mine into the programme, though. I am not happy about that.'

There was silence. Nick was shocked rigid by these revelations.

Craig glanced round, changing the subject. 'You two could stay on here, if you wanted.'

Carla came across to sit next to Nick. 'We've already signed up for another flat and paid the deposit, Mr Vincent. Anyway, I don't like this place and it has bad memories for Nick.'

Nick nodded and put his arm round her shoulders. 'The rent on our new flat is quite a bit cheaper, Dad. We have a lot of things to buy if we're going to set up home together.'

Craig grinned at them. 'I can't believe this is you, Nick, getting all domestic. But then, you always were the quiet one.' He looked round the room and frowned. 'Whose furniture is this?'

'Ma gave it to me and Steve.'

'You'd better take it all with you. I'm not clearing the damned place out. Oh, and another thing. Does Robbie know about you two?'

'Not yet. I'll phone him tonight.'

His father studied them again, his head on one side. 'Well, you certainly have all the signs of being in love and you look like a decent girl, Carla. I hope it works out for you both.'

After his father and the door installer had left, Nick let out a long sigh of relief.

Carla smiled at him. 'Relieved to have Steve off your plate?'

'Very. But I'm shocked. I had no idea he was in so deep. Anyway, that's enough about him. Let's ring Robbie, then Ma. Get it all over with.'

Her mobile phone rang. When she ended the call, she said, 'They want me to go into work for a couple of hours. Someone didn't turn up.'

'Shall I take you home afterwards?'

'No need. I give another girl a lift sometimes, so she can return the favour. I'll be all right.'

When she'd gone, the flat felt empty. Nick took out his phone, feeling a bit embarrassed. Would his family understand how quickly you could fall in love?

Chapter Thirteen

Early the next morning, as she was continuing to clear Fliss's house, Nell received a phone call from Edwina Richards.

'Nice to hear from you,' she said politely, not sure it was true.

Edwina didn't bother with idle chit-chat. 'I've been asking my great-aunt about your father and it seems we're more closely related than I'd realised.'

'Oh?'

'Yes. You and I are first cousins on my mother's side.'

'My father is your mother's brother? I have a great-aunt!' She had only hazy memories of her parents' families and once they moved to Australia, neither her mother nor her father would give her any details, though her mother had once said she had no siblings.

'Yes. You have an uncle too. Your father's younger brother and my mother are twins.'

'Good heavens! I can't believe this. And they're both alive?'

'Yes. Look, it's not the sort of thing to explain over the phone. This is my day off, so how about you and I meet for coffee? I'll tell you what I know so far and you can tell me what happened to your parents in Australia, then we'll take it from there. I haven't said anything about you to the rest of my family yet. I wanted to be sure it wouldn't upset anyone. Now, there's a café on High Street and—'

'Why don't you come here for coffee instead?'

Silence for a moment or two, then, 'OK. What time?'

'About ten-thirty?'

'Fine.'

Edwina disconnected without another word and Nell set her phone down gently. She was eager to find out what the quarrel had been about, why her father had been so adamant about never again getting in touch with his family. Once she knew, she could make up her own mind about whether she wanted to get to know her relatives.

Surely Edwina would have some information that would solve the mystery? It had upset Nell ever since she was a child to know she had relatives in England she could only vaguely remember. Only, unlike friends who were also 'Poms', Nell didn't know where the families were or anything about them, apart from Fliss.

And when she had later asked Fliss, even her aunt had said that it wasn't good to dig up the past and she must respect her parents' wishes.

Nell continued to clear things out. It was obvious that at some stage or other Fliss had done quite a bit of clearing out, as old people often did, because some of the bedrooms were empty of everything but furniture. It would only take her a day or two to go through the rest.

She even tiptoed into the front part of the attic, but she'd remembered correctly: the bedrooms there were bare. She didn't linger, because apart from the safety aspects, the smell seemed to be getting worse by the day.

Mid morning she tidied herself up and waited for Edwina to arrive, wondering what her cousin would be like out of police uniform. Would she still be stiff and officious, or would she be more friendly? And what were the rest of her Chaytor relatives like?

The doorbell rang and she hurried to open it, standing for a moment staring at her visitor, who stared back equally intently.

Edwina definitely looked different now she wasn't in uniform. She was quite a bit taller than Nell, looking fit and strong, but was more relaxed in posture today. She had grey eyes and naturally blonde hair, slightly wavy and tied firmly back in a ponytail.

'Do come in. We'll sit in the kitchen, if you don't mind. The house isn't in a very good state. But you must know that already. Do I call you Edwina or do you shorten your name?' She switched the kettle on, had the mugs and some biscuits out ready.

'My friends usually shorten it to Eddie. Look, I don't actually know the whole story of the quarrel, so we'll have to compare notes and see if we can fill in the gaps. Just black coffee, please, and no biscuits.' With hardly a pause she continued, 'Can I ask what happened to your father? Did he stay married to your mother? He's the family mystery and was almost never mentioned when I was a child. All I know I picked up by eavesdropping.'

'Yes, they did stay married. They were fairly happy

but not . . . well, not deeply in love.'

'Did he make a success of things? My brother and I often wondered, but Fliss would never talk to us about him.'

'She wouldn't tell me anything about my English relatives, either. Well, that's not quite right. She'd talk about previous generations, but not about my parents' cohort. Did you see a lot of her?'

'No. She was angry with my mother and uncle and I think it was because of the quarrel. We used to visit her sometimes when I was little but after your father left, my parents weren't made welcome at her house. She hadn't a good word to say about my father from then on, so he may have been involved in some way too.'

She waited a moment then went on, 'After I left home, I used to drop in occasionally to check that she was all right. I've had to break into houses where old people have died on their own and I didn't want a relative of mine to be found like that. She was always pleasant enough but we weren't really close.'

Nell sighed. 'I don't think I've got anything much to add. My father said I was "better not knowing that bunch of cheats and liars". When I cleared out my parents' house, there were no family photos from England, not even an entry in an old address book.'

'How did they die?'

'Dad got stomach cancer in his early sixties and died quite quickly. My mother seemed to fade away after that. She hated living on her own, but my ex refused to let her live in our house, even though he'd moved out by then, and I had the three boys to look after so I didn't fight for it. And then she was gone, too.'

'I'm sorry.'

'I gather your father is still alive, Eddie.'

'Very much alive.' She gave a wry smile. 'He's a prickly old sod. I suppose Denning told you about that. He didn't waste any time getting on good terms with you, did he?'

Nell frowned at her. 'If you bad-mouth Angus, our conversation will be over. And just to set the record straight, he isn't short of money.'

'Then why the hell does he drive that old wreck around? It's a danger on the roads. I'm not picking on him like my father does, honestly, but I've seen what happens with unsafe vehicles.'

'Angus has been working all hours in the day on an important project, and wasn't thinking about his car. Anyway, he's bought a new one now. It's still second-hand but it's in good condition. I made sure of that. He was supposed to be getting it today. They were going to deliver it and take his old car to the wreckers for him.'

'About time. You seem to know him well. I didn't think he'd been to Australia and you haven't been to England since you were a child. I can't understand why—' she broke off abruptly.

'Why Angus and I have got together? In a nutshell, we fell in love.' It was the first time she'd said it to anyone and the words came out more easily than she'd expected.

Eddie looked at her in amazement. 'But you've only been here for a couple of weeks.'

'Lightning can strike quickly sometimes.'

Her cousin got such a sad look on her face, Nell felt sorry for her. 'Anyway, we were talking about my father and his quarrel with his siblings. What the hell happened?'

'I think my uncle's friend was involved. Please don't be offended, but I did wonder if your mother might, you know, have had an affair.' She waited, head on one side.

Nell wanted to say that her mother couldn't have done that, but something stopped her. Once or twice she'd heard her parents arguing and a man's name had been tossed to and fro, and not politely. 'Was he called Mike?'

Eddie stared at her. 'Yes.'

'They argued about a guy called Mike more than once.'

'That's a possibility, then. As far as the Chaytors were concerned, Uncle Bob simply vanished and as he'd praised Australia a few times, they wondered if he'd gone there. My mother tried to find him but her letters to people he'd known and the place where he'd worked were returned with "no longer at this address" on them. It wasn't as easy then to find someone as it is now that just about everyone's on the Internet.'

'And your mother didn't try again later, when technology improved? After all, my father was her older brother?'

'By then she and my uncle had decided to let sleeping dogs lie because Bob hadn't tried to contact them, had he? It's been, what, about forty years? I think Mum's always hoped he'd turn up one day, though.'

'I'm surprised Fliss didn't say something to her. She's known where we were for over twenty years, because I wrote to her, then we kept in touch, first by letter then by email. I let her know when my parents died as well, naturally.'

'I saw her computer. It was nearly an antique. She was thinking of getting a new one, but then she died suddenly. I didn't like to fiddle with it.'

'I wonder why she kept quiet about Dad.'

'She could be close-mouthed when she wanted to. After she died, I contacted her lawyer to ask if he wanted me to clear out her house, in case there were family things there. But he said it had been left to another family member from Australia and it would be up to that person to do it.'

After a thoughtful pause, she added, 'We wondered who it was, maybe even your father. My father said I should contest the will because I'd been keeping an eye on her, but as far as I'm concerned, it was her property and her choice who to leave it to, so I let the matter drop.'

'If there's anything you want, you're welcome to it.'

'I'll have a poke round when you've taken what you want, if that's all right. I'd like a memento. There's a little statuette I rather like.'

'The 1930s woman?'

'Yes.'

'Take it. I have one similar in storage in Australia.'

'Thanks. Is it all right if I ask Mum and Dad whether they want anything? He's been looking into the family history since he retired.'

'Of course. But they'd better come and look round soon, because the purchaser is going to bulldoze the house.'

'Thanks. Much appreciated.'

'I've always envied people who grow up with families around them. They don't know how lucky they are to have people to turn to, people who care about them. When I had my problems with Craig, I was on my own. My parents refused to get involved, said only I could sort out what I wanted. They weren't very good grandparents, either, didn't seem interested.'

'Hard for you.'

'Yeah. Well, I got through it. Am I going to meet the rest of the Chaytor family?'

'I'll have to talk to them and get back to you. I'll bring Mum and Dad round the weekend after next, if that's OK. They're coming over from Fleetwood for her friend's 70th birthday bash. Maybe on the Saturday afternoon? I'll have to check with them.'

She hesitated, then added, 'I doubt you'll find my father easy to get on with, though, especially if you're living with Denning. Dad's dead against people with titles.' She looked at her watch. 'It's been nice talking to you, but I have to go now.'

'You will get back to me about your family, though, as well as your parents? I really do want to meet them.'

Another of those searching looks, then a nod. 'Yes.'

And with that, she had to be satisfied.

To Nell's surprise, her middle son rang her soon after Eddie had left. Her delight in hearing from him made her forget for a moment that he wasn't supposed to have her phone number. Then she realised that Craig might also have got hold of it.

'It's lovely to hear from you but how did you get my number? We were supposed to be sticking to emails.'

'Robbie gave it me. Don't get angry with him, Ma,' Nick spoke as if he could guess what she was thinking. 'He wouldn't have told me if it wasn't special circumstances.'

'How special? You're all right?'

'I'm fine. Never better.'

'It must be about Steve, then.'

'No, it's not, and never mind what he's doing. Dad's dealing with that. I'm not spoiling this phone call talking about my stupid brother. Ma, I've met a girl and we're engaged.'

'What?'

He laughed. 'Took me by surprise, too. I'll email you a photo of her.'

He spent the next ten minutes telling her about his Carla and how wonderful she was, ending up, 'So we're getting married in a month's time. Just a quiet registry office wedding. And no, she's not pregnant. That was the first thing Dad asked. He's a cynical sod, isn't he?'

'Then why the rush?'

'We want to be together. She's the one, Ma, she really is. But her family's Italian and they'd go mad if we lived in sin. In this day and age, would you believe? So we aren't even telling them we're getting married till just before the wedding, because they'd hold things up and insist on a big family party. We both think that sort of thing's a waste of time and money. We love one another so much and that's what matters. It's incredible.'

'I can hear the love in your voice,' she said softly. 'If she's the one, you go for it, Nick. Look, is it OK if I just send you a present? I'd love to be there but I simply can't face that horrible flight again so soon. Do you mind?'

'Not at all. We'll do a face-to-face call another time. Now, enough about me. How's the house?'

So she explained briefly about that. 'But I've found somewhere else to live, and I'm getting a nice lot of money for the house from a developer.'

'Good for you.' He chuckled. 'I'd like to see Dad's face when he hears.'

'I don't intend to tell him anything and you keep what I've told you to yourself. Now, fill me in about Steve. I'll only worry if you don't.'

'He got into more trouble, so Dad's paid his debts and found him a job in the country.'

'Your father did?'

'Yeah. Steve isn't happy about the job, but he was desperate, so he had to agree.'

'What exactly happened?'

'Nothing you need to worry about. I told you: Dad fixed it and put the hard word on him. Got to go now, Ma. Bye.'

Nick had never sounded so grown-up, or been so protective of her. She might ring Craig and— No, she wouldn't! Let him deal with Steve. He wouldn't let anything really bad happen to one of his sons, if only because it would reflect badly on himself. No, she was wronging him. He did care about the boys, as much as a selfish man like him could care about anyone.

She realised she was still holding the phone, which was purring gently in her ear, so put it down. She could understand how Nick felt about his Carla. The same *coup de foudre* had struck her when she met Angus. She'd been instantly attracted to him and fallen in love so quickly it took her breath away even to think of him.

She wasn't going to tell her sons about it yet, though.

She realised she was smiling like a fool, so told herself to stop wasting time. She grabbed a quick snack then went back to work.

There wasn't much more to clear out now, after which

she had to decide what to keep and what to sell. She wasn't keeping a lot. The objects had little sentimental value for her, so the Chaytors were welcome to anything they fancied.

She was sure Angus would let her store the stuff she was doubtful about. There were one or two pieces of furniture that might be worth selling carefully at auctions or to dealers, and some china and small silver items. Well, she thought they might be worth it. She wasn't an expert, had only watched antiques programmes on the TV.

Was she doing the right thing, moving in with Angus?

She smiled involuntarily at the thought. Of course it was the right thing to do. If her son could dive in at the deep end of love, so could she.

Angus was the one. No doubt about that. It was strange how certain she felt.

She'd rushed blindly into marriage the first time, young enough to be sure that everything would work like a dream. This time she didn't feel she was blinded by her love, but was quietly sure they could be happy together. And if there were problems, they could fix them.

And oh, the deep joy of that!

Steve seriously considered running away. Only where would he run to? He had no money left now, none at all, and no way of earning more without his father's help. And whatever his father said, he did not want to get into drug dealing.

Only why did he have to go and work in the country? He was a townie, had never had anything to do with life in the bush.

241

His father came into the living room. 'Ah, there you are. Owen's car has just drawn up outside. He told me he wanted to have a chat with you before you leave, but I am telling you now that if you don't take his offer, I'll throw you out immediately. What I've arranged for you is the best chance you're likely to get to turn your life around.'

'Yeah, yeah.'

'Do not talk to me like that.'

Steve blinked in surprise. 'Like what?'

'"Yeah, yeah",' his father mimicked. 'That tone of voice is an insult in itself. Is that how you talked to your mother?'

'It's how you talk to my mother.'

'I don't . . . do I?' He looked at his son in shock.

Steve nodded, but didn't push his luck by saying anything else.

'How she's put up with you lately I don't know. I should have got involved earlier. I owe her an apology for that.'

The doorbell rang and Craig rushed to answer it, returning with a giant of a fellow, dressed casually in jeans and a faded sweatshirt. It had ASPIRE written across the front. Steve hoped this Owen wasn't a member of the holier-than-thou squad.

'This is my youngest son.'

Owen studied him, the scrutiny going on for so long that Steve felt uncomfortable, then before he knew what was happening, Owen had felt his bicep.

'Not used his muscles much, has he?'

'No. He hasn't used his brain much, either.' His father glared at him. 'If he has one.'

Owen grinned. 'Right then, lad, listen carefully. I've

242

helped quite a few young fellows in the same sort of trouble as yourself, and most of them did well out of our programme. It's not easy; it's hard work. But if you're not prepared even to give it a try, if you're thinking of running away, save us all a load of trouble and do it now.'

Steve's father let out a snort and both men waited for Steve to say something. But what was there to say? He had no choice but to go with this Owen fellow.

'Um . . . what sort of work is it exactly? Dad didn't say.'

'Farm work, basically, but we also help a charity by restoring old farm machinery for Third World countries. So if you have a mechanical turn of mind you might move on to that later.'

'Um. No. I'm not mechanical. Well, I don't think I am. Except for computers. I'm good with them, built my own.'

Another pause, then. 'Well, you won't be using a computer for a while. Grab your things and let's go. We've a long drive ahead of us.'

'Where exactly is your farm?'

'Inland from Albany. Not near any town you'd recognise. We're ten miles from the nearest town, actually, which has a population of two hundred and seventy-six and one pub, which is also the general store.'

Steve's heart sank. Oh, hell. There'd be no nipping out for a beer, then, because his father was going to sell his car to help pay for his debts. He'd be trapped in the middle of nowhere.

At the door Craig put his hand on Steve's shoulder so he turned round, though all he really wanted was to get the hell out of there.

'If you graduate from the programme I'll help find you a job.'

What as? A farm labourer? Steve thought. He thought it wise to say, 'Thanks.'

He walked out behind Owen, not looking back.

Chapter Fourteen

Winifred was both excited and nervous about the garden-sharing meeting. She'd arranged to meet Dan at the senior citizens' centre a little early. He'd said the local newspaper might be sending a journalist to report on it and they might want to talk to both of them, but she hoped they wouldn't.

She was going early not only to support Dan, but because it always felt better to arrive without having to rush, not to speak to the press.

Janey had realised how nervous she felt and the dear girl had offered to skip a tech class to go with her, but she'd turned that kind offer down. Janey mustn't miss her classes. And anyway, Dan would be there at the centre.

Winifred had been to the centre before to attend computer classes for seniors. This time she went by taxi and hang the expense. Molly's lawyer had called yesterday to say they'd obtained probate and the money would be paid into Winifred's account within twenty-four hours.

So now she would be able to afford a computer of her

own and anything else she fancied too, like a new winter coat. She didn't have expensive tastes but she had been making do on a small income for so long that Molly's bequest seemed like a fortune to her.

Of course, she'd only have the money that had been in Molly's bank account till she sold her friend's house and its contents. She'd never sold a house before, had been born in her present home and never lived anywhere else, but she was sure her friends would help her sort that out.

Sometimes she wished she'd been able to lead a more interesting life, but she'd done her duty and accepted what fate brought her, and that was a comfort to her. She'd never allowed herself to mope, even during her mother's difficult final months. Well, what was the use? It wouldn't have changed anything, would it?

'We're here, madam.'

She jerked abruptly out of her thoughts and paid the taxi driver.

'Ah, there you are, Winifred.'

She turned to smile at Dan. 'Yes. Here I am, arriving in style.'

'What were you thinking about? You looked deep in thought.'

'As you know, I've been left a little money, enough to make my life more comfortable. I was thinking of buying a computer. Will you help me to do that?'

'Of course I will. Now, come inside and settle yourself. You're sitting at the front table with me and I'm hoping you'll agree to be our guinea pig.'

'Exactly how do I do that?'

He patted her hand. 'Nothing difficult about it. You just

have to be the first one to offer your garden and let us practise on you how best to organise the scheme. We won't do anything you don't like, I promise.'

'Oh. Well, I suppose I could manage that.'

'You've managed to hold your life together through two wars and other hard times, Winifred Parfitt. You can do anything you choose to.'

She could feel herself blushing at this compliment. 'Do you really think so?'

'I wouldn't have suggested it otherwise.' He chuckled as he added, 'I thought Dawn was running this meeting, but she says you and I are in charge and she'll just act as our adviser behind the scenes. In other words, she's tricked us into taking over the project, Win.'

Panic filled her. 'I've never organised anything as big as this.'

'Me neither. But we'll cope.' Dan gave her one of his cheeky grins. 'After all, they can't shoot us if we do something wrong, can they?'

By now Winifred was feeling more like running away than going inside the meeting hall, but she could hardly do that – even if her stiff old legs would run, which they hadn't managed to do for years. So she squared her shoulders and moved forward.

They were the first two there, but a young woman followed them inside, pushing a little boy in a shabby buggy.

'Is this the garden-sharing group?' she asked, so breathless and hesitant it was clear to Winifred that the younger woman was even more nervous than she was.

'It is. Do come in.'

'Who's this, then?' Dan smiled down at the little boy sitting sucking a lollipop.

'This is Howie. Say hello to the man, Howie.'

The child sucked the bright-red sweet even more vigorously and looked at the strangers suspiciously. Dan turned back to the mother. 'And you are?'

'I'm Izzy, short for Isabel. And I don't mean to sound negative, but it's no use me staying unless there'll be someone to show me what to do. I don't know anything about gardening, but oh, I'd love to learn. Fresh vegetables taste ever so much nicer and me and Howie like being out in the fresh air.'

Dan beamed at her 'I can help you. I'm not up to heavy digging these days, but I know a lot about gardening and I'd enjoy passing on my knowledge. And this is Miss Parfitt, who is generously going to share her garden with someone.'

'Pleased to meet you.' The young woman started to hold out her hand, looked down at it, then said, 'I'd better not shake. I'm all sticky from Howie. I don't usually give him lollipops, but it'll keep him quiet for ages.'

About a dozen people turned up, but there was no sign of Dawn, so Dan nudged Winifred and gestured to the platform. When they were both in place there, he stood up and said loudly, 'Good afternoon, everyone. Shall we begin now?'

Once people had shuffled and twitched into silent attention, he introduced himself. 'And this is Miss Parfitt, who has already offered her garden. Can I ask who else has a garden to share?'

Another middle-aged man and an elderly woman put up their hands.

'I'll start by explaining the ground rules. We can make up any rules we want, of course, but I have to emphasise that people who want to garden-share are not there to do the owners' work for them. They take over a portion of the garden to grow their own vegetables and fruit, whatever they choose. They keep their own portion tidy and pay for its use by giving the owner a quarter of what they produce.'

The elderly woman who had volunteered her garden stood up. 'I thought they were coming to help people who can't manage the gardening.'

Patiently, Dan went over the basic idea of the scheme again.

'Oh, I can't have someone digging up my garden and planting who knows what,' the woman said. 'I was told wrongly.'

She walked out without another word, leaning heavily on a stick and scowling.

As she was leaving another man came in and slipped into a seat in the back row. He was dressed in a suit and didn't look at all like a gardener, but when Dan summarised what they'd done so far, he raised his hand.

'Yes, sir?'

'I'd like to observe how this is done before I volunteer my garden for the scheme. Is that allowed?' He didn't offer his name, just folded his arms and waited.

Dan didn't like his tone, didn't like his face either, if truth be told, or the way he was alternately staring at Winifred and studying the other people in the room. Something about the man was wrong, but it was hard to put your finger on what it was, because the fellow had been perfectly polite and wasn't down at heel, far from it. Perhaps he was just too elegantly turned out to care about gardening.

Unfortunately, since this was a public meeting, Dan couldn't think how to tell him to go away. 'Yes, well, you must do as you see fit.' He turned to the older man who'd volunteered without all these ifs and buts. 'You're prepared to offer your garden, sir?'

'Yes, please. I live at the top end of Jubilee Road. The garden's far too big for me now but I don't want to move out of my house. I'm Stanley Packer.'

By the end of the meeting Winifred and Stan had each taken on three garden sharers and the single trial had become two.

Dan arranged to meet the young woman called Izzy and the husband of another woman, who'd come to put his name down because he was at work. The third person sharing it, of course, would be Janey.

The well-dressed man intervened. 'I wonder if I might come along tonight as an observer?'

Dan couldn't see any way out of letting him do that. 'Perhaps you could introduce yourself, as the others have?'

'Oh, sorry. I'm John Smythe.'

'Do you have a business card?'

'Sorry, no. I don't carry them.'

Now that didn't sound right. Everyone who dressed like a businessman carried cards, at least in Dan's experience. 'Well, perhaps you have a mobile number?'

'I'm afraid I use one provided by my employers, so I can't use it for private purposes.'

He didn't volunteer a landline number, either, which was another black mark against him in Dan's opinion. 'Well, we'll see you tonight, then, with the others.'

'Number 5 Peppercorn Street, isn't it?'

'Yes.' Dan followed the man to the door and something made him take note of the car registration. As Smythe closed the driver's door a piece of paper blew out, and something told Dan not to draw it to the driver's attention.

He waited till the car had vanished from sight to pick up the paper. It was a brochure for a property developer and had 'Is your garden too big for you?' in large red letters across the front. Inside it informed people with houses on large plots of land that their houses might be more valuable than they'd realised and Real Houses Ltd would be glad to send a representative to assess their home's value. In small letters at the bottom, it mentioned Nolan Ltd as 'the premier builder for infill housing'.

Aha! Dan thought. He hadn't heard anything good about Gus Nolan. Any company associated with him would probably cheat people out of the full value of their property. There was no mention of anyone called Smythe, though.

He shoved the brochure in his pocket and went to invite Winifred to share a pot of tea with him in a nearby café.

When he showed her the brochure, she hardly looked at it. 'I've seen this before. Several letters from this company have been pushed through my door, and they've phoned me too. They won't leave me alone.'

'Persistent devils, aren't they? Smythe's desire to observe is beginning to sound even more fishy to me. I'm sorry I agreed to let him come tonight. I wish I had someone younger and stronger to keep an eye on him. I'm even starting to wonder whether I should have got you into this project, if they're going to use it to pester you.'

'Perhaps we could ask Angus to come along tonight as well.'

'Good idea! Do you think he will?'

'If he's free.'

When they'd finished their tea, he called a taxi for her on the mobile phone his sons had bought him. 'I'd take you back myself, but I've arranged to visit a friend on the other side of town and I was enjoying our chat so much I've left it a bit late to get there.'

He beamed at the phone as he switched it off. 'I didn't want this, but they insisted, and I have to admit it comes in useful at times.'

'Well, you don't have your ear glued to it like many of the younger folk do,' she said. 'Silly, they look, walking down the street, talking loudly to thin air.'

'I agree. You should get a mobile phone, Winifred. Very useful, they are, for people our age, and not just for calling taxis. You can call for help wherever you are.'

'Oh, I will now that I can afford it. I'll do it this very week. I'm sure Janey will help me choose one and you can both teach me how to use it.'

She smiled all the way home. Her smile faded when she went into the house, though, because she found a plain envelope on the floor of the hall.

She stared down at it, noting that it didn't have a postage stamp and that her name was printed on it in untidy capital letters, as if someone had written them with their left hand.

She decided to handle it carefully. She put on her kitchen gloves and picked it up by one corner, using scissors to cut along the top. When she pulled out the letter inside it, she groaned. More threats!

WE HAVEN'T FORGOTTEN YOU
GET OUT OF THAT HOUSE
YOU DON'T NEED IT
OTHER PEOPLE DO

She clutched her chest, as she always did instinctively when her heart started pounding, and sat down on the nearest chair.

'You silly old woman,' she muttered. 'They want you to get upset. This is only a piece of paper.'

When she'd calmed down a little, she got out the card the police had given her and dialled the number of the detective, explaining what had happened. The woman at the other end asked if she was in immediate danger. When she said she thought not, they told her someone would get to her as soon as they could.

She knew there were more important cases for the police to deal with, but she was worried about Janey and little Millie getting caught up in this, so she phoned Angus and asked if he could come round and advise her.

'What's the matter, Miss Parfitt? You sound upset.'

'I got another threatening letter.'

'Are you on your own?'

'Yes.'

'I'm coming round straight away to the back door. Don't let anyone else in. And put the kettle on.'

She let out a shaky breath as she set the phone down, but she felt better knowing that Angus was on his way.

She had a sudden image of the man at the meeting, the one Dan had mistrusted. Was he connected with this? She might be old, but she wasn't stupid, never had been, and she didn't think she was losing her marbles. The smarmy creature must have some ulterior motive for wanting to 'observe' what they were doing.

And he'd have known she wasn't at home. Had he told someone to deliver this?

Why did they feel they had the right to bully people into selling their houses? This was her home!

It was wrong, very wrong. Money made people do terrible things.

She didn't often swear, but she did now. She banged her clenched fist on the table for emphasis and said loudly and slowly, 'Damn you, whoever you are! I'm not giving in to your threats!'

Angus switched on his own security system and ran across his untidy grounds, cursing as he tripped and nearly fell over a tree root hidden in the long grass. He went into Miss Parfitt's house via her back garden because when he'd repaired her fence he'd fitted one panel that appeared to be fixed in place but which could be moved easily by unfastening a hidden catch.

Of course, he'd obtained her permission to create this shortcut so that he could come and help her, if necessary.

And it had been necessary. Already.

As he ran towards her house, he could see her face at the window, pale against the darker background. She vanished and opened the back door.

'Thank you for coming, Angus. So silly of me to have panicked, but it reminded me of the night I was mugged and the time they burnt down my summer house. I was worried they'd . . . do something else.

'I have Janey and Millie to think about as well as myself now. It's so lovely to have them living here, but oh, Angus, what if I've brought them into danger?'

'Your friends will make sure none of you is hurt.' He gave in to the temptation to hug her. She felt fragile against him, thin and brittle with age, for all the liveliness and intelligence in her eyes.

At first she was stiff, then she relaxed against him. He guessed she wasn't used to being hugged.

He was glad she'd turned to him. She'd not only been a close friend of his great-aunt, but had been kind to him many a time when he was a small boy visiting Dennings. She was a feisty old lady, and he admired that, hoped he'd be as lively at her age.

'Show it to me.'

She pointed to the envelope and paper on the kitchen table. 'I've only touched the top corner of it.'

He let out a choke of angry sound as he leant over the table to read it, not touching anything. 'Damn them! Don't let them bully you into selling.'

'I won't.'

'Did you call the police?'

'Yes, but they couldn't come straight away, because it's not an emergency.'

'I disagree with that. The letter was planted to be waiting for you when you returned from that meeting, so it's my guess someone must have known you were going out, and even where. Can you think of anyone?'

'Well . . .' She explained about the man at the meeting.

'Pity you couldn't take a photo of him.'

'I'm going to buy one of those modern mobile phones

that take photos as well as make calls. I've seen them on the TV and wished I had one.'

'Excuse me, but can you afford it? There are monthly costs to pay as well as the cost of the phone itself.'

Once again she told someone about her inheritance. It felt so good not to have to depend on the kindness of others for everything. 'I'll ask Janey to help me choose one.'

'Let me do that instead. I probably know more about them and can get you a better price. In fact, why didn't I think about it before? I'll give you one if you'll help me test my new apps.'

She looked at him doubtfully. 'I've never even used an app, though I've guessed what they are from TV programmes.'

'That's exactly why you'd be so useful to me. I bought several cheap mobile phones to give to people who would test some computer programs for me – the sort we call apps, which help people to do small tasks. I've designed a whole suite of them especially for oldies and others who don't know much about modern media. They'll help people understand what to do and will extend their skills. I'm nearly ready to go public, but I need to do some testing first.'

He beamed at her. 'If I bring you one of my phones, will you work through the apps for me and make a report?'

'I'd love to, Angus. Life has become so interesting lately! If I can only stop these people from pestering me, I can try all sorts of new things before I die. I'm going to buy a computer too. And as soon as I can.'

He had to give her another hug. 'I'll help you buy one. You'll soon learn how to use it.'

His smile faded as he added, 'But I'll definitely come here later to take a good look at this Smythe fellow. I don't like the sounds of him.'

'You won't like the looks of him, either. Dan didn't, and he's a good judge of people.'

Chapter Fifteen

Two detectives turned up at number 5 just as Angus was about to go down the road to Nell's. They introduced themselves as Mike and Tony, and though they seemed pleasant enough, he decided to stay on and make sure they took Miss Parfitt's worries seriously.

He was relieved to see them examine the note with great care and discuss it in relation to the other note.

'I put it in a polythene bag to stop it getting touched by anyone here,' she told them, sounding anxious. 'Was that the right thing to do?'

'Definitely,' Tony said. 'We'll take this new note to be analysed, Miss Parfitt, though unfortunately these days most crims are careful about leaving fingerprints. Have you any idea at all who might be doing this?'

As she hesitated, Angus stepped in. 'It has to be someone who wants her to sell her house, don't you think? They could fit three modern houses on to this piece of land.'

'That had occurred to us,' Mike said. 'But we'd rather

the lady answered our questions, if you don't mind.'

'Sorry. I just worry about what's happening to her.'

'Angus only said what I should have told you.' Winifred sighed. 'I hesitated because I can't point the finger at anyone specific. No, wait a minute. What about this man who's coming tonight?' She explained about Mr Smythe.

'It wouldn't hurt to take a look at him,' Mike said thoughtfully. 'Preferably without him seeing us. There's a push on at the moment to find better ways to protect seniors and I, for one, am right behind it. If anyone tried to hurt my grandma, I might find it hard to keep to the letter of the law.'

Angus nodded in approval.

'Would you object to us hiding inside the house tonight and taking a quick look at this fellow?' Tony asked. 'We can't stay for the whole meeting, but we can come and see if we recognise him.'

'I wouldn't mind at all.'

'You could park your car on my land, out of sight,' Angus offered. 'And there's a way into the back garden from my grounds that I can show you, so if anyone's checking the house beforehand, they won't see you coming in.'

'Thank you, sir. Good idea. Now, you'd better keep all your doors locked and your downstairs windows closed whenever you're here on your own, Miss Parfitt.'

'It's like being in prison,' she muttered.

Janey arrived home just then from college, out of breath and looking worried.

'What's wrong?' Winifred asked at once.

She ignored everyone else in the room, she was so upset. 'I think my father is stalking me. There's a court order that says he's not to contact me or come near me. I don't know what to do because I can't prove it's him.'

She burst into tears and let Winifred put an arm round her. 'I'm so worried he'll hurt Millie. I wouldn't put anything past him. Why does he hate me? He's never cared about me, not even when I was little.'

'I thought Paul was going to walk up the street with you.'

'He isn't always at home to do that, and I can't hang around in case he gets back, can I? He might be out all evening. Besides, I thought I'd be safe enough in the daytime. Only . . . well, I didn't feel safe at all today because the van followed me up the street, moving slowly and keeping about a hundred yards behind. If someone chased me, I couldn't run fast with the buggy. Luckily, today someone came out of a house further up the street and stopped to talk to a neighbour, so I nipped into the path that leads to the next street and waited till the van had driven off before I came back to this house. I don't think they know I live here now, but it's only a matter of time till they find out where I am, isn't it?'

'This is another situation that needs dealing with,' Winifred told the detectives. She introduced Janey and they listened as the girl talked about her father.

'Don't worry,' Mike said. 'We'll spread the word that Dobson is possibly contravening that order and we'll keep an eye on the situation from now on.'

'Why are you here, anyway?' Janey asked. 'Has something else happened?'

Angus explained the new developments to her and she grew angry. 'Just let anyone try to hurt Auntie Winnie while I'm here!'

'We'll look after each other,' Winifred said. 'And I shall keep my poker handy.'

Mike grinned. 'I didn't hear that. Just make sure you only use the poker in self-defence. We'll be back later to take a look at this other fellow. Who else is coming to the meeting this evening?' The two men listened intently, nodding now and then.

Angus followed them to the door. 'I'll see you out and show you the rear fence panel that opens on to my garden. Miss Parfitt, I'll be back later to keep an eye on your meeting from start to finish, in case these officers get held up.'

As they reached the back fence, he said in a low voice, 'I hope you're taking this seriously. Miss Parfitt isn't the sort to exaggerate, nor is Janey.'

Tony nodded. 'I know about that young woman's former problems because I used to work with the man who raped her, and he wasn't liked in the area, I can assure you. I'm glad he's in jail and I can assure you that he won't be having a comfortable time there, because no one likes a cop who's gone bad.'

Mike frowned. 'What I don't understand is why Janey's father should be stalking her. You'd think he'd want to protect her.'

'I wondered about that,' Angus admitted. 'During the inquiries he always sided with her attacker, who is his best friend, and he even tried to give evidence that she'd led the fellow on. Fortunately her mother spoke up on her behalf.'

'What is it with sods like that, attacking young women? They're scum.'

'I did hear Dobson's wife has run away from him. Apparently he's been beating her for years as well.' Tony

262

scowled. 'I can't abide domestic violence. My sister married a bad 'un first time round. Took her a while to admit what was happening. I had to throw him out for her in the end.'

All three men were silent for a moment or two, then one of the officers asked, 'Um . . . while we're chatting, we need to ask: is Miss Parfitt to be trusted about getting the details accurate, do you think?'

Angus looked at him in surprise. 'She has all her wits about her, if that's what you're getting at. I reckon she has a sharper brain than most people half her age.'

'Glad to hear that. It was my impression too, but you have to check. So . . . we'll come round the back way tonight through your property, then once we've had a good look at the fellow who's supposed to be observing the garden-sharing meeting, we can slip away through the front door without any of them seeing us.'

After they'd left, Angus hurried home to get his car. He was late picking Nell up and hoped she hadn't been worrying about him.

He'd have to get back to number 5 in time to keep an eye on the meeting. Pity. He'd been looking forward to a romantic, leisurely outing. Well, that pleasure was only postponed.

Angus found Nell in the back garden studying the plants.

'Found any rare treasures?'

'I don't even recognise half of them. Is there anything you'd like to dig up and take to Dennings? There are some plants with pretty flowers over there.'

He did a quick tour of the rear and front gardens with her but said, 'I'm not really an expert, either. Tell you what,

I'll ask old Mr Trouton to come and check whether there's anything worth rescuing. He used to be the gardener at Dennings till he grew too old and he'll love poking around here. He'll know what's worth saving, if anyone will.'

He pulled her to him suddenly and kissed her soundly, then stood for a moment breathing deeply. 'You're a witch.'

She chuckled. 'I am?'

'Yes. I miss you when we're apart and I've been dying to kiss you ever since I got here. How did you make me fall in love so quickly?'

'I've missed you too, Angus.'

A couple of lads walking past the house gave loud whistles at the sight of the embracing couple and Angus let go of her, taking a hasty step backwards. 'Let's stop entertaining the neighbours and get some food. Would you mind if we made it a quick snack? Miss Parfitt has had another of those threatening notes, so I want to keep an eye on this meeting she's arranged for tonight with some people who might be sharing her garden.'

'Oh, poor woman! Yes, of course, you should keep an eye on her. In fact, I'll come too.'

'Good. We'll watch from inside her house, unless you have a better idea. We won't go outside unless we're needed. After the meeting ends, we can go back to my place and . . .'

She finished for him, '. . . make up for lost time.'

They walked into town hand in hand, their steps matching without any effort. Neither of them said much, but he couldn't stop smiling and he could see that she was looking equally happy.

It felt so good to be a twosome again.

* * *

As Paul turned into Peppercorn Street, he saw a scruffy-looking blue van further up the road and stopped dead. Was it the same one? He had to squint to make out the details of the number plate at this distance, but it confirmed his suspicions. It was the same van and the occupants must be watching this block of flats again, thinking Janey still lived here.

She said it was her father and his cousin. All Paul knew was that it was definitely the same two men as before.

He wondered what to do about it. Seeing a van parked regularly nearby wasn't enough reason to call the police. He sighed. He'd better not stand out here staring at it or he'd make them suspicious.

It was only as he turned into the car park of his block of flats that he saw the big silver car with its boot open and realised his mother and Kieran had returned from their honeymoon. He'd missed his mother more than he'd expected to, but he was glad she'd found someone new to love. His father had left them in the emotional sense long before his sudden death.

Paul hugged his mother and found himself swept into a hug with Kieran as well, because his new stepfather was a touchy-feely sort of person. He returned the hug shyly, not yet used to this, but liking it.

His mother linked her arm in his. 'Come inside and tell us what you've been doing.'

'Before we do that, could you have a look at that blue van further up the street, Kieran, and take note of its number? I think someone is stalking Janey.'

'What? I thought we'd sorted her problems out when we put that sod who'd assaulted her in jail.'

'She says it's her father following her now. He keeps hanging round the flats, so I let her through to the back one day to make him think she still lives here. Go on. Take a quick look at the van.'

Kieran's expression was grim but he strolled to the front of the car park and pretended to look down the street, as if expecting someone.

Paul turned to his mother. 'Sorry to dump this on you as soon as you get back, but Janey's really worried.'

'It's all right, darling. Just tell me quickly how you've been on your own, then you and Kieran can discuss what to do about Janey.'

'I've been fine. I told you I would be. I got tons of studying done and I tried out one or two recipes from that book you gave me. And I didn't leave things in a mess.'

Kieran soon joined them in the flat. 'I'll find out who the van belongs to from a friend with connections. The passenger looks like Janey's father to me.'

'I'd forgotten that you'd met him.'

'Yeah. Lovely fellow. He smashed up her printer rather than let her take it with her when she left home.'

'How's she getting on at Miss Parfitt's?' Nicole asked.

'She loves living there and she's going to have a share in Miss Parfitt's garden.' Paul sighed. 'She texted me earlier. Even the garden sharing isn't going smoothly, because some fellow they don't like the look of is hanging round.' He went over what had happened.

'Looks like things haven't settled down as well as we'd expected in Peppercorn Street,' Kieran said. 'Thank goodness for Angus Denning to keep an eye on Miss Parfitt. He's a great guy – well, he is if you can get him to forget his computer for an hour or two. Talk about single-minded. I interviewed him once for a piece on how the current generation of owners of Grade I listed houses are managing to fund the ongoing maintenance, and I learnt as much about computers as about listed houses. I found it all very interesting, though.'

'You said you might go back into journalism,' Paul ventured. 'Is that still the plan?'

'Yes. With your mother's librarian skills behind me, I can do even better in-depth articles now that I've more or less recovered from the accident. In the meantime, the rents from these flats will keep the wolf from the door. But I'll not be trotting round the world at the drop of a hat, or probably at all.' He hugged his new wife and Nicole beamed at him. 'I've got too much to keep me in England now.'

Paul smiled and nodded as he listened to their tales of the honeymoon trip. It was great to see how much they cared about one another.

He went to bed early to give the newly-weds some time together. That sort of thing would be easier once they moved into the new house. The flat felt rather cramped with the three of them here. He'd never understood why his stupid brother had burnt down the family home.

The psychiatrists could give it any fancy label they chose, but he reckoned the overuse of steroids had driven William crazy. He'd looked up steroid abuse online and he wasn't at all sure his brother could ever be fully cured. He would never trust William again, anyway.

He lay down on the bed with a mystery novel, but his mind was darting round like a demented grasshopper and he couldn't get into the story, so he put the book down and allowed his thoughts to wander.

It felt strange to see his mother madly in love. But nice. She deserved some happiness.

Inevitably, he thought about the car that had been lurking in the street. He'd become good friends with Janey and was worried about her safety. They had to do something to stop her father going after her.

She was just a friend, though, not a girlfriend. Well, she was older than him in more ways than one after having a baby. They got on well, though, as if they were cousins or something.

He wasn't into dating yet, not in a serious way. He'd been out with one or two girls, but his crazy brother had usually managed to spoil any budding relationships, and since William had been placed in a psychiatric hospital, the girls at school had avoided Paul too.

There was plenty of time for dating when he was older. At the moment he had his sights set on studying medicine, and for that you had to get really top results in the final exams.

No, serious relationships could wait till he'd got over the first big hurdle to the life he wanted: entrance into a medical school.

Dan was the first to arrive at number 5. He parked his little old car in the unused drive and got out a home-made sign saying: GO ROUND TO THE BACK FOR GARDEN-SHARING MEETING.

Having stuck that to the front door to save Winifred answering the door, he walked round the house and stood surveying the garden. He and Winifred had already studied it and worked out roughly where they could divide it. That was before the summer house had been burnt down. Eh, that blackened patch was a real eyesore.

Once he'd have grabbed a spade and made short work of turning over the earth. Now, he had to leave hard physical labour to younger men and husband his own energy carefully so that he could at least keep his own allotment going. If he didn't have that to go to, he'd be stuck in the house all day and that'd drive him mad.

'Hi, Uncle Dan.'

He turned round, pleased that Janey now called him that automatically. 'Hello, lass. Ready to get into some gardening? There's still time to plant a few things.'

'I'm looking forward to it. I still remember what my granddad taught me. I just wanted to warn you that Auntie Winnie has had another of those threatening notes. She's a bit upset, whatever she says about it. I'd like to strangle the people who're doing this to her.'

'I'd help you!' He swung round as he heard a noise by the back fence, but it was only Angus and Nell coming across from the big house to join them.

'We thought we'd hide ourselves indoors before the meeting starts,' Angus said. 'Don't hesitate to call me outside if you need help of any sort, though.'

'Those two detectives are in the house as well,' Janey said. 'They arrived a few minutes ago and went to look out of an upstairs window. Only they're not staying long. They just want to see that man who's pushed his way in.'

As she spoke there was the sound of a car drawing up in the street and Angus tugged Nell quickly back indoors.

A stranger came round the corner of the house and hesitated. 'Er, I'm John Grainger. My wife represented me at the meeting and told me to come here tonight.'

'Dan Shackleton.' He held out his hand. 'Pleased to meet you.'

Before he could introduce Janey, there was the sound of a squeaky wheel and Izzy came round the corner, pushing little Howie who was fast asleep in the buggy.

'Am I late, Mr Shackleton?'

'Not at all. We haven't started yet.'

He heard footsteps on the garden path and exchanged glances with Janey. It'd be their so-called observer, damn the fellow. Strange that he hadn't heard a car pull up.

Smythe came round the corner, as elegantly dressed as ever. Dan didn't bother to introduce him beyond saying, 'Mr Smythe wishes to observe before he decides whether to offer his garden as a share. Now, let's get started.'

Inside the house, Angus exchanged startled glances with Nell. 'What the hell is he doing here?'

'And what did Dan call him? His name isn't Smythe, not unless he was using a false name when he arranged the sale of my house.'

'I'll just nip upstairs and alert the detectives to the fact that he isn't called Smythe.' He ran lightly up the stairs and found Mike staring down into the garden from behind the net curtains and Tony peering out of one of the front-bedroom windows.

Mike turned round. 'Miss Parfitt didn't say she was selling her house.'

'You recognise that fellow, then.'

'Who? Jeffries? Yeah. He hasn't been working in Sexton Bassett long, but he's doing a lot of work for Gus Nolan, who isn't my favourite person. I take it Jeffries is the one who's calling himself Smythe?'

Tony came to join them. 'He'd already parked in the street, must have been checking out who came tonight to make sure there was no one who'd recognise him. Good thing we came in the back way. He knows me by sight.'

'Dan apparently took an instant dislike to him.'

'I don't like the look of him myself. Unfortunately, using a false name isn't enough for us to question him, unless he uses it to trick someone out of money.'

Angus went slowly back downstairs again and put his arm round Nell as they continued to watch out of the kitchen window, hidden by the net curtains.

Dan had the two young women putting in stakes and stretching twine across to mark out the three areas. He kept an eye on them as he and John Grainger discussed something with much gesticulating.

Winifred sat on a bench alternately watching them and smiling at Howie, still asleep in his buggy by her side. Millie's cot alarm was near the kitchen door and they'd already checked that it could be heard easily.

Smythe was standing to one side looking sour and bored. Good. Serves him right, Angus thought.

There was the sound of footsteps coming down the stairs and Nell glanced round.

Mike poked his head round the kitchen door. 'We'll slip out the front way while they're all occupied at the back. I don't think it'll be long before Jeffries leaves. Did you ever see anyone look so out of place and fed up?'

Ten minutes later, Jeffries pulled out his mobile phone, pointed to it and called goodbye to Dan and Winifred. As he walked away from the group, he began talking into his phone, unaware of the observers in the kitchen.

Although he was speaking quietly, his voice could be heard clearly through the open window as he came closer. 'Have to do something quite soon or those gardening fools will be there all the time and we'll have lost our chance to nudge her out of this place. No, I'd prefer not to know what you . . .' His voice faded into the distance.

Nell grabbed a pencil and scribbled down the words they'd overheard. She studied them for a moment, then looked at Angus. 'That sounds rather ominous. What did he mean by "nudge", do you think?'

'He'd better not do anything to upset her. I bet you anything it was Nolan on the other end.'

'But what can we do to prevent them?'

'Nothing at the moment, except keep our eyes and ears open, and warn Miss Parfitt who that fellow was. I think I should upgrade her security system, and connect it to my mobile phone as well. Your job is to nag her to remember to switch it on – and to remember to take her personal alarm with her when she goes out, even just into the garden.'

When the two new garden sharers left, Winifred, Dan and Janey came inside, beaming at their waiting friends.

'That went well, don't you think?' Dan asked. Then he saw their solemn expressions. 'What now?'

Angus spread his hands wide in a helpless gesture. 'Smythe isn't that fellow's name. He's called Jeffries and he's an estate agent working closely with Gus Nolan.'

'He sold my aunt's house for me,' Nell said.

'Oh dear!' Winifred sat down abruptly. 'I didn't like the look of him, but I told myself I shouldn't judge a man without proof.'

'Well, it's not exactly proof that he's going to commit a crime, but it's certainly suspicious. But we can't do anything without proof.'

'We heard him talking on the phone on his way out and I wrote it down.' Nell pushed the piece of paper towards the three of them.

Winifred looked stricken. 'I shouldn't have brought Janey and Millie into danger.'

'I think it's a good thing I'm here,' Janey said. 'At least you won't be on your own at night . . . and nor will I.'

Dan was frowning. When the others looked at him, he said abruptly, 'How about I move in here temporarily as well? I'd not be any good in a fight, but the more people around the place, the better.'

'Good idea. There are bedrooms to spare,' Janey said at once.

Winifred looked at him uncertainly. 'I can't ask you to do that, Dan. You might get hurt.'

'You didn't ask me. I volunteered. Anyway, I don't think they're the sort to knock people around. Pinch their wallets, yes. Cheat them out of their money, yes, but not actually hurt someone physically.'

'I was mugged,' she reminded him.

'You were on your own then. You mustn't go anywhere on your own till this is settled.'

Silence hung heavily in the room, then Angus said slowly, 'I think it'd be an excellent idea for Dan to move in, Miss Parfitt. Unless you wouldn't enjoy his company?'

'I always enjoy his company.' She turned to her friend. 'And now I come to think of it, I'd welcome you staying here for another reason: Janey's father.'

'You're right.' He pretended to flex the muscles on his scrawny old man's arm and that made them all laugh, easing the tension. 'I'll go home and get my things.'

'I'll be upgrading that security alarm tomorrow, as I promised,' Angus added. 'That'll make all three of you safer.'

Winifred moved towards the fireplace. 'I shall definitely keep my poker handy.' She picked it up and hefted it in her hand. 'I'll find you a poker, too, Janey. Dan? There's another one somewhere, because we used to have fires in the bedrooms in winter.'

He grinned. 'No need. I have a lead-weighted walking stick that used to belong to my granddad. I'll bring it with me.'

'But the detective warned you not to use violence except as the last extreme,' Nell protested. 'If you threaten these people, they may hurt you.'

'I will not give in to their underhand behaviour,' Winifred said firmly. 'I intend to have the means to protect myself. They've made me very angry indeed. My mother always said a lady should control her temper. And I have until now. Well, mostly. But I'm not letting anyone spoil my lovely new life.'

As Angus and Nell walked back to Dennings, he said quietly, 'What a courageous woman Miss Parfitt is. She can't weigh more than about fifty kilos wringing wet, yet she's brandishing a poker and refusing to be daunted. I think Jeffries may get a nasty surprise if he pushes her too far.'

'I hope he does – get a nasty surprise, I mean, not push her too far. And that Nolan fellow as well. How can they think they'll get away with it?'

He stopped and stared at her. 'You've put your finger on something that's been puzzling me. All I can think is that they must have bought someone in the town hall.'

'I suppose so.'

'We can get more help now. I saw my friend Kieran's car parked outside his flats, so he must be back from his honeymoon. I'm going to put him on the trail of official corruption. He loves to chase it down.'

'Who's Kieran?'

'He was an investigative journalist, very well known in the UK till he was badly injured in a road accident. It's taken him a while to recover, but if anyone can find out exactly what Gus Nolan is doing, it's him.'

They reached the door of Dennings and he disarmed the security system, studying a small panel. 'Ah. It seems someone was walking round my garden tonight. Let's get the recording up and see if we can recognise them.'

But the CCTV recording showed only shadowy figures of two men with no distinguishing features, except that they moved like younger men.

'This is all very strange,' he said thoughtfully. 'Definitely a case for Kieran. And for my trusty electronic gadgets.'

He pulled her towards him. 'But in the meantime . . .'

Chapter Sixteen

When Nell woke up the following morning she turned instinctively to Angus for a cuddle. But his side of the bed was cold and no sounds were coming from the adjoining bathroom. He must have got up early.

She wrapped her dressing gown tightly round herself, because although it was officially summer in the northern hemisphere, this time of morning felt chilly to her. She'd laughed out loud the previous days when someone said on the TV news that it was going to be a 'hot one tomorrow' and then added, '23 degrees'. That was a winter temperature in Western Australia.

Yawning, she wandered along to the kitchen, where she put the kettle on before going into the office.

As she'd guessed, Angus was working on his computer, but didn't seem to notice her come in. She watched him for a moment, loving the rumpled hair with its frosting of silver, and the slight signs of a beard. He was frowning and fiddling with some sort of electrical diagrams using a drafting program to amend the chart.

'It's the extensions to the security system at Miss Parfitt's house,' he said suddenly, without turning round. 'I'll give them till eight o'clock to get up, then I'll have to wake them. I need to get started early, because it'll take me all day. I intend to cover the gardens more thoroughly. I don't usually do this part of the job myself, I pass it on to a guy I know. But I'm qualified to do it and I'm making an exception for Miss Parfitt. I don't want any strangers going into her house until I've revamped the system and covered her garden.'

'She's not going to like your arriving if she isn't awake.'

'With a small child in the house, I bet they are awake.' He grinned at her. 'Remember what it was like?'

'Oh boy, yes. Why the urgency now, though, Angus?'

'Because I don't think those sods who want her land will wait long to cause more trouble. As the garden sharers get going, there will be people coming and going at all times. I intend to be ready for trouble. I'm putting a few cameras into the system and we'll spot any intruders, inside or out, yes, and record them as evidence.'

'Are you interested in breakfast before you go?'

'Some more coffee and a piece of toast would be great, if you've got time.'

He held out an empty mug, and as she took it from him, he turned to his computer again. She smiled. Talk about a capacity for intense concentration! He could have won an Olympic gold medal for it.

After a quick shower, she got dressed, then investigated the fridge, grimacing. There wasn't much in it, so she made them both cheese on toast. He'd probably forget to eat once he started work so she wanted to give him a good start to the day.

They'd have to organise the housekeeping better from now on. Perhaps that should be her job. Well, judging from how he was focused on his work, it'd have to be. She was very careful to eat a balanced diet, both for health and because she put on weight easily. Besides, she enjoyed cooking. She'd have to transfer what was left of her food staples and cooking equipment from Fliss's house to here today. And they were certainly needed.

She looked at the size of Angus's fridge and shook her head. She'd bring the old fridge from her aunt's, too. All the ones she'd seen in England so far were tiny compared to Aussie ones, which was difficult if you ate a lot of fresh food and needed more storage space. But two smaller fridges would solve that problem.

Angus left his computer and ate his breakfast quickly but with relish. 'I'd forgotten how good cheese on toast is. What are you going to do today?'

'The smell at my aunt's house is getting me down, so I thought I'd pack and move my personal things here – if that's all right with you?' She cocked her head on one side, waiting.

'You know it is.' For a moment he turned his full attention on her and his gaze felt as warm as a caress.

It took her a few seconds to remember what they'd been discussing. 'I – um, need to do some shopping as well. It's like the children's nursery rhyme. "When she got there, the cupboard was bare".'

He grinned and chanted the last line back at her. '"And so the poor dog had none". I looked it up on the Internet once and the verses get sillier and sillier as it goes on. You'll need some money, then, Mother Hubbard. How about we go half and half on the living expenses till we see who eats the most? If it's me, I'll pay extra.'

He fished in his pocket, muttered in annoyance and went to hunt around his desk, continuing to mutter as he tossed papers and miscellaneous pens aside.

She stood by the door, smiling as he pounced on his wallet and brandished it with a triumphant cry. He passed her a wad of notes without even counting them.

'Don't you want to—'

But he had begun packing pieces of equipment into cardboard boxes and seemed oblivious to her continuing presence in the doorway.

With a wry smile she gave up and went back to clear up the kitchen and prepare for a domestic day. She wasn't going to take over all the domestic duties, she would never do that again, but she didn't mind organising things at the start of their life together. She knew she was a good organiser and she enjoyed making order out of chaos.

What's more, if she'd managed to train a group of lawyers to follow her filing and storage systems, she was sure she'd soon convince Angus that her way was better in the kitchen.

Nell's mobile phone rang as she was opening the back door of her aunt's house. She glanced at the phone. Nick.

'Hi, darling! Hold on while I close the door. I've only just arrived home. There. Now I can talk in comfort. How are you?'

'I'm fine and so is Carla. Look, Dad's giving me stick

because I won't let him have your phone number and I had to promise him I'd let you know he needs to talk to you.'

'Is there a real reason he needs to call me or does he just hate not being able to?'

'He says it's about Steve.'

'Hmm. Well, in that case I'll see if a friend can help me phone Craig without revealing my number.'

Nick chuckled. 'You really meant it about getting away from Dad, didn't you?'

'I certainly did. And about time, too.'

'You did it for us, didn't you?'

'Did what?'

'Put up with Dad interfering in your life so that we could have a stable home.'

'You're not usually so perceptive.'

'I'm learning, Ma. Carla's teaching me a lot. I wish you could meet her. She's great, very liberated but not aggressive with it. I've never met anyone as wonderful.'

She listened, smiling, as he talked about the woman he loved. That was the second of her sons sorted out with a life partner. There was just Steve left and he had a long way to go before he grew up, let alone found a partner. He was definitely a slow maturer, only she couldn't think of what else she could have done to turn him into a more sensible person.

After a while she interrupted Nick's talk about what he and Carla were planning. It might be the end of his working day in Australia but it was still morning here. 'I have to go now, love. I've got to clear this house out so that the buyer can demolish it.'

'Where are you going to live? You didn't say exactly.'

She hesitated, then decided it was about time she stopped

concealing the existence of Angus. 'I'm moving in with a guy I've met.'

Silence greeted this, so she waited.

'That's a bit quick, isn't it?' Nick said at last.

'No quicker than you and Carla.'

'Ah. Yes. Point taken. Does Robbie know?'

'Not yet. I've only just decided to do it. You're the first of the family I've told.' She waited again.

'What's his name?'

'Angus Denning. You'll like him.'

'I'm going to meet him, am I?'

'If things continue to go well, yes. He's a great guy.'

'I hope they do go well, then, and that he doesn't let you down as Dad did. But be careful, Ma. He may be interested in your money.'

It was her turn to be silent for a few moments, then she said sharply, 'I shall ignore that remark, which implies either that I'm stupid enough to fall for a con man or that there's no other reason for a man to love me than money. Your father's influence is still showing and you're treating me like a fool. Tell Carla to put some more work in on your development.' She ended the call.

When her phone rang again, she could see it was Nick calling so didn't answer.

But she couldn't get the thought of Steve out of her mind. What exactly had Craig arranged for him? What had their youngest done that was so bad?

The only thing she could think of was that he'd been into drugs. That would have freaked Craig out, she knew. He had a thing about drug taking. Well, so did she. Surely Steve wouldn't . . . ?

But she couldn't stop thinking about her youngest and by the end of the day, she'd decided to ask Angus's help in phoning Craig without revealing her number.

It just might be the truth that he needed to talk to her about their son.

The two men watched Janey walk slowly up Peppercorn Street. She went right past the block of flats.

'I told you she'd not notice us if we used another car,' Lionel gloated. 'We'll buy your friend a drink or two.'

'I wonder where she's going?' Wayne said. 'The street's a dead end.'

'There's a path leads out of the turning circle at the top. She must go down that. I'll follow her on foot another time and grab her in the next street. These upper parts are usually quieter. The rich sods from the big houses are all out at work. You can drive round to pick us up.'

'I don't know about forcing her to come with us, Lionel. It doesn't seem right.'

'It seems right to me. We need a woman to look after us and she might as well make herself useful. She cost me a lot over the years.'

But at the top of the street, Janey went into a big old house, using a key.

Lionel thumped his hand down on the dashboard. 'The sneaky little bitch! I bet she's moved up here to another flat. She must only go down that narrow passage when she notices us following. Well, we'll come in your car next time and if she does . . .'

'I'm not at all sure about this, Lionel. We could pay a woman to do some housework and—'

'I'm not paying when I can get it for free.'

'But we'll have to feed her.'

'No, we won't. She gets money for being a single mother. We'll have some of that too.'

'But the police—'

'Will change that order if she asks them to, and once we have the baby, she'll do anything we tell her. It's her weakness, that baby is, just as *she* was my stupid wife's weakness. You'll see.'

When Wayne didn't say anything, he changed the subject.

'Come on. We've just got time for a quick pint. I'm buying today.'

In Australia, Steve finished his day's work, did his allotted share of the clearing up after the communal evening meal, and went back to his room, feeling exhausted. The work here seemed never-ending. It had occurred to him several times that this was how his mother's life had been, caring for three children without any help, day after day.

Why had he never thought of that before?

His steps slowed and he sighed as he reached his room, which was part of the old shearers' quarters. All the guys were lodged here. The 'rooms' were more like cupboards, but at least he had some privacy in the narrow space.

He studied his hands as he went inside. They were already rough with manual labour after only a couple of weeks but there were good sides to it as well. He'd always enjoyed being out in the open air.

What was the use of studying at university, though, if you ended up shovelling pig dung? He'd been stupid, hadn't known when he was well off. It hadn't taken him long to realise that. But he'd had to promise his father to stay here for three months in order to get his debts paid.

And anyway, he had nowhere else to go till he'd saved up some of the pittance they were paying him here.

He winced as he knocked his arm against the edge of the narrow metal locker. He already had a big bruise on it where he'd stumbled into the side of the tractor this morning. And he'd gashed his leg the other day. A farm was a dangerous place to work unless you paid attention every minute, Owen had told them, and he was right.

Steve flung himself down on the bed, closing his eyes.

What was that?

He frowned as he heard a whimpering sound outside. It could only be a small animal and it sounded in distress. When the noise went on and on, he went to look for it to see if the poor thing was trapped somewhere.

To his surprise, he found a puppy lying just outside his room. When it saw him, it pressed back against the wall, as if afraid of him hitting it. It was small and shivering visibly, so he made soothing noises and picked it up to comfort it.

It huddled in his hands, then began licking his fingers. When he bent closer to study it, it took a swipe at his nose with a small pink tongue. Then it shivered again and whined softly, sounding so pitiful he cuddled it close to his chest.

He didn't know what to do to help it, because his mother had never allowed them to have pets. Whenever they'd asked, she'd said she couldn't cope with one more creature to look after.

He'd resented that as a child, hadn't even thought of her

side of things. But Nick pointed out rather forcibly when he grumbled about her leaving them that she deserved some time for herself after raising the three of them without any practical help from their father.

Hell, that lesson was certainly being rammed home now. He supposed that was the point of him being here. He'd thought a lot about his mother during the first few semi-sleepless nights as the drugs worked their way out of his system, angry at her for getting him into this.

Only, he'd done it himself, hadn't he? You didn't have to be Einstein to work that out.

The puppy shivered again, so Steve carried it to the kitchen of the main house, where the other guys sat in the evenings, those who were feeling sociable, that was. There were only four of them here at the moment and Matt always disappeared the minute the evening meal was over. He hardly spoke to anyone, even when they were working together, seemed to hate the world. He was a very strange guy.

Dix and Logan were still sitting in the kitchen. They were playing draughts because Owen didn't allow them to watch TV during the week and they weren't allowed access to computers at all.

Steve hesitated in the doorway. He hadn't been exactly friendly to these two and now he needed to ask their help.

They looked up and Dix grinned. 'Come and join us. We won't kill you. Most guys keep to themselves at first. I did too.'

'Oh. Right.'

The puppy chose that time to whimper again.

'What the hell have you got there?'

'A puppy. It was crying outside my room. It seems to have lost its mother.'

Logan got up and came to study the pup. 'Poor little thing. I think the mother was killed this afternoon in an accident. Didn't you hear the shouting? She got caught up in some machinery. Owen was really upset. She was his favourite farm dog. He's found people to look after the other puppies, but he must have missed this one.' He touched its little head gently but didn't take it off Steve.

'Better tell Owen,' Dix advised. 'He'll know what to do with it. He's good with animals.'

Steve wasn't going to let them see that he was rather nervous of Owen, who had been scornful about his physical condition, and his idiocy in getting into drugs. But there was no one else to ask, so he took a deep breath and went along the corridor to the main house, where he knocked on the door as per house rules.

'Come in.'

He found Owen and his wife Megan sitting near a wood fire in a comfortable room, looking relaxed and happy. 'I found a pup, or rather it found me.'

Megan immediately got tears in her eyes. 'Oh, no! I thought we'd found them all. I was so upset I mustn't have counted properly.'

Owen came across to examine the tiny creature and sighed. 'It's old enough to survive but only just, and it'll still need a lot of looking after. I don't have the time because we're still a man short. Got any more friends willing to get up in the night and feed a pup, Megan?'

She shook her head. 'No. I'll have to do it myself.'

'You've enough on your plate and I'm not having you run yourself ragged at this stage.'

Steve supposed he was referring to his wife's very obvious pregnancy. How women walked around and did things with such a load in their bellies, he couldn't figure. And his mother had gone through it three times! He waited, stroking the puppy.

Owen stared at him then at the pup. 'We'll either have to put it down or you can look after it, Steve. I'm not loading anything else on to Megan.'

'Me? I don't know anything about animals.'

'I can show you what to do,' Megan offered.

'As long as you only show him,' Owen said. 'You are not taking on a pup, Megan. You've only got a month to go before the baby's born.'

Steve stared down at the puppy, which swiped a lick at his chin and stared up at him trustingly with its big brown eyes. Kill it? No way. 'I'll look after it as long as you show me how.'

Owen clapped him on the shoulders. 'Good man. I'll find you some bedding and puppy food.'

It was the first time Owen had said anything positive to Steve.

'You'll need plenty of old newspapers,' Megan called after them. 'It's not house-trained yet.'

At the thought of cleaning up poop after the little dog, Steve nearly said he'd changed his mind, then it shivered again and huddled closer. No, he wasn't going to let anyone kill it.

Owen took him through to the big farm storeroom. 'She'll need to cuddle up to you at first. She's been with

288

the other pups and her mother ever since she was born, so she'll fret if you leave her alone.'

'Oh. Right.'

'I'll get you a waterproof sheet to cover your bedding.'

'Yuk.' Again he wondered about giving her back. No, he couldn't do that. Especially not when she was cuddling up to him like this. 'Does she have a name?'

'Not unless you give her one.' Owen carried the stuff across the yard to Steve's room, gave him some rapid instructions and left him to it.

As Steve stared down at the pup he was still holding, she peed all down his front.

'Oh, hell!' He held her out but it was too late.

All he wanted to do was give her back to someone, but once again she gave him 'the look' and made a little mewing sound. He was a sucker, that's what he was, a stupid sucker.

He'd had a book when he was little with a puppy called Taffy in it. He'd loved that story. It seemed as good a name as any.

'Come on, Taffy,' he said. 'Let's get ourselves cleaned up.'

He didn't get much sleep, because Taffy peed on him again, then started whining for food.

Owen came for him at six o'clock with a puppy crate. 'I'll find you jobs near the house this morning. She'll need a hot-water bottle to keep her warm. Wrap it in this old towel. We don't want her getting burnt. You can leave her in your room but come back to check on her every hour.'

'What have you got me into?' Steve asked Taffy when they were alone.

She didn't answer; was too busy clearing the plate of

puppy food and then pooping all over the clean newspapers he'd just spread out.

It didn't occur to him for several days that Megan would never have allowed Owen to kill the puppy. But by that time, Taffy and he were best mates.

And at least she'd stopped peeing in the bed and was starting to recognise her name.

He'd always wanted a dog. Funny how things turned out.

Just let them try to take her away from him now.

Chapter Seventeen

Winifred watched intently as Angus explained what he was doing and how the improved security system would work when it was finished.

'I haven't forgotten about getting you a computer,' he said. 'I just have to install these special apps on it, then I'll bring it over. I'm designing a system to help elderly people understand what to do, one small step at a time.'

'What a good idea. When they told us what to do at those computer classes, it was as if they were speaking a foreign language. And the tutor looked at us as if we were stupid when we asked questions. But how are we to guess the meaning when these are new ways of using old words, or else completely new words? Someone needs to tell us what they mean before they start using a computer word.'

He stared at her in surprise, head on one side. 'That's a very helpful comment already. I was aware of that, but I wonder if I've started far enough back. Maybe I should put a list at the beginning with explanations of each word.'

'Better to have them available to print out as guidelines on pieces of paper,' she said. 'There were so many differences, I forgot half of them between one class and another. It's not that older people are stupid, Angus. It's that some of us don't have the foundations for using the new systems.'

He nodded slowly. 'You are going to be so useful to me in putting the final polish on my Golden Oldie Apps.'

'I am?'

'Yes.'

She beamed at him, then heard the post drop through the letter box and went to pick up the letters from the hall floor. She came back frowning and threw the post down on the table with an angry huff.

'Something wrong?'

'Yes. These aren't real letters; they're more rubbish from people pestering me to sell the house. I get several a week.'

'Mind if I look at them?' He picked up the envelopes. 'I think one of them's a real letter.'

He studied today's offers to sell while she opened the other letter. 'These two seem to be from different estate agents in Sexton Bassett, but I haven't heard of either of them, even though they've got addresses in town. Mind if I keep them?'

'Be my guest. I usually throw them straight in the rubbish bin.'

She was still frowning, so he ventured to ask, 'What's the other one about?'

'It's from a social worker at the council, wanting me to enrol for the seniors' programmes. Look at what they're doing!' She flicked the paper with one scornful finger.

'What do they think we are, children? I don't want to go and be entertained by amateur singers who should have taken singing lessons before they opened their mouths in public. And as for someone playing the spoons, the mind boggles.'

'Playing the spoons? You're joking.'

'No, I'm not. See. It's printed here.' She offered him a list of morning entertainments.

He studied it, agreeing with her comments. 'What rubbish they're offering.'

'I'm glad it's not just me. Angus, I'm not conceited but I'm not stupid, either. I'd be bored to tears by this so-called entertainment.'

She showed him a second sheet of paper. 'And I do not want to go into their medical programme.'

'Well, I can understand not wanting to go to concerts like those, but what's wrong with the medical programme? It never hurts to get a check-up.' He didn't say especially at her age, but he thought it.

'Once you let officials get their hands on you, they find ways to take over your life. They think old equates to stupid.' She screwed up the paper and threw it away. 'I go to my own doctor when I need to and that's enough for me. She doesn't pester me to join things. I've never been a joiner and I'm not going to start now.'

He'd never heard her speak so sharply. 'It's getting to you, isn't it? Especially the way these people are pestering you to sell.'

She nodded, blowing her nose good and hard. 'What if they try to burn down my house? They already burnt the summer house.'

'I don't think they'll go that far.'

'I'm beginning to think they might.'

He put his arm round her and gave her a quick hug. 'We'll catch these bullies for you.'

'And then what? Another one will pop up and start nagging all over again. What it amounts to is they want to take my home away from me. This place is far more than just a house or an asset to me.'

He'd never seen her so down in the dumps. That upset him. He wondered what he could do to help. He'd discuss it with Nell. She might have some ideas.

He'd discuss it with Kieran too, who had some useful connections.

When he left Winifred's house, Angus hesitated for a moment, then went out the front way and hurried down the street.

Kieran's car was parked at the flats, so he knocked on the door and as Paul opened it, asked, 'Is Kieran at home?'

'Yes. Come in.'

Kieran was sitting chatting to his new wife, holding a mug of coffee, looking so cheerful Angus hesitated to dump a problem on him.

'Hi. Sit down. There's one more cup left in the cafetière.'

'No, thanks. I have to get back. It's just . . . well, I need to see you about something quite urgently.' He explained what was going on with Winifred and saw Kieran's eyes brighten with interest, not irritation, thank goodness. He should have remembered how much his friend used to enjoy unmasking scams and villains.

'It'll be Nolan behind it,' Kieran said confidently.

'Who else could it be? But he's been very clever about not quite breaking the law.'

'He shouldn't be harassing an old lady to sell, though. Or inventing bogus companies. I'll have a think what to do and get back to you. There's usually a way to track down a trail of events.'

'And Janey? She needs help, too.'

'Paul's already told me about her problems and I got a friend to look up the owner of the van. It's someone called Wayne Dobson and he lives in a smallholding on the other side of Swindon. I have his address. Janey told Paul her father went to live with him when he lost his job and his house was repossessed. He was a fool letting his mortgage payments lapse for so long.'

'I'd rather catch him when he comes into Sexton Bassett to stalk Janey than out in the country. There's nothing illegal about living on your own land. In fact, we might find it useful to bring the police in on this and have her father tracked officially.'

'I'll arrange a meeting with a detective friend of mine. If Dobson is contravening a court order, they'll want to fix that.'

'I can't understand why he's stalking his daughter, unless he's hoping to get to his wife through her.'

'Or he might be just crazy enough to blame Janey for his friend being jailed and want to punish her. There are some warped people in this world.'

'That poor girl's had a hard time during the past year.'

'She's got her baby, though,' Paul put in. 'She loves Millie. Look, I can come straight home from school every night until we get this sorted out and walk up the street with her. Janey's safety is more important than clubs and chilling out with friends.'

'I can do it sometimes to relieve you, so that there's always someone here,' Nicole said. 'I don't work standard office hours, so we can co-ordinate who does what.'

'Thanks. I'll let Janey know.' Angus stood up to leave.

'I'll walk you out,' Kieran said. As he opened the front door, he said in a low voice. 'What we need is something to track that car.'

'Leave it to me. I'm the gadgets man. I'll find a way to stick a tracer on that car.' He set off briskly up the street.

When he got home, he sniffed in delight and headed straight for the kitchen, where something was bubbling on the stove. Nell was sitting at the table reading as she waited for him.

'I'm so glad to come home to you.' He pulled her up into his arms for a kiss.

Then he sniffed again. 'Whatever that is smells wonderful. I'm ravenous.'

'Just a stew with crusty bread.'

It was like paradise to sit and have their meal together, but every paradise seemed to have its serpent and when she told him about Craig needing to speak to her about their youngest son, he could only be glad the time differences prevented her from calling her ex straight away. He had other plans for tonight and anything to do with her ex made her edgy and tense.

'Could we contact him tomorrow, first thing?' she suggested. 'The times will coincide nicely then.'

'Whatever suits you. You can use my phone to call him. It won't show my number.'

'Thanks. Now, are you interested in apple pie and ice cream for afters?'

'It's my favourite. Is that home-made? Oh, I think I've died and gone to heaven.'

She chuckled. 'It's only an apple pie.'

'I can cook quite a few things, but I have to confess to having a leaden hand with pastry.'

He pretended to yawn. 'And after that, I'm so tired, I think we should go straight to bed.'

'Yeah, right. You look exhausted.'

But she didn't protest when he put that suggestion into action. And he didn't seem in the least tired.

Nell wasn't the only one worrying about phone calls that evening. Janey fiddled around with the food on her plate till Winifred insisted on being told what was worrying her.

'I'm still worrying about phoning my mother. I don't know what to say to her. Everything seems to be in a bit of an upset here and I don't want to add to her worries. Besides . . . we never did talk easily. She hardly spoke at all, now I come to think of it, even to my father.'

'I think she'd rather have more worries and be in touch with you than think you're never going to call her again.'

'Even though I don't feel close to her?'

'I never felt really close to my mother or father. I did my duty, but oh, how I longed for a life of my own!'

Janey reached across to squeeze Auntie Winnie's hand. 'So you think I should call Mum, even if it's just a duty call?'

'Yes. And tell her about your father stalking you. He

may not be after you. Perhaps he's trying to find out where she is.'

Janey thought about that, then shook her head. 'No. He may want to find her as well but I'm pretty sure he wants to get at me. The main thing in his life was his friendship with that horrible man. And the cousin he's living with, Wayne, will believe anything my father tells him about me.'

She sighed as she added, 'The Dobsons always stick together. Well, the other Dobsons do, anyway. My father said I wasn't a true Dobson when I told him I was pregnant. He hit me when I blamed his friend, then threw me out. He was always hitting me, though I never saw him hit my mother.'

'He sounds to be a very stupid man. You must have got your brains from your mother's side.'

'She never talked about her family.'

As the girl fell quiet, Winifred said gently, 'Call her, dear. You know it's the right thing to do. I'll keep my eye on Millie.'

Janey went into the other sitting room, which felt cold and lonely. She rang the number with fingers that trembled, then waited. A strange voice answered and she explained that she wanted to speak to her mother.

'Hang on. I'll fetch her.'

A minute later there were faint noises, then her mother said, 'Janey? Is that really you?'

'Yes. I said I'd call, didn't I?'

'I didn't dare hope.' Her voice broke and she gulped audibly.

Janey waited a moment then said, 'So . . . how have you been?'

'I've been fine, considering. People are ever so kind here.'

'That's good.'

'I should tell you that I've changed my name. I'm now Hope Redman.'

'You've gone back to your maiden name again. Was Hope a family name, too?'

'No. It's a promise for the future. I never did like the name Dorothy.'

'Oh. Well, Hope is a pretty name. I like it.'

After an awkward silence, her mother asked, 'How's Millie?'

'Thriving. Perhaps you'd like to come and see her sometime?' She regretted the offer as soon as it was out.

Her mother burst into tears. 'Thank you, Janey, thank you so much. I'm s-sorry to weep all over you again. I can't tell you how much I want to see her. Can I take a photo? I've got a new mobile phone – well, it's not exactly new, but there's this guy who wipes old ones clean and donates them to the refuge. Mine takes lovely photos. I'll give you my new phone number.'

'Of course you can take a photo. But only if you give me a copy,' Janey said as she noted the number her mother read out.

'I'll have to find out how to organise a meeting. It might be safer for you to come to me.'

'If it's not too far. I don't know where you are.'

'We're not allowed to tell anyone without permission. There might be someone who could pick you up. They like us to have visitors.'

'We'll do that, then. Only . . . I have to tell you, I think Dad is stalking me.'

'What?'

'You know his cousin Wayne has an old blue van that has a name on the side? I keep seeing the van in Peppercorn Street and it drives along slowly behind me.'

'But your father isn't supposed to come near you.'

'Tell him that!'

Silence, then. 'I'll have to go now, Janey. There are other people wanting to use this phone. If you call me on my mobile, we can chat for longer next time. If you have time, that is. And . . . I'll tell the warden here about your father, see if she can help. Maybe someone can talk to him.'

'OK.' As if anyone could change her father's mind when it was set on something. Janey shivered, and not from the cold.

The anxiety she'd felt when she first moved into the Peppercorn Street flat had returned with a vengeance, only this time it was her own father who was frightening her, not his horrible friend Gary.

Why did her father hate her so much? What would he do to her if he caught her somewhere on her own? Hurt her, she was sure. He'd enjoyed hitting her when she lived at home. That wouldn't have changed.

But most of all she was afraid for Millie. How could she protect her daughter?

She went slowly back into the kitchen where Auntie Winnie was talking softly to the smiling baby.

Janey related her conversation, mentioning her father but making light of the situation, trying to hide how worried she was. Auntie Winnie had enough worries of her own.

She didn't sleep well that night, though, she kept worrying, wondering what he was up to.

*　*　*

The next morning, Nell nerved herself to phone her ex. For some reason, even talking to him made her feel less sure of herself. Angus had offered to leave her alone while she did it, but she asked him to stay with her.

'Hello?' Craig's voice sounded cautious.

'It's me. Nell.'

'Ah. You got my message, then. Hang on a minute and I'll get something to write your number down. It's not showing.'

'That's deliberate. If you need me you can send a message by Nick or Robbie.'

Angus scribbled something down, an email address, one with no clues about the sender, then the words USE THIS?

'Hang on a minute. You can also use my friend's email address.' She read it out to him.

'What friend is this?'

She took a deep breath. 'A guy I'm seeing.'

'Oh. That was quick.'

'Was it? Anyway, I'm ringing about Steve. What I do is none of your business.'

'You're turning very sharp lately.'

'Glad you think so.'

'OK. Let's talk about Steve. I wanted you to know that I caught him with drugs, and forced him to go into a rehab programme in the country.'

'Steve was into drugs? Oh, Craig, how awful! Hard drugs?'

'He was just starting, not in deep yet.'

'How on earth did you persuade him to go into a programme?'

Craig made the little grunting sound that always

betrayed he was angry about something. 'He'd lost his job, was in debt and hadn't any money. It was do as I told him or go on the streets. And I've had to pay some of his damn debts.'

'You did the right thing, I'm sure.'

'Yeah, well, no wonder they call it tough love. It's tough on the one doing it, too. How's your aunt's cottage going?'

'I've sold it. Look, I have to go now, Craig. Keep me informed about Steve.'

'Just a minute. There's something else. Did you know Nick was getting married?'

'Yes.'

'Jenny and I are going to the wedding.'

That was typical of Craig, trying to score over her. 'Good. Nick ought to have some family present. I'm glad you're there to look after our sons.' She didn't add 'about time' but it felt as though the words hung in the air between them. 'Well, if there's nothing else, I'll get on with my day.'

She had a little cry against Angus's shoulder after she'd shut down the phone.

'Tell me,' Angus prompted. 'A trouble shared . . .'

She explained about Steve. 'I ought to be there.'

'Actually, I don't think so. Not if you want him to learn to stand on his own feet. At least your husband's dumped him with someone who has expertise in that area.'

'I wish I knew who it was.'

'It's a bit the same with me and my son. I worry about Oliver backpacking to all these remote places, haven't a clue where he is half the time. But it's his life and I can only pray he'll return safely.'

'You're right, really. It's why I left them. Nick's found

302

himself a woman and Steve . . . well, at least he's away from those horrible people he was hanging out with.'

She dried her eyes, then drew herself very upright. 'OK. I'm going to sort out your kitchen today because it's in need of a thorough cleaning and reorganising.' And because she always cleaned things when she was upset. It usually helped.

'Joanna did that too,' he said softly and added, as if he'd been reading her mind, 'cleaned things when she was upset, I mean.'

'Did she? Very sensible if you ask me, makes positive use of negative energy.'

'You don't mind me comparing you to her?'

'No. I like the loving way you speak about her. I'm sure I'd have liked her, too.'

'You're an amazing woman.'

'Yes, well, see what you think about me when I show you how the new kitchen system works, and when I throw a hissy fit if you disrupt things.'

'Should I be trembling?'

'You certainly should.' She punched him lightly on the arm. 'Stop teasing and let me get on with it. Later, we'll also sort out a schedule for who cleans what when. I warn you, I am very efficient.'

'Then it won't take you more than a day or two. After that . . . ?'

'I'm coming into your office and sorting that out.'

A look of alarm flitted across his face. 'I don't think—'

She held up one hand. 'Trust me. I'll improve your efficiency out of sight.'

A wry smile slowly replaced the alarm. 'Other people

have tried to organise me and gave up.'

'Tell me that in two weeks' time.' She laid one hand on his arm. 'But I hope you know that I'm ready to drop things at a minute's notice if I can help in any way with Miss Parfitt and Janey.'

'I know. Oh, and Mr Trouton will be pottering around your aunt's garden tomorrow. Leave him to get on with it if you bump into him. He's about eighty-five, refuses to tell me exactly how old, but says it does him good to do a bit of gardening now and then.'

'Good for him. I've moved into quite a community on Peppercorn Street, haven't I? I thought such communities were extinct.'

'Those of us whose families have lived on the street for a generation or two look out for one another when we can. I'm hoping we'll manage to pass that attitude on to the people who move into Cinnamon Gardens and Sunset Close.'

'I like Cinnamon Gardens as a name for a little side street, but I'm not keen on Sunset Close. It's too trite for words. They should have stuck with the spice names.'

'They were going to build a whole series of longer streets leading out of the town centre at one time with spice names, but the economy slowed down in the last quarter of the nineteenth century, and then there were two world wars, so things stayed mainly as they were, except for that dreary post-war housing estate to the east of the town. All the streets there are named after former mayors.'

'I prefer spice names.'

'Yes. The one I liked best in the list I once found in the town archives was Saffron Lane.'

'Oh, that's lovely. Very evocative.'

After a moment or two she made shooing movements with her hands. 'You've soothed my savage breast after my encounter with Craig. Thanks. You can get back to work now and leave me to complete the cure by attacking the dirt and chaos here. Oh, and when you have time, I need the fridge from my aunt's house bringing up here.'

He saluted. 'Yes, ma'am!' Then he walked off smiling.

She was smiling too.

Chapter Eighteen

Three nights later Winifred, who was sleeping upstairs in her old bedroom for security purposes, was jerked abruptly out of a pleasant dream by the sound of smashing glass and the shrilling of her modified alarm system from the garden. Well, she thought it was the outside one.

She lay for a few seconds with her heart pounding, wondering what had happened to make it go off, then remembered with a sigh of relief that she wasn't alone.

The door to her bedroom opened and Janey came in with a sleepy Millie in her arms. She whispered, 'Are you all right, Auntie Winnie?'

Dan came to join them. 'Don't put the light on or we won't be able to see out of the window. We need to check that they've gone away again. Have you heard anything from inside the house downstairs?'

'No. The first thing I heard was the alarm. But I stood and listened at the top of the stairs and I couldn't hear anything inside.'

'I think from the direction of the sound it must have been the kitchen window they broke to get inside.'

Janey put Millie down on the bed next to Winifred and moved across to the bedroom window. 'I can't see anything from here at the front. Well, I won't if they've broken into the kitchen. They may be inside the house, but the upstairs alarms haven't sounded so they can't have even started up the stairs.'

'Oh dear! What do you think we should do?'

'I'm going to watch out of the window for a few moments – and listen carefully. Dan, will you listen at the top of the stairs. If they start moving up the stairs, the other alarm will sound and you can run back in here and lock the door. We'll leave Millie on the bed and if necessary, we can wait here for help to come. The first alarm will already have gone through to Angus and the police, so someone will be on their way here.'

There was silence for a moment, then Winifred whispered, 'Can you see anything, Janey?'

'No.'

'Dan?'

'No.'

Suddenly they both heard the kitchen door bang downstairs. It always rattled in a certain way, so there was no doubt.

A few seconds later Janey saw a man come running round the house and flee down the front path. He went on to the street and vanished from her view.

She waited but no one else appeared. When she tiptoed across to join Winifred at the bedroom door, she heard no sounds of movement downstairs. But there was now an ominous smell of burning.

'Oh, no. He must have set something alight before he left.'

Winifred went across to pick up Millie. 'We have to get out of the house.'

'No, wait. The burglar has gone now, so I'm going to switch off the alarm from up here, creep down and check what's burning and put it out if I can. I can't see any light from flames, so the fire can't be spreading quickly.'

'Don't do it. It's too dangerous. We should just leave the house as quickly as we can by the front door.' Millie whimpered and Winifred cuddled her closer.

'No, I'll be quite safe going down because I can run back up quickly if I see anyone. You two get ready to follow me outside, if I call. Can you manage Millie on the stairs?'

'I can do anything to save this little darling.'

'Stay by the door, but be ready to lock yourself in the bedroom if you hear me shouting that there's still someone here.'

'It's too risky.'

'We have to find out what's on fire. Anyway, Angus will have heard the alarm and he'll be on his way. He'll be here any minute.'

Janey went outside the bedroom and joined Dan on the landing, listening for sounds downstairs.

'Have you heard anything?' she whispered.

'Not since the back door banged.'

There was a strong smell of something burning, or charring perhaps, but there was still no sign of flickering light under the kitchen door, which there would have been if there were flames.

'Let me go down instead, Janey.'

'No, Dan. I can run back up much faster than you can.'

She guessed that the man who'd broken in must have been told to set a fire, as another warning to the owner to sell.

Still, she'd take great care.

She switched off the alarm at the top of the stairs and began to creep down, ready to flee back to the bedroom at a second's notice.

As soon as the alarm was triggered at number 5, another alarm went off at Dennings. Angus woke up and within seconds realised what it was.

'What's that?' Nell asked sleepily.

'Trouble at Miss Parfitt's.'

'Oh, no,' she sat up.

He picked up the hand piece from beside his bed and studied the display. 'Someone's broken into her house. Only the downstairs alarm at the back has been triggered so far.' He swung out of the bed. 'I'd better go and investigate.'

'Won't the police be attending?'

'You can never be sure whether they're in the middle of something else or not. I bet I'm closer and quicker.' He was pulling on his jeans as he spoke and by the time she got out of bed and grabbed her clothes, he was fully dressed.

'Wait for me. I won't be a minute.'

They hurried to the back entrance of the big house and he set his own alarm system before leading the way through the darkened gardens.

'I could wish for a full moon tonight,' he muttered as he stumbled over something and fell.

As he stood up, he glanced again at the hand piece linked

to the alarm system and frowned. 'They've switched off the upstairs alarm system at number 5, so I think the intruder has probably gone. But let's hurry, just in case.'

Millie began whimpering and it took Winifred a few moments to quieten her. She stepped back a little way into the bedroom, trying to keep the noise the baby was making from echoing down the stairwell. She kept an eye on the stairs the whole time, ready to slam and lock the door.

But Millie settled down and everything remained quiet downstairs. All she could hear was the sound of the wind gusting outside.

When someone hammered on the back door, she waited for Janey to answer it or call up, but all remained quiet. This person had come openly to the house, so surely it couldn't be a burglar?

There was the sound of the back door opening and then silence. She prayed it was Angus.

Time seemed to tick by so slowly. Where was Janey?

She jumped in shock as a man's figure appeared at the foot of the stairs.

'Miss Parfitt! Janey? Are you there?'

She sagged against the door frame as she recognised Angus's voice. 'I'm here, Angus. And so is Dan.'

He ran up the stairs. 'Are you all right?'

'Yes. Haven't you seen Janey? She went downstairs to check what was on fire.'

'I smelt burning but it was some rags in the sink, and it wasn't causing any danger. But there was no sign of Janey. Let's put the lights on and search.'

'Shall I take the baby, Miss Parfitt?' Nell had joined

311

them at the top of the stairs and lifted Millie gently out of her arms. 'Do you want to sit down?'

'No, I want to go downstairs and find out what's happened to that girl.'

'She definitely didn't come back up,' Dan said. 'I was standing here watching the stairs the whole time. She didn't cry out, either. I'd have heard her.'

Winifred started down the stairs, not trying to rush it, she never did that because she didn't want to fall.

Dan followed.

Angus was now going round the ground floor, switching on lights and calling out for Janey.

Inside the kitchen Winifred pointed. 'This chair has been knocked over.'

Angus bent over it. 'There's something on the edge of it. Looks like blood. No, don't touch it, Miss Parfitt. The police will want to examine it.'

Winifred fought back panic. 'She's hurt. Someone's hurt Janey.'

She led the way into the kitchen, her heart fluttering wildly, and sank into a chair. 'It's my fault. They came to frighten me, I'm sure. But why would they have taken Janey away?'

'I don't think it's your fault at all. Maybe it's her father and nothing to do with you selling your house? He's been stalking her.'

'I still don't understand why he'd take her away?'

'No. Neither do I.' It seemed a stupid, irrational act.

'I'm going to phone Kieran and ask him to go out to the smallholding. If they've taken her, they'll probably be going back there.'

After a quick conversation he ended the call.

A couple of minutes later a siren sounded outside.

'Thank goodness! That'll be the police. You stay here with Nell and Miss Parfitt, Dan.'

He ran to open the front door.

Angus nearly groaned aloud when he saw who had arrived.

Edwina stared at him. 'Are you going to let us in? The alarm went and I presume Miss Parfitt needs help.'

'Sorry. I was just surprised to see you.'

'It was mutual.' Then she saw her cousin standing behind him and her expression softened a little. 'Are you all right, Nell?'

'I'm fine, but Miss Parfitt has had intruders and they lit a fire. Janey saw someone running away, so thought it was safe to go and investigate and now she's missing. Why don't you come into the kitchen and we'll tell you what we know?'

Angus let her do the talking since he could never speak to Edwina Richards without them disagreeing about something or other.

'I'll have a look round outside,' the male officer said.

'There will be CCTV recordings of whatever happened out here,' Angus said. 'I've only just fitted modifications to extend the security system. Miss Parfitt is an old friend of my family.'

Edwina nodded, as if accepting this.

'I phoned a friend to ask him to go out to the smallholding where Dobson is staying,' Angus said. 'Kieran Jones. You may know him.'

'The famous journalist? Yes, he phoned the station to

313

say he was doing that. I thought he'd been badly injured.'

'He's been rehabilitating himself, but he's not gone there alone, just in case there's trouble. We didn't dare wait for the next police vehicle. If that brute Dobson took Janey there he could hurt her. He's vicious.'

'I sat in on interviews with her mother in the women's refuge,' Edwina said, 'so I know quite a bit about him and vicious would be a good word to describe him. I'm sorry we're not staffed to respond more quickly but it's been a busy night.'

When explanations had been made, Edwina said abruptly, 'If you can get the recordings from the CCTV cameras, Mr Denning, I'll have them checked.'

'They're on thumb drives. I've left some spares here in case there were any problems. It'd be better if you or your colleague watched me access them and I'll let you remove them from the system yourselves, just to prove I'm not doing any substitution.'

'We may not have agreed about some things, but I don't suspect you of doing anything illegal.'

'No, but a court might not believe me if that sod gets a good lawyer. Better to be safe than sorry.'

'You're right. I'll call in and ask if there's been any sign of the girl.'

She went into the next room and spoke in a low voice to the people on night duty at district headquarters, coming back to say, 'The police haven't got anyone out near the smallholding so they're contacting the nearest unit. I hope your friends get there quickly.'

'Why don't you put the kettle on, Nell, and make us all a cup of tea?' Winifred suggested. 'I'm busy holding this young lady and shall continue to do so till her mother comes back.' She cuddled the sleeping baby and added, 'There's some cake in that tin next to the kettle. Dan, will you get it out, please?'

'Miss Parfitt is well known round here for her cakes,' Angus told Edwina. 'And she's very generous about sharing them.'

Nell exchanged glances with her cousin Edwina, hoping she could get the message through to humour their hostess, and received a slight nod in reply.

'Thank you,' Eddie said. 'We'll be happy to accept your offer, Miss Parfitt. We've been on duty for a few hours and I for one am parched.'

Nell got things ready following Winifred's instructions. She kept an eye on the old lady, but her colour had come back and she seemed to be deriving comfort from holding the baby. Dan was also looking better now. He'd been very pale and breathless at first.

As she worked, she prayed that Janey was all right.

Janey's head hurt so much she kept her eyes closed for a moment or two. Which she soon realised was a good thing because someone was talking.

She tried to work things out. The last thing she remembered was tiptoeing down the stairs and opening the kitchen door. She was sure she hadn't made a sound, or heard a sound, either. She definitely hadn't seen anyone.

Now she was in a car. How had that happened?

There must have been a second thief and he'd been waiting for her in the kitchen. But why was she now in a car? She listened intently.

'Come on, Wayne. Surely you can drive faster than that?'

Oh, no! It was her father's voice. Fear shivered through her. Why had he captured her? What about Millie? She hoped he hadn't got her daughter as well. She listened but could hear no baby sounds. That was good news, surely? It must mean Millie and Auntie Winnie were safe. Dan would have had time to warn them if anyone had tried to go upstairs.

She quickly realised the other speaker was her father's cousin Wayne, a sullen man, as big a bully as her father. His wife had left him years ago.

'If I go any faster, Lionel, the police may stop us for speeding, then we'll be in trouble. I don't know why you had to bring the girl along.'

'I told you. I want her to get them to take that stupid court order off me.'

'Well, they won't do it.'

'They will if she asks them, if she says we've made friends again.'

Janey's heart sank. Had her father gone mad? Of course she wasn't going to ask to have the court order lifted. She didn't want him coming near her. That would be bad enough. But she had a daughter to protect. She didn't want him to touch Millie with even one fingertip. Her child wasn't growing up being thumped and hurt.

Her father went on grumbling. He was always complaining about something. 'Janey might have done that more willingly if you'd got hold of the baby too, like we planned. But you didn't expect such a loud, fancy security system, did you? So you didn't wait to see what would happen, just ran like a frightened rabbit.'

'I ran to save myself and you'd have done the same if you had any sense, Lionel. I saw at least one CCTV camera. You've made a damned mess of it, as usual. You always were hasty. I don't know why I let you talk me into this. When we get back you can pack your things and get out, yes, and take her with you. I'll manage my farm without your help from now on, thank you very much.'

'I'm not going anywhere and if you try to force me to leave, you'll regret it. I know things about you and I'll tell the police. What about those lovely green crops down the back that bring you in some nice money? They wouldn't like it if they found out about those.'

There was absolute silence, only the sound of the car's motor. Janey peeped through her eyelashes. They must be out of town now, because she could only see tree branches being blown about by the wind in the moonlight. No roofs or street lights. So there'd be no one round here to help her if she screamed for help. She'd better go on pretending to be unconscious.

After a few minutes, Wayne asked suddenly, 'Shouldn't she be waking up by now? You haven't killed her, have you?'

'Of course I haven't. She's still breathing. I know how to hit someone to knock them out.' Lionel sniggered. 'As my wife will be able to confirm when I get her back as well.'

'Dorothy's gone into a refuge. They never come out of those places. My damned wife didn't.'

'Dorothy will if she thinks her precious daughter is in danger.'

Silence, then Wayne said obstinately, 'Well, I still think that girl ought to have woken up by now.'

'Ah, shut up. She'll be coming round all too soon. You'll see. I'll give her a good shaking when we get back. That'll bring her out of it.'

What made Janey pretend to wake up sooner than she'd planned was her father's hand lingering on her breast, tweaking it. That shocked her rigid and made her feel sick.

'Get your hand off my breast, you filthy pervert!' she yelled.

His answer was a smack across her face that made her head spin.

The car pulled up just then and he jerked her out of it, throwing her to the ground. She curled up, sure he was going to kick her.

Kieran answered the phone. When he realised what Angus was telling him, he put the call on speaker so that Nicole could listen in. Paul appeared in the bedroom doorway, looking worried.

'I have his address, Angus. I'll go after Janey straight away while you deal with the police.'

Nicole leant forward. 'Is the baby all right? She'll ask about that.'

Angus said simply, 'Listen.'

The sound of a baby howling indignantly came through the phone.

'As you can hear, Millie's fine. Miss Parfitt and Nell are taking care of her. Dan's OK too. Look, is there anyone you can take with you, Kieran? There are two men involved and Dobson is a big fellow, brutal with it.'

'I'm going with him,' Nicole said at once.

'So am I,' said Paul.

Kieran rang the police to tell them he was going after Janey.

'Do not put yourself at risk, Mr Jones. We're sending a police car out to the smallholding as soon as we can.'

There was another of those infuriating, muttered conversations, then the officer added, 'I think you're closer to it, though. So as these men could hurt the girl, we'd be grateful if you could go and keep an eye on things. Stop them taking her anywhere else, if you have to, but otherwise don't intervene.'

'I won't stand by if Janey is in danger.'

Kieran ended the call and swung out of bed, grimacing at his stiffness and limping slightly as he grabbed his clothes. Since the accident he usually warmed up the muscles in that leg before getting up. No time for that now.

Nicole was already nearly dressed and Paul had vanished, presumably to put his clothes on.

Kieran shook his head ruefully. Fine rescue squad this was. A man with a bad leg, a slender woman and a gangly teenage lad. But the numbers would make a difference, he was sure, and one car could box in another and stop anyone escaping. That at least he could do. It didn't matter if his car got damaged. It was only a tin box, nothing as valuable as a human life.

They were in the car within minutes and he began programming the satnav. Then he set off, driving as fast as was safe in the windy night.

Wayne swung round and stared at his cousin. 'Why did she just call you a filthy pervert? What did you do to her?'

'Nothing.'

'He touched my breast.' Janey tried to roll away from

him but he yanked her to her feet.

'What? I'm not having any of that in my house, whatever you threaten.'

'Aw, she's lying again. She always was a liar.' He kept hold of her arm and slapped her across the face again with his free hand. 'Not another word from you, you damned troublemaker.'

Janey tried to pull away from him, but couldn't. 'I'm not lying, Wayne. I'm not.' She forced a sob, hoping to soften his heart. 'He did touch my breast. He's sick in the head.'

Wayne didn't move. 'I saw enough to believe her. I'd never have thought it of you, though, Lionel. Not that. Not after what our uncle did to us.'

'I'm not like him. I was just tormenting her a bit, making her pay for what she's done to me.'

'Normal men wouldn't even think of doing that,' Janey said, rubbing her breast with her free hand and forcing another sob.

'Let go of her,' Wayne ordered. 'This has got to stop. We'll dump her in the town centre and deny we ever saw her.'

'No. She owes me for bringing her up. She's mine to do what I want with.'

'Not in my house, she isn't.' Wayne suddenly swung his fist at his cousin, who had to let go of Janey to defend himself.

When Wayne yelled, 'Run for it, girl!' Janey didn't need telling twice. She took off at top speed, heedless of the fact that she was wearing only her slippers.

She hadn't a clue where she was heading because though she'd been to Wayne's smallholding before, it'd been years

320

ago and in the dark everything looked different. But any risk was better than staying with Lionel.

Sobs escaped her and they weren't forced this time. She felt sick with disgust and horror. How could she have a father like him?

When she fell over, she scrambled to her feet and was running again within seconds. Branches whipped in her face, but she ignored the stinging pain. Something trickled down her forehead and she brushed it away from her eyes impatiently.

Finally she saw lights ahead and when she got closer, stopped for a moment and glanced over her shoulder to make sure he wasn't coming after her. This was still a minor country road and she wasn't going to knock on any doors unless she knew who was inside the house. What if they didn't believe her? What if they handed her back to him?

On the other side of the house she saw moving lights and limped up a small slope. Beyond it was a wider road and two or three cars passed by while she watched.

If she could get to it, she could flag down a car. They'd take her to a police station, surely?

She thought of Millie and that helped her move on. She had to walk more slowly now, because her feet were hurting badly.

She still couldn't hear any sounds of pursuit so picked her way more carefully. Her slippers were torn, not much protection.

Everything hurt.

Kieran followed the satnav's instructions, driving as quickly as he dared, but it took him a full twenty minutes to get there, even though there was hardly any traffic on the roads.

The house was dark but a car was parked in front of it and when he got out of his vehicle to examine it, he found that the motor was still warm.

He took firm hold of the weighted cudgel that looked like a rounders bat. He'd carried it before in self-defence.

He knocked on the front door, but there was no answer.

He knocked again, sensing someone behind him and sidestepping quickly. But it was Paul, his young face grim in the moonlight.

Kieran tried the door handle and it turned.

He felt around for a light switch and caught a man in its sudden brightness. Dobson. Creeping towards the back of the house.

'Stay where you are.'

'Who's going to make me?'

'I am.'

'And I'm with him,' Paul said.

'I'll be photographing it all on my phone,' Nicole said from behind them.

'I'll call the police if you attack me,' Dobson blustered.

'They're already on the way. Where's the girl?'

'What girl? There's no girl here.'

There was a sound from the room at the end of the short corridor, a groan.

Was it Janey?

Paul pushed past so quickly he took everyone by surprise.

When Lionel tried to follow him, Kieran used a trick he'd learnt while on a story assignment in the Far East to send the bigger man sprawling. He used some handcuffs he shouldn't have been carrying to clamp Dobson to the stair rail before the man realised what was happening, then went to investigate.

'Is Janey all right, Paul?' Nicole called down the corridor.

'It's not Janey. It's a man. And he's hurt.'

He knelt down and checked the man's vital signs quickly but the injured man was conscious. 'What happened to you?'

'Lionel beat me up. They need to lock that sod up! He's into incest now as well as violence.'

'I'm damned well not into incest,' Dobson roared from down the hall, yanking at the handcuffs, making the banisters shake about. 'She's not my daughter.'

There was silence for a few moments, and it seemed to echo with the implications of that reaction.

There was the sound of a struggle but when Kieran ran back into the hall, he found Dobson bent double, gasping for breath and Nicole standing over him.

'My fist happened to connect with his belly,' she said. 'My foot will connect with something a bit lower if he gives us any more trouble.'

In spite of the seriousness of the situation, Kieran grinned at her. 'Atta girl!' Then he got his phone out and called an ambulance.

Paul had been going round the house, banging doors open and looking into every room. 'She's not here.'

Kieran went back into the kitchen where the injured man was lying with his eyes closed. 'Do you know what happened to the girl?'

'He started feeling her up – his own daughter! – so I thumped him and told her to run for it. Did she get away?'

'Looks like it. Well done.'

'I'm not into hurting women and I'm sickened by incest. That sod was touching up his own daughter.'

'She's not my daughter, I tell you!' Lionel yelled again.

'I hope that's true,' Nicole said sharply. 'It'll be a load off her mind, if it is.'

'Bitch.'

She raised the meat mallet she'd snatched up before they left home. 'Shut up, you.'

A couple of minutes later the police arrived.

Kieran went out to meet them, explaining what they'd found. The officers' voices were grim as they checked the injured man.

'He's not going to die but he's been badly hurt.'

One man went back into the hall, raising his eyebrows at Kieran. 'Who handcuffed him?'

'I did. I had, um, an ornamental pair.'

The officer grinned. 'Well, they are highly polished, that's for sure. But I'd better put one of our own restraints on him before we haul him off to the station. Wouldn't like you to lose your, um, ornaments, Mr Jones.'

'The girl is still missing, the one he kidnapped. The injured man said he told her to run for it when he started fighting Dobson, and he hasn't seen her since. Can you put out an alert for her?'

'Yes, of course. This fellow can wait a few minutes while I call it in.'

Chapter Nineteen

Janey limped to the side of the main road and flagged down the next car to contain a woman, sighing in relief as the driver stopped.

All she wanted to do was burst into tears, but she held herself together somehow and quickly told the elderly couple what had happened. 'Have you got a mobile phone? Could you please call the police, then? Please.'

'I'll do that,' the woman said. 'Get in and we'll take you home or to the police station.'

Janey got into the car, relieved to be sitting down, aching all over now.

'George, drive on. I can phone while we're moving. We don't want to give that man a chance to attack us as well as this poor girl, do we?'

He drove off slowly and she dialled 999, speaking clearly and crisply. She was put through to the police, explained again, then handed the phone over to Janey.

After she'd given her name and details, the woman on

the phone asked, 'Can you please tell us your daughter's name as identification?'

'Millie. She's called Millie.'

'Good.'

'Is she all right?'

'We have no warnings out for her, so she must be. We only knew that you had been taken from your home. Where are you?'

'I don't know.' She turned to the woman. 'Do you know where we are?' Her voice broke on the final words and she smeared away the tears that were escaping her control.

'Give the phone back to me.' The woman gave their location and agreed that they'd take Janey back to Peppercorn Street, where the police were already waiting for her.

'Thank you for helping me,' Janey said. 'I'm so grateful.'

'We were happy to do it,' the woman said.

'Anyway, we'd been having a boring evening,' the man said. 'This'll make a great story to tell our friends.'

Great story! Was that all he thought it was? Janey wondered. It had been like the worst nightmare of her whole life.

She shuddered, hating the thought of how her father had touched her, then she let her eyes close as she rested her head against the car seat.

She'd be all right once she'd seen Millie, she told herself. And surely they'd lock her father away now after he'd kidnapped her?

Surely she'd be safe now?

Angus suddenly needed a minute to himself. 'I'll go and look out of the front room window to see whether there's any sign of Kieran or the police.'

No one answered. Edwina was talking quietly to Winifred and Nell was listening to them.

He didn't switch the light on, but stared out of the window blindly, relishing the brief respite. Then something caught his eye, a flash of movement in a car. He didn't move but suddenly all his senses were on alert again and he watched carefully.

There was definitely someone in the car, someone slumped down. What was anyone doing sitting out there at this time of night? It must have been the moonlight glinting on a wristwatch that had caused the flash of light. He screwed up his eyes and managed to get the car number, then went back into the kitchen.

'Officer, I think there's someone in a parked car watching the house.'

Edwina jumped to her feet, licking cake crumbs off her fingers. 'Show me.'

They moved carefully into the front room, staying a little way back from the bay window. After a few moments the person moved again.

'Can you keep an eye on the car and I'll call in to see who it belongs to.'

Before she could do that, however, another strange car pulled up outside and Janey tumbled out of it, running towards the house, looking as if she'd been beaten or worse.

Angus ran to the front door, just as Janey crashed it open. He managed to slow her down. 'Millie's all right,' he said, guessing this would be her first worry.

'Oh, thank goodness!'

'Who brought you here?'

'I escaped and flagged down a car.'

Edwina joined them. 'I'd better go out and speak to them. Oh, damn! That other car's driving off.'

'We have its number,' Angus reminded her.

'Yes. Can you look after Janey? I'll speak to the people who picked her up.' She went outside, taking his agreement for granted.

'Come on, love. But keep quiet, if you can. You'll wake Millie if you go rushing into the kitchen and Nell's only just got her back to sleep. Your daughter has very powerful lungs.'

He put an arm round the girl's shoulders and walked into the kitchen, saying, 'Look who came to join us.'

Janey stared round the room. 'Where's Millie?'

'She's in my bedroom.' Winifred stood up and came across to give Janey a big hug. She held on to the shaking girl, making shushing noises as Janey struggled not to weep.

Dan stood beside them, patting them indiscriminately on the shoulders, first one woman, then the other.

'Just let me see Millie,' Janey begged. 'I'll be all right once I've seen her.'

She stood for a moment in the doorway of Winifred's bedroom, then tiptoed across to the bed, where Millie lay fast asleep, spread-eagled in her usual starfish manner. The child looked rosy and well.

Janey drew in a long, sobbing breath and turned. 'Thank you for looking after her.'

'We were happy to do that. You know I love her as if she really were family.'

Janey sniffed and managed a near smile. 'Yes. I know.'

Winifred put an arm round her again at the door and led her across to a chair in the kitchen. 'Soon you must have a shower and we'll tend to your poor feet—'

'My feet?' Janey looked down. 'Oh, yes.'

'But first, how about a cup of hot chocolate and a piece of cake?'

'I know I'm home when you offer me cake. Thank you, Auntie Winnie. I love you.'

'I love you, too, dear.'

'I'll put the kettle on,' Dan said.

Edwina had come back, staying by the hall door and listening. She and Nell smiled at one another, seeing the tender little scene, then she beckoned to Angus. 'They're taking Janey's father down to the police station. I need to get some sort of unofficial statement from her, just to be sure what happened.'

He looked into the room, where Nell was bathing Janey's face with a damp cloth, Dan was brewing a pot of tea and Winifred was cutting a piece of cake. 'Give her a minute or two. The fussing will help her recover.'

'You've got a big bruise on your face, Janey,' Nell was saying, smoothing the girl's tangled hair from her forehead. 'Did he hit you?'

'Yes. He always does. And he touched me.' She pointed to her breast. 'There. My own father!'

Edwina muttered and came forward. 'He's in custody and his cousin has accused him of the same thing, but he's claiming he's not your father.'

Janey stared at her, her face slowly brightening for all its bruises and scratches. 'He's saying he's not my father? Oh, I do hope he's telling the truth. It'd be the best news I could ever have. I'll phone my mother first thing tomorrow. She'll tell me if it's true or not.'

She stared down at the plate and piece of cake, murmuring, 'Not my father. Oh, please, let it be true.' Picking up the cake, she took a big bite.

Edwina looked at Nell. 'I'll have to ask you to stay here to look after Millie, if you don't mind.'

Janey looked up. 'What do you mean?'

'We need to get you to a doctor to check your injuries, then we have to take a proper formal statement. Do you trust Ms Chaytor and Miss Parfitt to look after your daughter?'

'I've had plenty of practice,' Nell told her. 'I've brought up three sons.'

Janey sighed. 'I'd rather stay here and look after Millie myself. Can't you take the statement here? I don't really need a doctor. It's just bruises and scratches.'

Angus crouched beside her, studying her bruised face. 'Better to do things by the rule book, Janey. It'll make things easier when he's taken to court.'

'Will you come with me to the police station, then?'

He cast a questioning glance in Edwina's direction and at her nod, said, 'Yes, of course.'

Edwina turned to Winifred. 'Thank you for your hospitality. We'll be in touch.'

'Look after her.'

'We will.'

As they walked out, Edwina murmured to Angus. 'My colleague will drive us. I'm going to check that car number plate on the way there. Do you mind coming in the police car? We'll arrange a lift back. It's just that I'd rather be able to say that I was with Miss Dobson from the minute she got home and you can bear witness to that, if necessary.'

'Good thinking. I'll do whatever you feel is best.'

She eyed him sideways for a few seconds, then said, 'We got off to a bad start, you and I, didn't we?'

'I think your father is to blame for that.'

'I suppose so. He'll never change. He's living in the past about that sort of thing.'

'Well, you're Nell's cousin, so I'm willing to wipe out the past and start again.'

'Yeah. Me, too.'

He wasn't sure what he was supposed to have done that needed wiping out, but what the hell! Life was too short to hold grudges.

'I can't believe how quickly you and Nell got together,' Edwina said suddenly.

'Yes. It took us both by surprise. I certainly didn't expect to find someone to love again.'

She didn't say anything else but concentrated on the response to the car number plate query.

He sat quietly and when he noticed how strained Janey was looking, he patted her hand and whispered, 'You'll be safe from now on. We'll make sure of it.'

When they got to the police station they were kept busy with interviews and writing statements for several hours. Janey also had to do a mouth swab for the DNA test.

At one stage Edwina came to see them, looking excited. 'Do you mind waiting a bit longer? Will the baby be all right? It's just . . . we've found something out that affects the bigger picture.'

'Any hint as to what?'

'Not yet. But I promise you'll both be pleased.'

'Is it all right if Janey makes a phone call?'

'Perfectly all right.'

He glanced out of the window. 'I see there's a café across the street. Perhaps we could grab something to eat, since we missed breakfast?'

'Of course. But please come straight back.'

As Edwina returned to the rear offices, he looked at Janey, hating to see her poor battered face. 'What do you make of that?'

'I don't know. But I don't think she'd lie to us, do you?'

'No. In fact, she's usually too blunt. Let's phone Auntie Winnie from the café. It'll be much pleasanter there.'

The detective now in charge of the case grinned at Edwina when she asked him how long it'd take to check Dobson's DNA to find out if he was the father of Janey.

'It just so happens we're trialling a new speedy DNA test from America. How about we put your samples forward for inclusion in the trial? The new test isn't yet validated for court use, so you'll still have to get a standard test done as well, which will mean taking more samples, but we can find out within a couple of hours what the samples show and it should give you some guidance at least. Actually, we've found it very accurate so far.'

'I'll owe you for that tip, David.'

'You can buy me a drink one night.'

She looked at him in surprise, then smiled. 'OK.'

'Friday next?'

That did surprise her. He was new to the area and not the best-looking guy on the planet, but then, she wasn't the most beautiful woman in the world, either. He seemed pleasant enough, so why not have a drink with him and see if anything came of it? Her father wasn't around any longer to deter men from dating her. 'Suits me just fine.'

When Angus and Janey got back, she explained and asked for another sample. 'Can you wait for the first set of results?'

'Yes.' Janey said. 'Oh, yes please. And I'll be praying it shows he's not my father.'

'Don't quote me on it, but I don't blame you,' Edwina said.

When she left them in the waiting room, Edwina went to grab a snack bar from her emergency stash and found David waiting for her again.

'Wayne Dobson's started singing nice and loudly to us,' he said abruptly.

'About what?'

'About what he'd hinted at before, being hired to cause trouble for the old lady Janey lives with. We need to track down that car you saw. It allegedly belongs to a Mrs Dorothy Dobson.'

'I doubt it. She's Janey's mother and she's in a refuge. She won't have had access to any vehicles lately. But I'm happy to phone and ask her about the car. I know the woman who runs the refuge, so I can probably get through to her more easily than you could.'

'OK. Go for it. I'll get on with the paperwork.'

She went to find him a quarter of an hour later. 'Dorothy Dobson says she's never owned a car or learnt to drive. Her husband wouldn't let her. I checked and there's certainly no record of her ever having a driving licence. What's more, she hasn't left the refuge for the past few days. Lots of witnesses to that. She says her husband's cousin owns a car like the one I described, though.'

David looked thoughtful. 'Curiouser and curiouser.'

'I wonder if this watcher ties in to the harassment of Miss Parfitt at number 5. Over the past few weeks, she's been mugged and had the summer house in her back garden burnt down. She's pretty sure someone is trying to force her to sell her home. A developer could get three modern houses on a piece of land that big. Angus may know something about it. He's a family friend. He's still here with Janey.'

'Let's go and talk to him.'

Angus confirmed the harassment, explaining about the way he'd nearly caught the mugger in the first incident, and the security system he'd extended for Winifred. 'I've also got the latest brochures from two estate agents I've never heard of in my car. They were posted to her. Janey may be able to tell you about other incidents.'

He went out to get the brochures and Janey joined them to discuss the ongoing harassment.

'There's one developer who's been warned before for hustling old people in this town and buying their houses at knock-down prices. He's made a lot of money from small developments,' Edwina said thoughtfully. 'He's the one doing that new one they've called Cinnamon Gardens.'

Angus nodded. 'My partner just sold your aunt's house to him, but willingly. You must have seen what a bad state it was in. I helped her hold out for a decent price, though.'

'She was lucky. He isn't usually generous. Unfortunately we've never been able to pin anything dishonest on him and his developments go through the planning procedures very quickly. I'd guess he has someone in the council helping him navigate the shoals of bureaucracy.'

'I'm dealing with a similar case on the other side of town, only this time it's the son of the house owner who came to us to report harassment to his elderly father,' David said thoughtfully.

'Who'd have thought a kidnapping could suggest links with this sort of thing?' Edwina shook her head. 'Perhaps Nolan's getting too confident.'

'I think I'll go and have another word with Lionel Dobson,' David said. 'He's very eager not to be charged with incest and to get off as lightly as possible from the kidnapping charges, so I'm sure he'll co-operate.'

'Who'd be stupid enough to hire him to harass anyone?' she asked scornfully. 'He's not the smartest person in town, goes at things like a bull at a gate. I doubt even Nolan could be that stupid.'

They looked at one another thoughtfully.

'Maybe it's his cousin who's being hired?' David said slowly. 'Wayne Dobson hasn't got any police record. In fact, he lives a very quiet, private life.'

'Hmm. Well, however loudly this Dobson sings about his cousin's doings, I'm still going to charge Lionel with assault. Have you seen Janey's face?'

'Yeah. He's only about twice her size, the sod.'

'Can I sit in on your interview with him?' she asked.

'Be my guest.'

They took their places in the interview room, with Lionel opposite them together with a bored-looking duty lawyer.

After the preliminaries, David waited a moment to ask

his first question, studying Lionel thoughtfully. Then he said quietly, 'We'd be grateful for your help in figuring out what was going on tonight, why your cousin wanted to go to Miss Parfitt's house.'

'How grateful?' Lionel asked at once. 'Will it be taken into account?'

'Oh, I'm sure everything will be taken into account.'

'Someone's paying Wayne to harass that old lady, someone who wants to buy the house. He wouldn't tell me who, though.'

'But *you* went there to kidnap your daughter.'

'She's not my daughter. I keep telling you that.'

'OK. Kidnap Janey.'

'Well, Wayne said since what I wanted would frighten the old lady as well as anything else, he'd help me to get Janey.'

The lawyer whispered in his ear, but he waved the man away and stared at the two police officers.

'Your cousin Wayne doesn't have a record, Mr Dobson. We checked. Why should we believe you?'

Lionel hesitated, then said, 'You could check out his smallholding. There's a valuable green crop at the back, though he's probably destroying it as we speak.'

'As in?'

'Marijuana.'

'Interview closed,' David said abruptly and led the way out of the room.

Edwina smiled as she left him talking to his inspector. This was getting even more promising.

He came rushing into the staff room. 'Let those two go home, but keep Lionel Dobson here. I'm going after his cousin.

336

We knew someone round here was growing, but not who.'

She went off to do as he'd suggested.

When they got to the smallholding, David smiled as he got out of the car and waited for a second car to pull up.

'OK. Let's go.'

They had to wake Wayne up and he was a bit dopey as he answered their questions.

'I think he's been smoking his own weed,' one man said.

It was all over in a few minutes, with two men staying to guard the crop till it could be taken away and Wayne refusing to answer any more questions till he got a lawyer.

'It's my cousin's crop,' he insisted. 'What do I know about growing that stuff?'

When they got back, further questioning elicited only the same responses. Each man was claiming the other was responsible for the illegal crop.

It was Edwina who thought of a way round this during a break in questioning. 'I wonder whether Janey's mother knows anything about this?'

'Do you think they'd let me come into the refuge with you, Edwina?' David asked.

'If I vouch for you.'

Dorothy, who was now insisting on being called Hope, had plenty to tell them after years of watching what her husband and his cousin were up to. She even knew the name of the man who came to take away the crops.

'Did they never guard what they said in front of you?' David asked in surprise.

'I don't think they even noticed me most of the time, and

that was the way I wanted it, so that I could protect Janey. Only I didn't, did I? Lionel's friend raped her. He was in on the marijuana, too.'

Edwina looked at her in surprise. 'That didn't come out in court.'

'Lionel said if I gave one hint about it, he'd maim me permanently. I believed him.'

'Will you testify in court about the marijuana now?'

'Yes. I hope they keep Gary in prison for even longer because of it, and my ex with him.'

'You've been very helpful, Mrs – um Ms Redman.'

'Any time. Will you be seeing Janey?'

'Yes.'

'Give her my love.'

'I will.'

'Have you seen the baby?'

'Yes. She's a lively little thing.'

'I'm hoping to see her soon.' It was the first time she'd really smiled.

When they were in the car, Edwina thumped the steering wheel. 'Why do women let men turn them into such meek, helpless creatures?'

'Beats me. I bet no one would do it to you.'

'You can be certain of that.'

'Good for you. Anyway, let's go back. We may have the DNA results by now.'

Chapter Twenty

Edwina knocked on the door of number 5, surprised when Nell answered it. She'd expected her cousin to have gone back to Dennings with Angus.

'I'm hanging around till things are sorted out,' Nell said in a low voice. 'Miss Parfitt is still a bit nervous. Mr Shackleton is going to continue sleeping here but he's a bit shaken tonight. Who did you want to see?'

'Janey. We have some news for her.'

'The DNA tests?'

'Yes.'

'Come in. She's been on edge, waiting to hear.'

Janey was sitting in the kitchen, where Winifred was doing some baking.

'Shall I leave you on your own?' Nell asked.

'No, please stay. You're involved in all this,' Janey said. 'What did the tests show, Officer?'

'Dobson can't possibly be your father . . . or even a distant relative.'

Edwina had expected Janey to burst into tears of joy, but instead the girl grabbed Winifred and waltzed her round the kitchen. Then she picked up her daughter and danced her round, too, smacking a couple of big kisses on her cheek. 'Isn't that wonderful, Uncle Dan?'

'The best news you and Millie could have.'

The baby grabbed her mother's hair and laughed at her.

Then Janey sat down. 'I'll have to talk to my mother. I don't know what I'll do if she won't tell me who my father is.'

'I could phone and see if she's happy for you to visit her. There's a room where you can talk privately.'

'I can drive you over there,' Nell offered. 'And Miss Parfitt can come along for the ride.'

'I've got a cake in the oven,' Winifred said. 'I'll be all right here with Dan to keep me company. We'll keep all the doors and windows locked.'

Hope was waiting for them in an arbour in the back garden of the refuge. 'I'll take you through,' the woman who'd opened the door said.

Janey took the baby out of her car seat while Nell got the buggy out of the car boot.

'I'll phone for a taxi when we've finished talking, Nell. I don't know how long I'll be.'

'All right. I'll get back to Miss Parfitt now.'

Janey walked forward across the smooth lawn at the rear, her mother's tense expression making her suddenly certain what she wanted to do. When the buggy got stuck in a soft patch near the edge of the lawn, her mother came forward and helped her push it into the arbour.

But Hope's eyes were on the child. 'She's beautiful and looks such a happy baby. You can always tell when they're loved and well cared for.' Her face crumpled and she began to weep. 'I didn't look after you very well, did I?'

For a moment Janey wondered what to say, then it came to her. 'Don't cry, Mum. You did your best and we had some good times when Dad was out of the house.'

'It wasn't good enough. I lost heart, you see, could only try to survive towards the end.'

'Well, you've a lot to look forward to now, we both have. Pick up Millie and get to know your granddaughter. We should look to the future instead of the past. We've both done enough crying to last a lifetime. To hell with him! We won't let him spoil our lives.'

'You're right.' When Janey put Millie into her arms, Hope hid her face for a moment by hugging the child.

'Perhaps you'll be able to babysit her for me sometimes,' Janey said casually.

Hope gasped and her eyes lit up with joy. 'Do you really mean that?'

'Yes. I have a lot of studying to do. If they lock him away, you can come out of here and get yourself a flat. And you'll be able to get another job easily, I'm sure. I'll help you find second-hand furniture and—'

Hope grabbed her and pulled her close and the three of them stood cuddling for a moment, till Millie wriggled and gave a little whimper.

'Sit down and I'll tell you,' Hope said.

'About my father?'

'Yes.'

'Is he still alive?'

'I don't know. He was going to Australia, said he'd send for me, but I never heard from him again. When I found I was expecting, my parents threw a fit and Lionel was the only one who was kind to me. So when he asked me to marry him several months later, I said yes.'

'I can't imagine him being kind to anyone.'

'It didn't last long. I soon realised he'd wanted a housekeeper and slave, and when I tried to stand up for myself after I'd had you, he beat me so badly I was in bed for days. After that he was careful not to be so heavy-handed – and to hit me where the bruises didn't show.'

'Why didn't you run away?'

'He made it seem as if it was my fault for being stupid. Gradually I lost heart, Janey. It's a common pattern of behaviour in abused women, they tell me. I did what he wanted and made sure you were looked after physically. I just . . . survived.'

'You used to hug me sometimes when he wasn't at home. When I was little. Not so much later.'

'No.'

'What was my father's name?'

'Adam. Adam Torrington.'

'I don't suppose you have a photo of him?'

'No. I burnt them all, I was so angry with him for not writing to me, not even to let me know he'd arrived safely. I regretted that later.'

'We can search the Internet. It isn't a common name.'

'Not yet!' Hope sounded panicky. 'I have to get myself together again, make a new life. What if you found him and he saw me like this?' She gestured to herself.

'All right. I'll wait.' But not too long. She wanted to see

her birth father, if that was at all possible. That'd make everything real about Dobson.

'I think I'll change my name to Redman, too,' Janey said.

'That'd be wonderful. We'd still sound like a mother and daughter.'

'We are a mother and daughter.'

Millie crowed with delight just then and grabbed hold of her grandmother's shoulder length hair, and after they'd disentangled her little hands from it – no mean feat – Hope changed the subject firmly. Janey didn't push to talk about her birth father again. At least it wasn't Lionel Dobson and she knew her real father's name.

Instead she told her mother about her ambition to become a doctor and Hope was delighted, offering to babysit any time she could, once she had her own home again.

'The people here managed to save the furniture, you know, when the house was repossessed, and they've put it in storage. There will be some of your things among it, I'm sure. And they're keeping an eye on the legal situation. The bank foreclosed on the house, but there will be something left after it's sold because we'd been paying off the mortgage for years.'

When Janey left, she was very thoughtful and pleased that she'd started building a bridge to her mother.

She was pleased too with her mother's new name and the class she was taking in assertiveness.

In fact, it was a long time since she'd felt so good.

When Nell got back to number 5, she saw a car she recognised parked outside the house. Instinctively she pressed speed dial for Angus, but only got his reply service. So she called Edwina and told her that Jeffries had turned up again.

'I'll be along in a few minutes. Don't put yourself in danger.'

She didn't know why she felt threatened by Jeffries visiting Winifred, but she did. Well, she'd not find out anything by sitting here. She got out of the car and walked into the garden, going round towards the back and peering round the corner of the house.

Why had Winifred let Jeffries inside? That didn't make sense.

Nell crept forward a little and peeped through the kitchen window. He was talking earnestly to Winifred who wasn't saying anything. The old lady was sitting at the opposite side of the table from him. Her expression gave nothing away, but her body language indicated that she was anxious.

'Psst!'

Nell looked round.

Angus showed himself briefly on the other side of the kitchen window, then made urgent gestures to her to get back.

Nell did this, puzzled. What was going on?

She waited, wishing she could overhear what Jeffries was saying. And where was Dan? Why wasn't he with Winifred?

When she heard the sound of a car pulling up, she walked quietly back to the front and intercepted Edwina and her colleague.

'Angus is there and he wanted me to keep out of sight, so

I think we might wait a minute or two before interrupting. Come and have a peep.'

Edwina did that and Angus made the same gesture to her, telling her to keep back and putting one finger to his lips.

'I'm tempted to march in,' she muttered to Nell. 'What the hell does he think he's doing?'

'I can't work it out, but he didn't seem upset.'

'He seemed almost triumphant,' Edwina said. 'Do you think . . .'

'I bet he's set a trap to catch Jeffries.'

'He shouldn't have done that and put an old lady at risk.'

Angus came out of hiding and walked across to them. 'I've got it all on tape, the way he's pressuring her to sell. And just now he threatened her. I think we've got enough to haul him in for harassment and misrepresentation. I don't want to leave her on her own with him any longer.'

'Did she agree to do this?'

'When I suggested it, she was eager to do something to end all the harassment. I wonder . . .' He looked at Edwina. 'How about you let me go in and frighten that prettified idiot a bit? Off the record. I know not to smash his face in, but I may be able to use threats you couldn't.'

Edwina looked at her colleague, and he rubbed his ear. 'I didn't hear what your friend said, Eddie, and I think we've got a call from the station to answer before we can deal with this.'

Nell watched her cousin's face and could see that Edwina was torn as to whether to allow this or not. 'Let Angus have a go,' she urged.

Edwina turned and went back to the police car without

another word. Her colleague winked and said, 'We'll take a little drive round the block.' Then he followed her.

Angus made some adjustments to a gadget, blew a kiss at Nell and walked into the kitchen.

She watched through the window as he spoke to Jeffries. Annoyed that she couldn't hear him, she bent low and moved closer.

'And tell your friend Gus Nolan that my friend Kieran and I have looked into his business dealings online and we've found some very interesting irregularities. He's walking rather close to the legal line.'

Jeffries looked at Winifred, but she was smiling now.

'Did you manage to record what you wanted, Angus?' she asked.

'Record!' Jeffries looked round as if searching for a microphone.

'Tsk! Tsk!' Angus wagged one finger at him. 'Old people are using technology too these days. In fact, Miss Parfitt's house has one of the most complex and effective security systems it's possible to buy, now that I've extended it. It also covers the garden. I have the same system at my place.'

He waited, then added softly, 'I'll be sending some of the information I've collected to the police. They're already worried about the way you're harassing some of the town's older citizens.'

'I was just trying to help Miss Parfitt.'

'You were trying to persuade me to sell you my home at a knock-down price,' she snapped. 'I was only stringing you along because that's what Angus wanted.'

Jeffries breathed deeply. 'I'm sure it's illegal to record people's private conversations.'

'I'd love you to sue me about that.' Angus gestured to the door. 'But I think the best thing you can do is go away and we'll leave the police to look into Nolan's dealings. Go right away and do not come near this house ever again, or I shall take action.'

Jeffries edged towards the back door as if expecting to be attacked. When he stepped outside, he nearly bumped into Nell and yelped in shock.

She flourished one hand towards the path. 'Get out!'

She followed him to the front gate, just as the police car returned. He didn't run to his own car, but he certainly walked very quickly.

Edwina came to join her. 'Did Angus thump our friend?'

'Didn't touch him. But he did make a few things clear.'

'I wish I'd been a fly on the wall.'

'I think it was still being recorded.'

'Good. Now, if I can just check that Miss Parfitt is all right, I'll leave you in peace. But I will be pursuing other investigations.'

In the kitchen Angus was holding Winifred close and her shoulders were shaking.

'What the—'

Then Winifred turned round and they could see that she'd been crying with laughter. 'You should have seen him deal with that horrible man!' She laughed again. 'Oh, Angus, I shall chuckle about this for years. Dan, do come out of hiding and join us!'

He opened the door from the front hall and came in, and he was smiling too.

Angus turned to the police officers. 'If anyone else has any trouble with being nagged by Nolan to sell their houses, I can help you fix up a surveillance system.'

Edwina wagged her finger at him warningly. 'Leave us to take care of him now, Angus. I promise you we will.'

He saluted her. 'Shall do.' Then he turned back to Winifred. 'Now about this app of mine that you're going to test . . .'

'Dan wants to test it too.'

When Janey came home, the girl seemed thoughtful, but not unhappy. Winifred could tell that at once.

She shooed Angus and Nell out and told them to take some time to work on their romance.

'Dan will be staying for a few more nights, so we'll be fine.'

Then she waited for Janey to tell her in her own time what had happened with her mother.

When Nell got back to Dennings, she found an email from Nick on her computer.

'Phone me, Ma. Whatever time it is. It's really good news.'

She did that immediately, waiting impatiently for the call to be answered. 'Nick? What's happened?'

He chuckled. 'Straight to the point, as usual. It's Steve.'

'Oh no, what now?'

'He's fallen in love.'

'Steve has?'

'With a dog.' He explained about the pup and added, 'I think he's enjoying an open air life, too. He never did settle easily to studying and bookwork, did he? But Dad threw a hissy fit when he tried to do a gap year before going on to study in TAFE.'

'Are you sure of this?'

'Yes. Dad was so amazed he went down to see his friend Owen and find out what was going on. Dad's very full of himself for sorting out Steve, you know what he's like when he feels he's scored over someone. But it was the pup that did it, Ma. And the way you brought us up, I'm sure.'

Tears of joy came into her eyes. 'I'm so glad.'

'So, tell me what you've been doing? Tell me about your new guy. Dad is so miffed about that.'

When she put the phone down Nell was smiling, feeling as if she'd shed a heavy burden.

She went and kissed Angus. 'I think it's time now that we got on with our own lives, as Miss Parfitt just said. I love you, Angus. I think we're going to be very happy together.'

'I love you too, darling.'

'Coming to England, making the boys stand on their own feet was the right thing to do. But, best of all, I met you . . . and a cousin . . . and I'm going to meet some other relatives. Isn't life wonderful?'

Three weeks later, an Australian friend of Angus set up a computer to broadcast the wedding ceremony to Dennings.

Angus didn't tell her anything until it was nearly time for the wedding.

Nell stared at him in amazement, then sat down to watch Nick and Carla exchange vows.

Afterwards another camera took up the story at the small reception Craig had insisted on.

'Thank you, darling,' she said as the drinks and nibbles session ended and Nick escaped with his new wife.

Even Steve had been allowed up from the country, pup and all, to be present, because Craig wasn't having Carla's parents thinking no one on Nick's side cared. Her family had been invited at the last minute so that they couldn't change the arrangements.

Afterwards, Nell sighed and turned to Angus. 'Thank you, darling. You couldn't have done anything that pleased me more. It did upset me not being able to participate in my son's wedding. What did you think of Craig? He and Jenny were a bit overdressed, weren't they?'

'I may be a tad biased, but I didn't like the looks of him,' he said. 'I'd not buy a used car from him, that's for sure.'

She let out a gurgle of laughter. 'How did you guess? That was what he was working as when we first married. Before he made it into management.'

Angus grinned. 'No, Management with a capital "M".'

'I've not seen Nick looking so good for ages. Or Steve.' She mopped away some happy tears.

Angus frowned at her. 'I hope you're not going to weep all over me at our wedding.'

'I'm bound to. I always cry when I'm particularly happy.'

He rolled his eyes and pulled her close. 'I'll just have to get used to it, then. Because I'm definitely going to marry you and the sooner we do the deed the better.'

Another tear fell on his cheek and he laughed softly.

'I agree,' she said. 'The sooner we get married the better. I want a big, fancy wedding.'

He jerked in shock, moved his head back, then grinned. 'Phew! Don't tease me about things like that. Big weddings give me the horrors.'

'OK. But I'll feel free to tease you about anything else.'

And she did feel free, wonderfully free, happier than she'd been for many years.